## "DO... TO BE A PRINCE, ADRIENNE."

Nick tapped her chin. "I've done a lot of things in my life I'm not proud of. Someday, I'll tell you about them."

She kissed him lightly on the lips. Her thighs were brushing against his. He wanted to roll her over and bury himself in her goodness.

"Why not tell me now?" she asked softly.

He almost did it. He nearly told her right then and there who he was, and what he was doing on the island. But he simply couldn't make the confession, nor risk what Adrienne might do if she found out everything.

"It's getting late." He stood and offered her his hand. Pulling her up from the sand, he said, "What do you want to do tomorrow? Sunbathe? Swim? Sail?"

"No."

"Read?"

"Nope." She threw her arms around his waist, propped her chin on his chest, and grinned up at him. "Guess again."

# NANCY BERLAND
## Island Fever

**ZEBRA BOOKS**
**KENSINGTON PUBLISHING CORP.**

ZEBRA BOOKS

are published by

Kensington Publishing Corp.
475 Park Avenue South
New York, NY 10016

First Printing: February, 1993

Printed in the United States of America

*For my editor, Star Helmer,
who also pines for powder-white sand,
a pristine beach, and an exotic, remote
lagoon in the South Pacific—and
who brings out the best in me.*

# Chapter One

Adrienne Laurel hadn't expected to find her guide nearly nude.

And certainly not so outrageously gorgeous.

So now was as good a time as any to go to work.

Behind her, the ferry back to New Caledonia's big island gunned its engines and slipped away from Ile de Fleur's only dock. Adrienne dumped her luggage on the rickety wharf and dug in her tote bag for her camera. She had to get a picture of that guy, before he awoke.

Foster's instructions had been explicit. He wanted pictures of everything for her report on the undeveloped island, from the moment she arrived until she returned to Phoenix in six weeks.

"So, Nick Helton," she murmured as she peered through her lens, "I guess that includes you."

She focused on the scantily dressed guide who lay snoozing on the deck of his sailboat, the *Lorelei*. From Foster's briefing, Adrienne had expected him to be a crusty old fisherman. Boy, had she been wrong!

Steadying herself on the gently swaying dock, she let her focused gaze slide over his rock-hard body. He wore nothing but a skimpy pair of pale blue cutoffs frayed almost to the juncture of his thighs. That left—she tightened her focus—a broad chest, a narrow band of skin below his navel, and gloriously sculpted legs exposed to the blazing sun.

And to Adrienne's eyes.

Her camera lens fogged over. Still staring through her viewfinder, she blindly probed her bag for two things—a tissue for her forehead and a polishing cloth for her lens.

Meanwhile, her guide lay sprawled in his deck chair, sunglasses perched on the bridge of his straight, even nose. His arms were folded snugly across his chest, hands tucked into his armpits. His legs—dusted in a furry blond fuzz—were spread in idle relaxation. The hint of a smile curved his lips, as if he was dreaming about something immensely pleasurable.

Probably another beer, Adrienne thought with a loathsome sideways glance. Three crunched aluminum cans littered the deck of his sailboat.

Still, if her report on Ile de Fleur was positive, Foster would build his resort here. Then his well-heeled society matron clients back in Phoenix would gobble up this bronzed Adonis like so much beluga caviar. And who could blame them?

she thought, stuffing the tissue and lens polishing cloth back in her bag.

With the firm press of her forefinger, she tripped the shutter. Her camera whined as the film advanced to the next frame.

She lowered the camera, expecting the whine to nudge the slumbering hulk of a man from his nap. He didn't flinch a muscle. And he had plenty of them to flinch in all sorts of interesting places. A wicked little shiver shot over Adrienne's aching shoulders and down her arms. The hair on her arms stood up, and her parched throat tightened.

She blinked twice and looked again. In her fatigued state, she could be hallucinating.

No change. Slicked down in oil that glistened in the midday sun of the Coral Sea, Nick Helton smelled like coconut and looked like any woman's dream man.

If any woman could shake him from his sleep long enough to stir him to action, that is.

"Excuse me?" she said and waited for a sign of life.

He didn't move. He didn't speak. The only sounds Adrienne heard were the creaking of the rigging and the thudding of the hull, as the sailboat rocked against the dock.

She cleared her throat loudly and tried again. "Nick? Mr. Helton?"

Still nothing.

Adrienne resisted the urge to scream at him.

She didn't care if one look at his hard-muscled body shot a long-overdue load of hormones into her bloodstream. He could at least be civil—open his eyes and look at her.

Why hadn't he? Was he ignoring her? She had a growing suspicion he was. If she truly thought he was refusing to acknowledge her arrival, she'd throw a shoe at him.

Sea gulls hovering overhead mocked her with their plaintive cries. The September sun emerged from behind a cotton candy cloud. The rays bounced off the crystal clear water and shot shards of pain into her tired eyes. The glare nearly blinded Adrienne with its intensity. She shoved her sunglasses back over her eyes.

She had to rest her weary body soon. Get this Nick person to ferry her over to her bungalow on the leeward side of the island. If she didn't, she was afraid she'd pass out, right there on the dock, assignment or no assignment.

Her patience snapped. She'd been in and out of airplanes for almost twenty-four hours. She'd lost her grip on what time it was where. She knew she had left Phoenix yesterday afternoon, on the first of September. She'd flown to Los Angeles, then on to Sydney and Brisbane. Her final flight took her eight hundred miles east to Nouméa, the cosmopolitan capital of New Caledonia on the big island, Grand Terre.

Foster had given her the option of chartering a flight to Ile de Fleur from Nouméa. To facilitate the development of tourism, the French government had built an airstrip in the center of the island. But if she'd flown in, she would have had to hike halfway across the island to her accommodations. Drastically short in the stamina department, she'd opted for sea over air.

Mistake. The thirty-five-mile ride southeast of Grand Terre over choppy seas had bounced her until her head throbbed and her breasts were tender. And she couldn't seem to get her guide's attention for the life of her.

She wanted to peel off her crumpled cotton dress and soak her sticky body in a long, leisurely bath. Afterward, she would curl up beneath an umbrella on the beach with a good book. Next she planned a nap of her own, indoors on freshly laundered sheets.

A two-day nap maybe. Then she would get serious about her work. Begin cataloging the island's abundant species of flowers, for one thing. Even at a distance she could see splashes of hot pink and salmon in the lush tropical growth where the beach ended and the island climbed skyward to jagged mountain peaks.

She closed her eyes and drew in the drugging scent of sea and salt and rich organic growth. She would be living in a veritable greenhouse for six weeks. Unbidden, visions of her grandmother sprang to mind. Gracie cooing to her gardenias and singing to her hibiscus. Adrienne's chest tightened.

A shriek from the junglelike growth echoed over the water, setting off a chorus of birdlike sounds. Adrienne welcomed the intrusion on her melancholy thoughts and forced herself to focus on the sheer beauty of the island.

Foster was right. Ile de Fleur was a paradise. She would take full advantage of it. When she had her strength back, she would fish for her own dinner, dive for oysters, and taste the native foods. Foster had assured her the exotic locale would take the kinks out of her shoulders and the frown off her face. If she was lucky, after six weeks, she might stop jumping every time someone said boo.

Her private Shangri-la lay on the leeward side of the island, though, in a remote lagoon.

"Oh, ex-cuuuse me," she repeated, this time in a louder voice. She cleared her throat in pointed emphasis, wondering if her guide was a deep sleeper or plain old lazy.

Still no response. Not the flutter of an eyelash or the twitch of a toe.

She knelt to the wharf and, bending over, gave the rail of the gleaming white sailboat a hearty downward push. The craft rocked gently in the water.

The boat's lone occupant stretched languorously and glanced over his sunglasses. "Well, hello," he said. His sultry baritone voice echoed across the water. He rumpled his shoulder-length hair with an open palm. Yawning, he stretched that glorious body in a male show of sinew and muscles, then slowly hunched forward.

He propped his forearms on his knees and gave her a sizzling visual once-over. His gaze lingered at her breasts, then at her lips. She had thought she was too tired to feel anything. When her pulse cranked and sped like a starting lawn mower, she knew she'd been wrong.

"You are Nick Helton, aren't you?"

He grinned up at her. There went the pulse again. "Depends on who's asking, darlin'."

"My name isn't darlin'," she responded testily. "It's Adrienne Laurel."

"From Phoenix," he confirmed. "I'd about decided you weren't coming."

"My flight to Nouméa was held up in Brisbane," she explained while she tried to pinpoint the origin of his accent. Mississippi? No. Alabama? Huh-uh. Dallas? Maybe. "Foster said there weren't any phones here on the island. I couldn't very well call to let you know I'd be late."

"No sweat." He dug in the red foam ice chest by his chair for another beer. "Gave me an excuse to kick back and enjoy a few winks."

He popped the top on the shiny aluminum can. Tossing his head back so his hair brushed the curve of his rock-solid shoulders, he took a long thirsty gulp.

Adrienne found herself transfixed by the bobbing of his Adam's apple and the thickness of his corded neck. He wiped his mouth with the back of his hand, then gestured with his can at the ice chest. "Want a beer?"

"No, thank you. What I'd like is a ride to my bungalow. You will take me, won't you?"

He rolled his tongue around his cheek and shook his head. "I wouldn't touch that line with my best fishing pole, darlin'."

Adrienne decided he just might be the rudest man she'd ever met. Unfortunately, he was the only English-speaking inhabitant of the island Foster had unearthed in his research. Word was he could be hired to do most anything — for a price. So Foster had sent what he called a healthy check to cover his services.

Lucky for Adrienne, she needed rest and an occasional guide, not male companionship. She'd call the guy only when she absolutely had to, like when she delved into the finer aspects of her report for Foster.

Mentally, she tried to conjure up that list tucked away in her tote bag. Her memory, once razor sharp, was still addled. The doctor had assured her time and rest would restore what she'd always considered a rare gift.

She did remember she needed to sail around the island, explore the interior. Sample the native delicacies if she could persuade the dark-skinned, curly-haired Melanesians to cook for her. Fish, snorkel, scuba dive. Return to Nouméa, the French-speaking capital of New Caledonia, for a couple of days. The Paris of the Pacific was supposed to be delightful with its multitude of boutiques, gourmet restaurants, and continental customs.

She'd have no choice but to call Nick for assistance. That is, if she could pry him from his deck chair long enough.

She glared down at him. "May I please come aboard?"

"I was wondering if you were going to stand there all day." He shoved his sunglasses atop his thick, wavy hair, revealing eyes that could rival the sky for the most vivid shade of blue.

Moving with the languid grace of warm molasses, he pushed out of the creaky chair to offer his hand. The muscles in his forearms and thighs bunched with the effort. He was tall; he was imposing. The thought of touching his hand had Adrienne's insides twitching.

Avoiding the skin-to-skin contact, she thrust her suitcase into his open hand. Hiking up her skirt a few inches, she carefully stepped down from the dock to the sailboat that rode low on the water.

Another mistake. Before her foot touched the deck, the boat shifted, widening the distance from the dock. Nick grabbed her forearm for support. Losing her balance, she fell against him, her hand landing smack dab in the middle of his bare, fuzzy chest. His skin was hot and oily slick beneath her fingers. His muscles were hard and flexed at her touch.

She snatched her hand away, wiping the coconut-scented oil on the skirt of her dress with a trembling hand. "Excuse me. I . . . I'm not normally so clumsy."

He grinned down at her, focusing on her lips. "Don't apologize on my account, darlin'."

Adrienne's head was spinning, and not from fatigue. She hadn't touched the bare chest of a man in more months than she cared to count. She expelled a grateful sigh. Thank goodness she wouldn't have to contend with this cocky and disturbingly virile man on a daily basis. If she did, she wasn't sure she could unwind long enough to tackle the job Foster had sent her to do.

Besides, she didn't need his kind of distraction while she put the pieces of her life back together.

"If you brought more'n a couple of bikinis and sunscreen, you overpacked," he commented, tilting his beer at her suitcase. "Life's pretty easy on Ile de Fleur."

"I don't wear bikinis."

His gaze moved a hot path down her body and up again. He shook his head and mumbled something under his breath.

She didn't have to hear the actual words to catch the blatantly sexual overtone of his comment. Bristling, she shot him a chilling look. The last thing she needed was a self-assured, aggressive male. Especially one who had already proved he could send her libido soaring with a simple glance or a touch.

16

She fussed with her tote bag, with her hair, with the belt that cinched the waist of her cotton dress.

"Your boss was right," he observed, leaning back against the railing and regarding her with amused eyes.

"About what?" she asked wearily. But she was fairly sure Nick was about to tell her whether she wanted to know or not.

"You're tight as a tick on a hound dog's back."

"This was a mistake," she grumbled and cast her gaze around for an alternate mode of transportation to the other side of the island.

She glanced across the aquamarine water to the gleaming white beach that bordered the island. There wasn't another soul in sight, not even a spare boat.

She had two choices. She could trudge several miles around the island in the sand, carting her own luggage until she found her bungalow. Or she could grit her teeth and deal with Nick.

She pulled another tissue from her pocket, this time to blot the perspiration from her forehead. "Can we please get going?"

"No way, darlin'."

"I don't believe this is happening to me." She slumped into the second deck chair and hung her head. She was tired. She was hungry. She was hot. The events, the overwhelming demands on her personal stamina and constitution of the past two years weighed heavily on her shoulders. If she had the energy to cry, she would.

The balmy ocean breeze washed over her. She closed her eyes and pressed them with her thumb and forefinger. "Why not?"

"Simple. Low tide."

"And?"

"If I sail into that lagoon in the next hour or so, the coral reef'll rip my boat to shreds."

"So how long do I have to wait before we set sail?" she asked wearily.

"I figure we could get away in oh, say, four, five hours."

She heaved an exasperated sigh. "And what do I do until then?"

"Kick back, have a beer, relax."

He reached into the cooler and grabbed an icy beer. The can seemed to shrink in the expanse of his grasp. He stood and, legs akimbo, planted himself directly in front of her.

Adrienne's breath caught. When she looked straight ahead, her gaze collided with *that* part of him. Forcing herself to breathe, she looked up. He was so tall, she had to crane her neck to focus on his eyes. Hands on hips, he gave a slow, easy grin.

Like a coiled spring, she shot to her feet. The deck chair tumbled over behind her. She felt foolish and awkward. Nick's grin widened. She contemplated pouring the beer over his ruggedly good-looking head.

Instead, she clenched her jaw. She was a lady. She would act like one. She tilted her chin with a defiant air, determined to gather up what was left of her dignity.

It was then she saw it — a drop of perspiration sliding down over Nick's Adam's apple. Transfixed, she watched it snake a leisurely path down his neck and over his chest. The droplet wove its way through the fuzzy mat of golden hair the wind ruffled like spun silk.

Besides the coconut of his suntan oil, she was acutely aware of his personal scent. Musky, clean, taunting.

She swallowed over a lump clogging her throat. "Maybe I will have that beer," she squeaked between suddenly parched lips.

Still studying her with amused eyes, he wiped the icy particles and condensation from the can with a smooth swipe across the seat of his sun-bleached cutoffs. "Here," he said and handed the Australian beer to her.

She took a quick gulp. The tangy bite of ice and beer squeezed past the lump in her throat.

"You listen to Nick," he told her while he effortlessly repositioned her chair with a snap of his hand. "Before you know it, you'll be laid-back, island-style."

From behind the privacy of his reflective sun shades, Nick studied Adrienne Laurel.

He didn't care if she was a knockout. He didn't trust her. He didn't want her here. Furthermore,

19

the lady was about to drive him nuts with her fidgeting.

He had been awake when she'd first tried to get his attention on the dock. Hell, he'd heard the rumble of Murphy's ferry engines five miles before he'd docked. Playing possum, though, had given Nick the time to take a good long look at the elegant brunette. Time to decide if she was the sneak who had pried his whereabouts from his lawyer's receptionist in Los Angeles.

He'd gotten perverse pleasure from watching Adrienne's irritation grow. Especially after she had snapped that picture of him before he could duck out of the camera's range.

She could take all the pictures she wanted, though. There would never be any prints. The closest film processor was on the main island. The mail arrived and left on Murphy's boat. If asked, Nick's old buddy would pitch Adrienne's film in the ocean for him. And wouldn't Adrienne be ticked off if she lost her film!

She'd throw a fit. The woman was a beauty, but she was strung as tight as a tennis racquet. Frowning, he thought back. Had he been that uptight four years ago?

Yeah, he guessed he had been. He didn't like being reminded, either.

Adrienne lifted her hair off her neck and, eyes closed, piled wads of chestnut waves on top of her head. Damn, what a pose! She might be trying to let the breeze cool her neck, but she was making things a whole lot steamier where he sat.

When he had squinted one eye open and taken that first curious look at her, he'd almost fallen out of his deck chair. Her boss's letter left out pertinent details, such as the woman's age and marital status. Foster Trent had only written that Adrienne Laurel would need Nick's services and a well-deserved rest.

For some reason, Nick took that to mean she was a whole lot older. He'd conjured up a vision of some biddy with a shrill, grating voice. Wearing flip-flops and one of those billowy Mother Hubbard tent things. Tourists loved to buy the shapeless garments in the Nouméa Tontouta Airport so they could dress like the native women.

One glance at the exotic-looking travel agent — if that's what she really was — and Nick knew he was in trouble. While she stood up there on the dock, scowling down at him, he'd gotten an eyeful from behind his reflective lenses. He'd watched the wind mold the softness of her pink dress to the generous curves of her body. To her long, willowy legs. After he had revealed the fact he wasn't asleep, he'd knocked back half a beer trying to cool his ardor.

She lifted her can to her lips, the inner surface of her upper arm brushing against the fullness of her breast. She took a dainty sip. Nick stifled a moan. Before he knew it, his free hand, propped idly on his thigh, twitched and curved around the

21

fullness of an imaginary breast. Not an imaginary breast. *Her* breast.

Long unsatisfied desire had him tightening his hand into a fist. Perspiration beaded on his upper lip. He glanced over the *Lorelei*'s railing. He could jump in. Go for a short swim. Let the cool water deal with the embarrassingly heightened nature of his neglected libido.

But to do that, he'd have to stand up. Then even a fool would be able to tell what effect she had on him. And he had a sneaking suspicion Adrienne Laurel was no fool.

*Don't let her get to you like this! The timing of her visit's too coincidental. The planned duration of her stay, too damned long.*

*Use your brain, buddy.*

Okay, so he would pump the lady for information. Maybe in her weary state she would slip and tell him something.

He crushed the can with his hand and tossed it onto the deck. He needed something to do with his hands, though. He reached for another beer and popped it open.

"So, what brings you here?" he asked with a forced casualness to his voice.

She stared down at her drink for a long moment before answering his question with one of her own. "Didn't Mr. Trent explain my visit when he arranged for your services?"

"Only in the briefest of terms, in his letters." He shrugged. "But hey, forget it. Bottom line—I was just making conversation, lady." He glared at the little snip. "I won't make the same mistake again."

She sighed deeply and cast her gaze across the water. A brisk breeze lifted her long, wavy hair until it fluttered behind her like a silken chestnut sail tinged with auburn.

She turned back to him. "My boss is thinking about building a resort here. He'd like me to look over the island. Write a report."

At least he had her talking. "Why here?"

"Foster has owned his travel agency a long time. His clientele is pretty affluent. High-level executives. Chairmen of boards. People with demanding jobs and social positions. To cope with the pressure-cooker lives they lead, they have to get away now and then."

"And they'd be willing to pay big bucks to fly to a no-place island like this?"

"Foster seems to think Ile de Fleur could be perfect for them. You'd be surprised how often some frazzled client calls and pleads with us to find him a remote spot in the South Pacific. Preferably with a pristine beach, clean air, no phones, and someone to wait on him hand and foot."

"We've got the beach. We've got the clean air. We don't have any phones." He thought about the trusting natives serving as maids and bus boys, being tipped a dollar here, a dollar there when the whole island should be theirs.

Damn the French government for opening up

the island to tourism! Especially when Nick was making so much progress with the natives. "The other he'd have to import."

"What about the natives? Wouldn't they want to work as maids or cooks or chauffeurs?"

"I suppose a few would be lured by the almighty dollar," he allowed, "but I'd hate to see it come to that."

"Why? Foster would pay them well."

"Yeah, well," he grumbled, "maybe there are other considerations besides money."

Adrienne removed her sunglasses and frowned at him. Her eyes were huge, brown, and doelike, with thick black lashes that curled at the ends. She looked innocent. Too innocent.

"What considerations?"

He'd said too much. He searched his mind for a quick, flippant answer and came up short. "The natives have lived on this island in peace for hundreds of years. I'd hate to see outsiders cram a new way of living down their throats."

"They lived in peace? You call cannibalism a peaceful way of living?"

"That was a long time ago."

"And it took outsiders—the French missionaries—to get the natives to change their ways."

"Yes, but I'm afraid tourists might not be as well-meaning as the missionaries were."

"Surely you don't think Foster would allow—"

"I think," he continued, grabbing at a thread of

believable opposition, "you don't get what I'm trying to say."

"Why don't you just come right out and say it then?" she asked with an impatient sigh.

"The natives don't intermarry. Their blood is pure. They're proud of that. Now do you get my drift?"

"Oh, that," Adrienne said and, looking away, dropped the subject, which suited Nick just fine.

She reached into her bag, pulled out her airline ticket, and fanned herself with it. A pink flush colored her cheeks. Nick wasn't sure if the high color on her olive skin was from the heat or from him irritating her. He hoped the latter.

He was so accustomed to seeing the dark-skinned Melanesians who occupied the island that he was almost transfixed by the color of Adrienne's skin. And the texture. It was smooth and unblemished and would probably turn golden brown within a week. By that time, her blood would thin. Then maybe she'd loosen up a bit. The thought of her loosening up had erotic fantasies whirling in his head.

"You didn't come here just to write your report, though, did you?" he pressed, trying to catch her off guard.

She paused for a moment, as if trying to decide how much to tell him.

Uh-oh, that pause meant something. He had a good idea what that might be.

"I need a rest," she answered lamely.

25

So her boss had said. Nick was still skeptical. "From what?"

She rolled her eyes. "Just because I'm not a high-level executive doesn't mean I don't get stressed out."

Ordinarily he wouldn't be so nosy, but he needed facts. The only way he'd get them was to push her for details. "What from? Family? Job? Money? Love life?"

"That's really my business, isn't it?" she snapped.

He'd done it now. She was going to clam up on him before he could determine if she was connected to Mitch or Morgan.

If the parole board lost its mind, Nick's old partners could be released from prison any day. Or maybe they had already experienced their first taste of freedom in four years.

Nick knew Mitch and Morgan. It would be just like them to send a beauty such as Adrienne to pinpoint his location. To keep him busy until they arrived to exact the revenge they'd promised. Thanks to the brunette who had pumped his attorney's receptionist, Nick's old partners must know he'd lived on remote Ile de Fleur the four years since the trial. They would be curious as hell about what Nick's angle was for sticking around the place so long. If they found out about his project before he had the loose ends tied up, they could destroy all he'd worked to accomplish.

Nick wouldn't take any chances. Travel agent,

spy, whatever Adrienne was, she wouldn't get close enough to him to make him forget what Mitch and Morgan were capable of. And if he did learn those jerks had sent Adrienne-Laurel-from-Phoenix to watch him, he'd take care of her in his own way.

His gaze snagged on the front of her dress. Her nipples were poking at the soft fabric. He had to hold his breath to keep from expelling it in a sigh of desire. This secluded island life was tough on a guy.

But not as tough as soured friendships, he reminded himself.

He wouldn't let Adrienne get to him. He would stake his biggest, pinkest pearl on his resolve. She might be beautiful. She might make his heart pound like an angry surf. But she wasn't worth losing what he'd worked four years to build.

And, what was more important, his self-respect.

The beer did nothing to cool the rising temperature in Adrienne's fatigued body. Neither did the indolent smile this Nick person kept casting her way.

How could he just sit there for hours, doing nothing? Listening to the waves lap against the hull of his sailboat, the sea gulls cry as they dipped into the surf for an early dinner? Why wasn't he doing something, like cleaning the deck, or replacing the boards in the pitiful wharf?

"I think I'll take a walk," she announced and stood to stretch.

"Suit yourself."

"How much longer?"

He squinted at the sun sliding at a snail's pace to the western horizon. "I figure a couple more hours."

"A couple more hours, huh?" She pinched her forehead between her thumb and forefinger, trying to think. If she couldn't sleep, she might as well get one task out of the way. "Where are the natives?"

Nick's grip tightened on his beer can, his fingers making indentations in the aluminum. "Why do you want to know?"

"I thought I might drop by their village and say hello, since I'm going to be living here awhile. They are friendly, aren't they?"

"If by friendly, you mean they won't shoot you in the back with a crossbow, then shrink your head, yeah, they're friendly."

Adrienne shot him an icy look. "I had in mind taking some pictures."

"Bad idea."

"Why do you say that?"

"They're spooky as hell about cameras. They think those things will capture their spirit."

Adrienne tapped a finger against her lips. "Some Indians back in the States believe that. Well, I wouldn't want to get off on the wrong

28

foot. I'll leave my camera here and just chat with them awhile."

"That's going to be hard, darlin', seeing as how you don't speak their language."

"You could interpret for me, couldn't you?"

He leaned back in his chair and made a great show of getting comfortable. "I could, if I had a mind to."

"But of course you wouldn't," she mumbled, wondering how she was going to deal with his laziness for the next six weeks.

"Not when we'd have to hike a couple hours that way to find them." He gestured with his beer can to the opposite end of the peaceful island. "They spend the daylight hours working their crops way up there over those mountain peaks."

Adrienne could hardly blame him for not wanting to scale mountains, however small, in the present heat. She was limp as a rag herself. "Well, perhaps some evening when it's cooler you could take me to their village."

"I wouldn't count on it, darlin'."

This *darlin'* business was grating on Adrienne. By the smug look on Nick's face, she was fairly sure he knew it. She wouldn't give him the satisfaction of letting him know he was getting to her. She drew on her last ounce of patience and politely asked, "I take it there's a good reason why not?"

"Yes, ma'am."

"Well, what is it?" she prodded, annoyed.

A smug grin again. "They're a reclusive tribe. They don't take to strangers well. Matter of fact, they hardly ever stray from their fields or villages, except to fish, and that's mostly at night. You won't hear a peep out of them the whole time you're here."

Later, as Adrienne meandered barefoot down the beach to kill some time, she replayed her conversation with Nick about the natives.

She examined not so much his words, but the sudden change in his demeanor when she mentioned she wanted to meet them. For a brief moment there, his cocky arrogance had vanished. His body had tensed, and his voice bore a skepticism unwarranted by her request.

What she couldn't figure out was why he should be surprised she wanted to meet the islanders. Anyone sizing up Ile de Fleur's tourism potential would want to know if they were friendly or hostile.

Perhaps Nick wasn't aware of Foster's prior work. Maybe he didn't know her boss had earned a sterling reputation for respecting island culture while developing in the Caribbean. That would explain Nick's less than welcoming greeting and his skepticism.

Well, he needn't worry. The last thing she would do is hurt the locals. He'd learn that soon.

She glanced back at the dock. The *Lorelei* was

rocking in the incoming tide. Nick was still sprawled in his deck chair, his hands folded across his chest, his magnificent legs spread in idle relaxation.

She angled a path across the powdery beach to shoot a picture of a giant red hibiscus in the undergrowth. She lifted the camera to her face and started to adjust the aperture opening for a close-up.

That's when she noticed an overgrown path leading from the beach into a dense fern forest. She took a few cautious steps along the path. The air was thick, the humidity overwhelming. Sunlight barely filtered through the triple canopy growth. She pushed aside a giant fern to encounter another and yet another. The long, slender leaves caught in her hair and brushed over her bare arms.

Her foot came down on what felt like a garden hose. It moved.

She gave a startled cry and backed into a wall of ferns. The branch slithered away.

Shuddering, she backed out the way she came in and welcomed the breeze off the ocean. She said a prayer for the warm sand beneath her feet. She whirled around and took in a deep breath.

Nick was standing at the rail, hands on hips, glaring at her. She got the distinct impression she had caught him about to come after her.

"Don't ever go in there again," he yelled across the water.

31

"Why not?" she yelled back, expecting a well-deserved lecture on the hazards of snakes, biting insects, and wild animals.

He didn't answer her. Not then anyway. He waited until she returned to the boat. The moment she had both feet firmly planted on the deck, he grabbed her arm and spun her around.

"Don't ever go anywhere on this island without me again," he said, his voice dripping with venom. "Because if you do, I'll have you on Murphy's ferry out of here so fast, your head will spin."

He let go of her so suddenly, she staggered backward and fell into the deck chair. She couldn't move. She couldn't breathe. She could only sit there, speechless, watching Nick prepare to set sail.

Her heart clamored in her chest while she tried to make sense of what had just happened.

And then it struck her. Nick hadn't been worried about her welfare when she ventured into the fern forest. He had been worried about her seeing something.

What? And if she saw it, she wondered with a sudden chill, what would that hulk of a man do to her?

# Chapter Two

With the gentle breeze fluttering the white silk of the sails, Adrienne watched Nick angle his sloop toward a shallow dip in the coral reef. As he sailed into the lagoon, she looked over the side. Gripping the arms of her chair, she held her breath. The coral was so close to the surface it would tear a gaping hole in the hull if Nick veered a few inches to the right.

They cleared the reef. She relaxed. Almost immediately the winds diminished to a gentle breeze laden with the exquisite scent of a mixed bouquet of fragrant flowers.

Nick hadn't said a word since they set sail. He'd stood at the wheel, the wind whipping his hair while he expertly maneuvered the *Lorelei* around outcroppings of coral.

Adrienne had stayed glued to her deck chair for the hour's sail, too stirred up to nod off to sleep. She had watched Nick's anger dissipate until all traces of the madman were only a memory.

But what a memory! What kind of a man

had Foster sentenced her to work with for six weeks?

Forcing herself to concentrate on her assignment, she pulled her notebook from her carry-on bag. She jotted down a few observations about the exquisite aqua color of the water and its clarity. She also noted the way the ocean had changed hues, as if the varying depths had tie-dyed the unspoiled water. Although Adrienne knew better, she would swear she could dip her hand into the water and touch the bottom of the lagoon. She could close her eyes and draw in the unpolluted air and forget about exhaust fumes and ozone alerts.

Outcroppings of white boulders marked the entry to the lagoon on either side. Past the reef, the water was deep enough to accommodate the boat's deep keel for some distance. In shape the lagoon reminded Adrienne of a huge octopus head.

Foster would have to do something about access to the lagoon, though. Build a road across the island from the windward side maybe. Only a seasoned sailor like Nick could maneuver through that reef. Foster couldn't risk having his clients wreck on the sharp coral.

A shadow crossed her notebook. She glanced up. Nick was leaning over, one hand on the wheel, one offering her some binoculars. "What am I supposed to do with these?" she asked dryly.

"I thought you might want to take a look around." His eyes had lost that hard, resentful edge. He offered a faint smile, which Adrienne gathered was his crude attempt at a peace offering. Miraculously, Adrienne found herself returning his smile.

Maybe she'd been wrong. Maybe Nick really had been worried about her welfare in that fern forest and not something he didn't want her to see. She shrugged, took the binoculars, and slipped the brown-and-white needlepointed strap over her head.

She focused her gaze on the western, leeward side of the remote island and lost herself in the unspoiled beauty. No craggy mountain peaks here. Palm trees and tropical undergrowth bordered a narrow strip of blinding-white beach. Beyond, the terrain rose into softly rolling hills. There native grasses rippled in waves of gold. Trees, pines she thought, resembling cocktail picks dotted the distant landscape.

By the time they had set sail, the Trade Winds had churned up the tide on the island's eastern shore. Here, in the exotic lagoon, though, the current was practically nonexistent. All along the beach seashells littered the sand like jewels waiting to be plucked and treasured.

Adrienne spotted bougainvillea and a giant hibiscus. She lowered the binoculars and bit her lip to fight back a choking wave of nostalgia.

If only her grandmother could be there to

35

share the abundance of flowers and unspoiled beauty.

Halfway into the lagoon, Nick cranked the anchor into the water and inclined his head to the left. "See that bungalow over there?"

What Adrienne saw was a large, round hut, the steeply pitched roof blanketed with palm fronds. A primitive-looking hut. Not what she'd call a bungalow. "Yes."

"The Ile de Fleur Hyatt, darlin'," he said, pride evident in his voice. "And over there, to the right—" he pointed to a separate stall-like structure on the beach, also covered with palm fronds "—your very own bathroom, complete with a mirror and a shower."

"As long as that hut has a bed, it'll do," she offered charitably.

"That *hut,* as you call it, is not as primitive as it looks," he responded dryly. "The French built it during World War II and used it as a sighting post. It was made to look like the local huts, but the walls are wood and sturdy. You've got luxuries the natives don't have. Electricity. Hot and cold running water. A refrigerator stocked with enough food for a couple of weeks. You want anything, give me a call on the short-wave."

Give him a call if she wanted anything? The irony had Adrienne shaking her head while Nick lowered the dinghy into the water. For two years she'd been at the call of her sweet, ailing grandmother. Then Gracie's heart had finally given out and she'd slipped off quietly in her sleep. So Adrienne had returned to work full time at the travel agency.

Two weeks later, one of Foster's best clients had phoned her in a panic. "You've got to help me get the hell out of here!" the insurance company executive had declared. Then he'd issued a string of demands to arrange an immediate getaway and tension-diffusing vacation.

Foster had found Adrienne staring at her computer monitor, the phone glued to her ear. She couldn't move. She couldn't talk. Tears had streamed down her cheeks.

Foster had gently removed the receiver from her hands and told his half-frantic, half-confused client he'd call him back.

Later Adrienne had learned how close she'd come to cracking under the two-year pressure of constant demands on her physical and emotional stamina. Of propping up her grandmother after she'd been demoralized in the health-care scam.

Here no one would expect anything of her, and Nick, bless his craggy soul, would be the one at the beck and call.

"Grandma," Adrienne murmured into the balmy air, "if only you could be here to see this."

"What did you say?" Nick asked.

"Nothing. I was just thinking about my

37

grandmother." Adrienne pressed her hand over the familiar heaviness in her chest. "I lost her a few months ago."

"That's tough." Nick gazed out over the water and appeared to think for a minute. When he spoke again, his voice was thick with emotion. "I know how much my grandmother means to me. I don't know what to say, except, I'm sorry."

Considering his earlier behavior, Nick's empathy was surprising, but welcome. Strangely, he helped her past the latest in a continuing series of melancholy moments. Maybe the guy had a couple of virtues hiding beneath his cocky facade and hulking body after all.

"Thanks. I appreciate that more than you know."

Nick climbed over the rail, down the ladder, and stepped into the dinghy with the litheness of a lion. Holding onto the ladder with one hand, he smiled up at her. "Watch your step, Adrienne. When you let go of the ladder, grab my hand to steady yourself."

Adrienne? Not darlin'? That was more like it. She handed Nick her suitcase and her tote bag, then negotiated the ladder without incident. When she grabbed Nick's hand, she wobbled a bit and laughed.

He squeezed her hand and smiled warmly.

Something in his brilliant blue eyes struck a chord. She had seen this man before. She was almost sure of it. But where? she wondered as he helped her to her seat.

Nick handed Adrienne up from the dinghy to the dock. Feeling like a first-class louse for shoving her into her deck chair, he followed her softly swaying hips to the bungalow.

Never mind that he was cursing himself out big time. He simply couldn't help picturing her hips in a bikini cut high at the legs and low everywhere else.

He tightened his grip on her hefty suitcase.

Forget the bikini. He could picture her hips cupped in his eager hands while he buried himself in her exquisite body.

*Close your eyes, stupid. What you can't see, you won't want to touch.*

"Too late for that," he grumbled.

"Hmm?" Adrienne queried over her shoulder.

He snapped his gaze to her face. "Nothing," he muttered. "I didn't say a thing."

"Whatever," she responded with a puzzled look, then shrugged and moved on, still swaying those damned sweet hips.

Maintaining his cool, unaffected demeanor was tougher than hell. One minute she'd move a certain way, and he'd have an overwhelming craving for her body. The next, she'd look so pitifully sad, he'd feel like cradling her in his arms and asking her to tell Nick everything.

What had finally done him in was when she'd

39

fought back tears of mourning for her grandmother. Even though he knew Adrienne's story could have been concocted to throw him off guard, he'd felt a tightening in his chest and immediate sympathy.

He'd never forgive himself if Gran got sick and died before he had a chance to see her again. She was the one he missed the most. Her faith and trust in him had never wavered through the trial.

But being half a world away was better than staying in Georgia and subjecting his family to continued harassment and humiliation.

He put those thoughts aside and followed Adrienne down a flight of creaky stairs to the best and only accommodations Ile de Fleur had to offer.

Set back from the reaches of high tide, the thatched hut stood sentry over the northern inner curve of the lagoon. Nick ducked his head and followed Adrienne through the bungalow's open doorway. He'd swept the wooden plank flooring the day before, but as they walked, the sand gritted beneath the woven mats.

Well, Miss Priss would get used to the ever-present sand soon enough.

He pitched her tote bag and leaden suitcase on the bare twin mattress and watched for her reaction to the place. To the fact he hadn't, wouldn't make the damn bed for a woman who could be a snitch.

He had to hand it to Adrienne. If she noticed the lack of maid service, she didn't let on. She merely wandered about the bungalow, touching each piece of furniture as if to make it hers. She paused to run her hand over the smooth native wood of the chest of drawers. With its curved back, it fit snug against the circular wall.

"What a lovely piece of furniture."

"I ordered it from Nouméa. It's local wood."

In the confines of the twenty-foot diameter bungalow, Adrienne's perfume was getting to Nick. The island was full of fragrant flowers, but this scent was different. Subtle and elegant, while at the same time damned alluring.

Needing to do something with his hands, he clicked on the bedside lamp. In the waning light of day, the bulb cast a soft glow on the nearby pillow. Nick wondered how Adrienne would look with her auburn hair spread out across the ticking. Her lids heavy and her lips parted, while she welcomed him between her legs.

"I see the generator's working."

"And how." He turned and pretended to adjust the bamboo shades over the window. "Call me if it goes on the fritz. I had it overhauled, but the darned thing's fifty years old and you can never tell. Same goes with the water pump."

"It's really quite lovely here, Nick. Thank you for all you've done to make me feel at home."

"Don't thank me," he tossed over his shoulder. "Thank your generous boss."

"What do you mean by *generous?*" She sank into the hand-woven wicker chair one of the island women had loaned Nick for the duration of Adrienne's stay.

"Six grand."

Her eyes widened. "Foster's paying you six thousand dollars to be my guide?"

"Hell, no. He's giving me three. The balance was to be spent fixing this place for you."

She slipped out of her shoes and crossed her narrow ankles over the pink and purple floral cushion on the wicker ottoman. "Actually, Foster can be quite generous."

"I'll just bet he can."

"What's that supposed to mean?" she demanded.

"Surely you can guess."

Suddenly red circles colored her cheeks. "You're way off base, buster. Foster is my boss and a close family friend. That's all."

"My name isn't buster."

"And mine isn't darlin'. And I am not, I repeat, I am not Foster Trent's mistress."

"Did I say you were?" Nick feared this travel agent business could be a cover. Adrienne might be that brunette who waltzed into his attorney's office and sweet-talked the receptionist into revealing his whereabouts.

All the while Nick had worked to modernize the bungalow, it had grated on him that he might be laboring for Mitch and Morgan's little sneak.

Still, the French were opening up Ile de Fleur and a slew of other islands in the South Pacific for foreign investment in tourism. If Adrienne and her boss were on the level, better Nick be included in their site inspection. This way he might be able to steer them away from the natives until he was ready for the world to know what he knew.

Adrienne leaned back and closed her eyes. "I can't keep my eyes open another minute. Thank you for your help. Now, if you'll kindly leave . . ."

Nick didn't. Not right away. He stuck around and watched the lady until her hands were limp at her sides, her breathing shallow and even.

He paused in the doorway to take one last look at his charge for the next six weeks. She shifted in the chair until her cheek rested on the unpadded arm. In the morning she'd have wicker tracks on her smooth skin and one hell of a crick in her neck.

"Ah, hell," he muttered and retraced his steps. He'd pushed her around and insulted her. The least he could do was put the damned sheets on the bed.

He moved her suitcases to the floor, then ripped open the package of mint green percale sheets he'd mail-ordered from Sears. He found

Adrienne staring at him with red, unfocused eyes.

"I thought I asked you to leave," she murmured.

"You did."

"Then why are you still here?"

"Momentary insanity, I guess." He slipped one corner of the fitted sheet over the mattress.

"What are you doing?"

"What does it look like?"

"Making the bed. Foster said maid service wasn't part of the deal. I can do that," she protested and rose from the chair to wedge herself between Nick and the bed.

She looked up at him with full, pouty lips and, despite her fatigue, determined eyes. He guessed he was supposed to acquiesce and step back.

He didn't budge. He just stood there, close enough to feel her warm breath on the underside of his chin. To see her tongue dart out and moisten her full, lower lip. To die for a taste of her creamy, smooth neck.

The skin on her cheeks was flushed. She smelled all womanly. It could all be an act to seduce him. If it was, it was working, damnit. She hadn't been on the island half an hour, and already he wanted her.

She uttered her words on a sigh. "Are you going to give them to me?"

"Am I going to—what?"

"The sheets. Are you going to give me the sheets?"

"The sheets. Oh." He glanced down at his hands and felt foolish. "No."

"I've changed more sheets than most mothers change diapers." She gave a little laugh that bore the edge of hysteria. "I can do it with my eyes closed."

What all could she do with her eyes closed? he wondered, but he kept that thought to himself lest she belt him. "Oh?"

"Just give them to me, Nick. It's getting late. You really should be going before the sun sets. I'd hate to think you might crash on that reef out there because you took the time to make my bed."

Well, what do you know? Now she was acting considerate. "You're beat. I can spare a couple minutes. Sit."

Her shoulders slumped, as if to confirm his observation. "I don't have it left in me to fight. I will sit then. Thank you very much."

"You're very welcome." He turned his back to her, determined not to let her overstimulate him again. "After this, you're on your own."

"You have no idea how good that sounds."

"It'll be just you and the sea gulls."

"As long as they can't call my name."

"So, you're a loner, huh?" he asked, tucking one end of the pillow under his chin so he could slip on the case.

"Not usually, but I could stand a week or two all by myself."

"You've got it, darlin'."

"Where do you live?"

"Back around the island. Fishing's better there."

She narrowed her gaze at him and tapped a long, tapered finger against her rosy lips. "I have the strangest feeling we've met before."

Uh-oh. "That's supposed to be a man's line," he returned with a nervous chuckle.

"No, I mean it. It's in your eyes."

"I have one of those faces. You know, the kind everybody thinks they've seen before."

"But I'm almost certain . . ." she rubbed her eyes and pressed her hands to the small of her back ". . . it's probably just my imagination. How long have you lived here?"

"Several years. Look," he said, wiping suddenly damp palms over the seat of his shorts, "I got to be going. Sundown's on the way. Dark time's fishing time." He backed out the door and gestured toward the beach. "Shower's over there. Radio me if you need anything."

And he got the hell out of there before she took one more look at his face.

Nick gunned the dinghy's outboard motor and tore over the lagoon's quiet water to the sanctuary of the *Lorelei*.

He wasted no time. He went below and

46

yanked open a drawer in the galley where he kept his navigational maps. There were other islands in the South Pacific where a man could live without anyone asking questions. Where no nosy travel agent might recognize him and tip off the media back in the States.

He'd almost forgotten the panicky feeling of being hounded every time he stepped outside. Of having a microphone shoved in his face. Of being spit on and sneered at. Of watching his own parents and grandmother become recluses because the media hounded them, too.

He couldn't let that happen again.

But he didn't want to leave Ile de Fleur, damnit.

He gazed out the porthole at the familiar skyline. No skyscrapers here. No smog. Just a little island bristling with tall, short-branched pines on one side and majestic mountains on the other. This was his home now. And he'd made too much progress on his project to quit now.

All those efforts would go down the drain, though, if the press found out N. McKenzie Holton owned a luxurious sailboat. That he wiled away his days at the end of a fishing pole. God, they'd have a field day persecuting him, not to mention his poor family.

He pulled open another drawer and found the bulging sock with a knot in it. He worked open the knot and emptied the contents into his hand.

Pearls. Huge pearls. Two dozen of them. The best he'd found. As smooth as a woman's breast. As pink as nipples. As translucent as perfect skin. He closed his fist over them and knew what he was going to do.

He was going to stay on Ile de Fleur. If Adrienne recognized him, he'd keep her quiet until the papers came through from his lawyer.

How?

For starters, he could break her shortwave radio.

Dumb thinking. She had probably prearranged to contact her boss periodically with an update on her report. If Trent didn't hear from her, he might panic and send in private investigators or fly down himself.

Anyway there were other ways she could communicate with the outside world. The island wasn't that big—six miles wide by seven long. She could walk around it and hop on the ferry that docked weekly with his provisions.

Then there was the airfield in the center of the island. Once in a while a doctor from Nouméa flew over to treat the natives. Adrienne would hear the droning of the plane's engines when it circled. Before the doctor left, she could find the airstrip if she was determined. She'd already demonstrated she wasn't afraid to explore.

Aside from the problem of her recognizing him and resurrecting one of the decade's most sensational scandals, the secrecy of his pearl project was at stake. It didn't matter whether Adrienne was Mitch and Morgan's spy or a travel agent. Either way, Nick couldn't afford to let her find out why he was working so closely with the islanders. Even if she was the travel agent she pretended to be, if she found out about his pearl project, she might tell Foster about it in a shortwave call or a letter. In days the word could spread. Fortune seekers could be on Ile de Fleur in a heartbeat.

Nick had to keep Adrienne away from the native village. There hundreds of bamboo holding cages for the oysters were stacked everywhere. In no time she'd figure out some of the natives knew enough English to converse a little. She'd ask about the cages. The unsophisticated islanders would tell her anything she wanted to know. They'd talk about their lessons in pearl culturing.

Nick and the chief had agreed the only safe thing to do was keep a distance between Adrienne and the natives. To that end, he wouldn't let her wander about by herself. He was to whistle when he took Adrienne on sightseeing hikes. If the natives heard him whistle, they'd make themselves scarce.

If Adrienne managed to learn about the pearls, and she was connected to his old partners, she could get the word to them. They'd figure out that N. McKenzie Holton, alias Nick

Helton, was involved in a project that could make them rich.

After what Nick had done to them, they would not only fly down and put out his lights, they'd rip off those natives big time.

So Nick was stuck watching Adrienne like a hawk for six weeks.

How the hell could he do that when she lived on the lagoon, and he anchored on the other side of the island near his hut?

*Simple, you fool. Build yourself a hut on the lagoon near hers.*

"But damn!" he grumbled and pounded the galley counter with his fist. How could he keep the inquisitive lady from insisting on seeing the islanders?

He'd have to find a way to keep her busy.

The litheness of her graceful limbs, the silkiness of her long, wavy hair, the soft curves of her breasts sprang to mind. And the jolt that shot through him when she had flattened her hand over his chest.

Maybe keeping her occupied might not be so terribly unpleasant.

He had called off tonight's training session with the natives. He would rest at anchor just outside the reef, beyond Adrienne's range of sight. He would focus his binoculars on her and watch her every move. Tomorrow at high tide he'd sail back in and announce he'd decided to build himself a hut there in the lagoon. If she asked why, he would tell her he wanted to be closer to her so he could ensure her safety.

If he was crafty, he might even get the uptight lady to help him build the hut. Maybe that would help satisfy her curiosity about the island culture without the risk of a personal encounter with the natives.

The construction process would occupy the whole of a week. Two, if they dawdled.

That left four more — four whole weeks to play keep away. How much time could a guy eat up playing tour guide?

Adrienne watched Nick streak across the lagoon to his sailboat as if he couldn't get away fast enough.

"What's with him?" she wondered out loud.

Not that she cared. Nick Helton had already shown her he was as volatile as a warehouse full of dynamite. She didn't want or need a man who manhandled and insulted her.

But he did light some fires, didn't he? she admitted reluctantly.

Yes, but so had Brandon. That sleazeball had tricked her into thinking he was madly in love with her.

He had been oh-so attentive until her grandmother had taken ill. Until Adrienne had told him she was moving Gracie into her apartment so she could care for her.

"Yeah, well, good riddance to bad garbage," she muttered, yet the pain still gnawed at her. Brandon had only wanted to marry her for the worldwide travel freebies accorded those in the business. A lazy, good-for-nothing bum, much like her father. She couldn't believe she'd fallen in love with such a parasitic low life.

"No more bums. No more bad memories," she lectured herself. She stripped off her wrinkled dress, grabbed a towel, and headed for a much-needed private shower before she became one with her pillow.

Nick propped his elbows on the railing. Binoculars in hand, he adjusted the lenses so he could watch Adrienne's movements.

If she was only pretending to be tired, she would start looking around any minute now.

Ah, there she was, leaving her bungalow, the little rat. If she ventured into the dense growth beyond the beach, he'd hightail it back and intercept her. If she was Mitch and Morgan's snoop, he'd take her someplace a heck of a lot less comfortable than that bungalow. And he damned sure wouldn't make her bed this time.

There was an old prison not far from the airstrip. The place was a hellhole where the French had shipped their incorrigibles a century ago. A couple of cells were still intact.

He could lock her up there, if he had to,

until his project was finished. He could make sure she radioed some bland message to her boss every now and then. Maybe even convince Trent she wanted to stick around after the six weeks was up because of Nick. People did amazing things when held at knifepoint.

He zoomed in on the beach next to her bungalow and almost tumbled into the gently rolling surf. Bare feet crossed the stretch of sand from the bungalow to the shower stall.

He moved his binoculars up long, bare legs and saw . . . nothing. Something went thud in his chest. He swallowed hard. It wasn't true he didn't see anything. The most beautiful breasts he'd ever laid eyes on—full, bare breasts, with large, rosy nipples—swayed as she strolled leisurely on the beach. What looked like a towel was draped over her arm, obscuring the womanly part of her.

He felt a quickening in his groin and realized he was holding his binoculars in a death grip.

*Take it easy, man. It's just flesh.*

God, what flesh! He hadn't seen breasts that lush in years, maybe never.

What the hell was she doing walking naked on the beach? The natives were offended by nudity. If they saw her, there would be trouble.

*You idiot, you told her the natives lived at the other end of the island. You all but promised her absolute privacy.*

*Which you're invading, you jerk. What kind*

53

*of man leers at an unsuspecting woman with binoculars?*

A man in a heck of a hard way.

Hands trembling, he lowered his binoculars and forced himself to breath in, out. His heart thundered in his chest like native drums.

He wouldn't look at her anymore. He wasn't that kind of man.

The hell he wasn't! Greedily, he jerked the binoculars back to his eyes and licked the perspiration beaded on the skin of his upper lip.

Damn! She was in the shower now. That's what he got for his momentary lapse into gentlemanly virtue. All but her head and lower legs were obscured by the thatched cubicle he'd erected for her privacy.

He watched while she tilted her face up to the water. Eyes closed, she smoothed her hands over her wet, glistening cheeks, over the dark hair that descended in a gleaming satin band down her back. Nick strained but could only glimpse the upper curves of her breasts. Damn!

If she'd only get up on her tiptoes, he'd be able to see—

Smack! A wave broadsided the boat. One of those rollers created miles and miles away by an underwater landslide or a minor earthquake. Gallons of saltwater washed over the rail, slickening the deck. Something slimy wrapped itself around Nick's bare ankle. An eel? Hell!

He kicked wildly, teetering in the ankle-deep

water. Arms airplaning, he reached with his free hand for the rail.

Another swamping wave, and Nick was a goner. The last he saw of his binoculars, they were flying through the air.

That was at approximately the same time the ocean flipped his heated body into the evening swells.



What a hedonistic feeling it was to stroll across the beach, letting the humid night air caress her bare skin.

Adrienne slipped between the crisp, new sheets and nestled her weary head into plump, down pillows. Foster's clients might demand to be waited on hand and foot by servants. This was enough for her—quiet, absolute privacy. No phone. Luxury almost more than she could bear.

The undulating roar of the ocean drifted through her window. Although the lagoon's waters were quiet, the surf flung itself at the distant coral reef with regularity. She closed her eyes and drew in the drugging scent of salty air, of time-weathered wood, of the verdant growth not far from her bungalow. Insects and birds, and what else Adrienne could only guess, struck up a symphony of soothing, junglelike night sounds.

She picked up her mystery novel and opened

it. When she had read no more than a page, the words blurred before her eyes. Her eyelids drifted shut. She was vaguely aware of the book slipping from her fingers. Of visions of Gracie and Foster drifting through her mind. Of a tall, imposing man with a broad, bronzed chest.

Nick?

The hair was the same. Blond, sunstreaked, only cut in a short, conservative style.

Mmm. She snuggled into her pillow. Such nice hair. Did it feel as silky as it looked?

She fell into a deep, troubled sleep. Eyes, stark blue, stared at her. Unsmiling, they drifted in and out of her troubled subconscious. Why couldn't she see the rest of the face?

She awoke, feeling drugged. The morning sun slanted through her window, warming her cheek. For a minute she lay there, eyes closed, waiting for Gracie's call.

She shouldn't have slept so late. By now she should be up, cooking breakfast. Running yesterday's sheets through the laundry. Lining up the day's medications. If she were organized, she could squeeze in a couple of hours' work on the computer Foster had installed in her apartment after Gracie fell ill.

*Gracie.* Adrienne's grandmother's name rolled around in her head like an errant pinball. No more medication for Gracie. No more sheets. No more breakfasts on bed trays. Gracie's . . . gone.

**No!**

Adrienne rolled away from the window, pressing a closed fist to the overwhelming ache in her chest.

If only her grandmother had gone to a doctor sooner. If only those unprincipled scoundrels and their health-care scam hadn't robbed Gracie of her dignity and every penny she'd ever saved.

A burning anger forced the pain from Adrienne's chest.

If she ever got her hands on any of those jerks, she'd make sure they never forgot what they had done to her grandmother.

Adrienne's doctor's words reverberated in her head. *Let it go, Adrienne.*

Flopping to her other side, she looked out the window and focused on the cloudless, blue sky. She breathed deeply, trying to release the long-held anger over the humiliation Gracie had suffered.

That's when she saw it—the salmon hibiscus floating in a small hand-thrown pot on her windowsill. How lovely!

She scrambled to the window and looked out. Whoever brought her the flower had disappeared. One of the natives maybe?

She didn't think so. Nick said they kept to themselves.

That left only one possibility. Nick himself. She smiled, remembering how he'd taken one look at her slumped in the wicker chair and put her sheets on the bed. Maybe she had misjudged this man. Maybe he was more sensitive than she had—

She sat bolt upright, the blood rushing to her cheeks. What had she been doing when Nick left the flower on her windowsill? Had he been hiding in the shadows somewhere while she strolled across the beach to the shower wearing . . . nothing?

She thought about that awkward moment when she had insisted she could put the sheets on the bed herself. She had trapped herself between Nick and the mattress. He'd stood there, searing her with his gaze, making her feel vulnerable. Undressed.

The thought of his eyes watching her, actually seeing *everything* robbed her of her breath. What if Nick had left the hibiscus as a subtle message that he had been there and seen her—all of her?

## Chapter Three

Adrienne dug in her suitcase for the white tube top and shorts she'd bought at the airport in Phoenix. She shimmied into them, then grabbed a notepad, her book, and a tumbler of iced tea.

Her report could wait a few days. For the first time in years, she was going to get a tan, and she was going to start this morning.

At low tide, the lagoon's beach offered her a wide crescent of choices. She chose a spot in the middle where she could gaze out into the wide, open sea and daydream.

The sand, as soft and white as talcum, was a velvet cushion beneath her reclining body. She closed her eyes and catalogued the sounds of the tropics.

The screech of a bird. A parrot, maybe? The rustle of leaves, the flap-flap of wings as the bird took flight. The gentle lapping of the crystal-clear water at her feet. The plaintive cries of curious sea gulls soaring overhead.

Knees bent, she dug her feet deeper into the sand and sifted the softness through her toes. "Heaven. I think I'm in heaven," she murmured on a sigh of contentment.

"Are you talking to me, darlin'?"

Adrienne scrambled to her feet, sand and book and notepad flying. "Nick!"

He stood before her, brushing the powderlike sand from his legs and chest with his open palm. "I swear, Adrienne. I'll be glad when you unwind. You act like a damned squirrel."

"Why did you sneak up on me like that?"

"I didn't sneak up on you."

"You could have warned me you were here."

"I didn't think I had to make a formal announcement. Besides, you looked so peaceful, I hated to disturb you."

"Like last night?"

Grinning sheepishly, he stroked his broad, square jaw. "What do you mean, 'Like last night?' "

Resuming her position on the beach, she opened her book and pretended to look for the page she'd last read. "The flower. I'm talking about the flower."

"What flower?"

"Nick, really! The hibiscus."

He scratched the back of his head. "What hibiscus?"

She peered over the rim of her sunglasses.

"Are you telling me you didn't leave that beautiful salmon hibiscus floating in a little pot on my windowsill?"

Nick's expression hardened. "That's exactly what I'm telling you."

What kind of game was he playing? "I suppose it was one of the natives then."

Nick's gaze swept the lagoon and lifted to the rolling hills beyond the dense tropical growth that bordered the beach. "If it was, I'd be very surprised."

"If you run into any of the natives while you're fishing, you will ask who it was, won't you, so I can say a proper thank-you?"

"I'll ask all right," Nick grumbled and stalked off in the direction of the dock.

"Nick?" she called after him.

He stopped and pivoted slowly in an act of protracted impatience. "Yeah, what do you want, Adrienne?"

The morning sun slanted across his body, highlighting the magnificent swells of his pectorals, casting a thin, vertical shadow in between. The V of fuzzy chest hair ruffled in the light breeze. His swimsuit was aquamarine in color, like the ocean, and skimmed his hips in a narrow strip of Spandex. Adrienne's throat tightened. It didn't take much imagination to picture him strolling across the beach nude.

She forced her attention to his face and

found him scowling. "Are you upset about something?"

"It's nothing. I . . . uh . . . just have a couple of things to see to."

"But what are you doing here this morning?"

"You forget. *I* live here."

"No, I mean, what are you doing over *here?* You said you tied up on the other side of the island."

"Oh, that." He propped his hands on his hips and studied the sand before answering her. "I decided maybe I'd better keep an eye on you. Your boss is paying me a good bit of money to be your guide. He wouldn't like it if something happened to you."

"But what could happen to me here?" she asked, spreading her arms wide.

He shrugged. "Ask the person who snuck up on you and left you that flower."


Nick made a trip to his boat, then returned. From the look on his face, Adrienne could tell he was preoccupied with something. He didn't say what. She didn't ask.

She truly tried to ignore his presence. Yet every time she lay back and closed her eyes, her attention was drawn to him.

For the past ten minutes he'd been walking in small circles in the sand some fifty yards to the south. He paused, crouched down and drew something in the sand with his forefinger. Frowning, he drew two lines across the bottom, then looked out to his sailboat.

Adrienne found herself wishing he'd get back in the *Lorelei* and leave. As long as he was walking around in that skimpy swimsuit, she'd never be able to drift off to sleep.

"Nick?" she called out.

He answered without looking her way. "Yeah, what do you want?"

"What are you doing?"

"What does it look like?"

"If I knew that, I wouldn't be asking."

"Okay, I'm planning."

Curiosity lured Adrienne from her resting spot. She tugged the fabric of her shorts down and walked over. She could see now that Nick had been computing something in the sand. But she couldn't make heads or tails of it. "What is it you're planning?"

He lifted his gaze slowly up the length of her legs, leaving goose bumps in his wake. "My hut."

Adrienne was painfully aware that her nipples were tightening into little buds. Nick had to be able to see them poking through the thin fabric of her tube top.

She swallowed hard and cursed her voice, which had suddenly become squeaky. "That's not necessary. I'll be fine by myself."

"After that flower business, I can't be sure. And I told you, I don't want you wandering around the island by yourself."

The thought of Nick being able to watch her every move, night and day, unnerved her. "I'm sure it's a lot of trouble to build a hut, and I'll be gone in six weeks. Then you won't need it anymore. Why don't you just anchor in the lagoon at night?"

"I couldn't be here quick enough if you needed me. Besides, if it's not you, it'll be somebody else. Since the French have decided the almighty tourist dollar is more important than maintaining the local culture, it won't be long before people descend on us here like vultures."

"That's a harsh analogy."

"Look, your boss may have good intentions, but if he builds here, he'll destroy the unspoiled beauty of this island."

"Ah, but you don't know Foster. He'd only build a modest resort, in size. It would be posh, of course. But he'd leave the rest of the island in its natural state. Besides, there would be advantages for you."

"Such as?"

She examined her fingernails. "You'd have someone to talk to besides yourself."

"I have all the company I need."

"I'm speaking of women, Nick. I happen to think they would adore you."

"When I get the urge for lady friends, I sail over to Grand Terre."

"But don't you see? If Foster built here, you wouldn't have to do that. You'd also have a place to buy a decent meal. That reminds me. Was the fishing good last night?"

Staring at his feet, Nick dug in the sand with his toes. When he glanced up, he looked like the cat that had swallowed the canary. "As a matter of fact it was."

"What did you catch?"

"Oh, a couple of . . ." he ran a palm over his mouth, a smile stealing over his face, ". . . a couple of good ones."

"Are you going to have them for lunch, or dinner?"

"Only if I'm extremely lucky," he mumbled, and turned his back to her.


During the heat of the day, Adrienne sought refuge inside her bungalow from the searing tropical sun. No sense getting sunburned immediately.

Meaning to take a short nap, she curled up on her bed with her book. Late in the afternoon, she awoke, feeling almost human again. The nap was the first good sleep she'd had since Gracie had been ordered to bed by her doctor.

Adrienne looked out the window and

sighed. There was Nick, meandering around the same spot where they had talked earlier. While she slept, he had hauled in lumber, thick wooden poles, his lawn chair, and ice chest.

He was really going to do it! He was going to build right there and destroy her privacy. Irritation eating at her, she yanked the bamboo curtains over the window and slipped into clean shorts and a halter top.

She would sit outside in the shade of her bungalow and read. She would ignore him.

But he whistled. The piercing notes cut across the cove and grated on Adrienne, prompting memories she wished she could forget. Memories of a man who swore he couldn't find a job. Memories of her father. When someone found him work, he got fired within a week. He lay around the house, whistling, while Adrienne's mother labored days in a smelly tire production plant, nights and weekends as a grocery checker. By the time Louisa Laurel had turned forty, she looked a haggard sixty.

Later Adrienne's father had stolen his daughter's dreams as he'd stolen her mother's. Whenever Adrienne heard someone whistle she thought about him and the toll he had exacted from her mother. Even though he had been her father, and she loved him, she wished he hadn't talked her mother into marrying him.

Him instead of his absent friend, Foster Trent.

She opened her book and tried to engross herself in the mystery, but she kept stealing glances around the bend of the lagoon. Curiosity had her wondering exactly what was involved in building a native hut. Admiration for the male physique had her studying Nick.

Before long she gave up all pretense of reading. The scenery was too enjoyable to ignore. She was mesmerized by the bunching of muscles in Nick's arms, on his back, up his long, hard thighs.

He reached for a plastic container and drank from it greedily. Afterward, he splashed some of the liquid over his chest. Turning toward Adrienne, he smoothed his hand over his pectorals and grinned at her.

She ducked her head, pretending she hadn't been watching him. But she continued her vigil behind the privacy of her sunglasses.

Legs braced apart on the beach, he grasped one of the long poles in his hands and hefted it into the air vertically. He slammed one end into the sand with a dull thud. Next he positioned a square piece of wood across the top of the pole, adjusting the block a speck this way, then that.

Apparently satisfied with the results, he meandered back to his building materials and sank into his deck chair, whistling. Adrienne checked her watch. He'd been working five whole minutes, and already he was taking a break!

She watched him pull a beer from his ice chest. He popped the top and lifted the can to her in a toast, then drank deeply. Still pretending she wasn't watching, Adrienne turned a page in her book and checked her watch again.

Thirty minutes later Nick pushed out of his chair and made a big show of stretching the kinks out of his shoulders. Then he dug around in what looked like a canvass duffle bag for something. Finally he produced a sledgehammer.

Dragging the hefty tool behind him in the sand, he meandered a circular path around the positioned pole. He crouched down, stroking his chin with one hand. At last, he stood. Adrienne watched while he swung the sledgehammer in a wide arc and dealt a fierce blow to the block of wood.

A sharp thwack echoed across the water. The pole sank a few inches into the sand.

He slung the tool to one side and stood there, hands on hips, looking at the pole for a full minute. The pole was crooked. Adrienne could tell that. She ruffled the pages of her book with her thumb and resisted the urge to offer her help.

Three more minutes passed before Nick finally picked up the sledgehammer and dealt the pole another blow. Whack! Another blow. Whack! Another. By the time he had finishing setting the pole in the sand, Adrienne felt like screaming.

And then he took another break.

By sunset Nick had driven five poles into the sand in a slight curve. Only five. At least fifty more lay strewn about the beach. Adrienne guessed the poles would serve as a circular, outer frame for his hut. At five poles a day, he would take ten days to drive the hut's supports into the beach. Then who knew how long to construct the remainder of the dwelling?

She craved peace and quiet. She longed for privacy. On a sigh of disgust, she crammed a hat on her head and stalked across the beach.

"Well, hi, darlin'."

Adrienne gritted her teeth. "Hi."

"What can I do for you?"

"It's more like what I can do for you."

Grinning widely, he leaned forward, propping his elbows on his knees and lifting his gaze slowly up the length of her legs. "I'm all ears."

"Okay, here's the deal. I'll help you build your hut."

His grin faded. Adrienne wondered what he thought she was going to say and decided it was best she didn't know.

69

"I'm trying to get some rest," she explained in her most businesslike tone of voice. "I can't sleep. I can't even read for all your hammering. At the rate you're going, you won't finish for a couple of weeks." She lifted her chin. "I'm pretty good with my hands. I figure if I pitch in and help, we could finish in half the time."

"That's right friendly of you." He patted the beach beside him, his eyes dancing with mischief. "Sit down. Let's talk about how good you are with your hands."

"I have a better idea. Why don't I just show you?"

He leaned back and folded his hands over the taut muscles of his abdomen. "This is getting better by the minute."

"Oh, don't sit back, Nick. What I have in mind, we'll have to do together." Arm outstretched, palm up, she beckoned him with a crooked finger and the most seductive look she knew how to give.

He took her hand and practically leapt to his feet. Swallowing a grin, she led him to the meager beginnings of his hut. She pointed at the sledgehammer and spoke like a school teacher giving an assignment in simple terms that couldn't be misunderstood. "I'll steady the pole. You hammer."

"Huh-uh. I've worked all I'm going to for the day. Besides, *I* have a better idea."

She propped her fists on her hips. "What is it?" she asked irritably.

"This." He snagged an arm around her waist and pulled her flush against his sun-heated body. He took the palm of her hand and pressed it over the sweat-slickened curve of his pectoral. "I'll hold, darlin', and you stand there and feel the hammering in my chest."

She squirmed, but he easily resisted her efforts to break loose. "Nick," she said between clenched teeth, "let go of me."

"Huh-uh, darlin'."

The blood was pounding in her ears. "We . . . we have work to do," she sputtered, feeling weak in the knees.

"You, little lady," he said, bending to steal a quick kiss, "need to lighten up. Take life easier."

And he released her.

Adrienne stumbled back, pressing her fingers where he had imprinted her with the heat of his kiss. Fear skittered through her veins. Fear he would come after her. Fear he wouldn't.

He took a step toward her. She gulped in a lungful of air and dug her heels into the sand. He would not intimidate her by his sheer size.

She lifted her chin and leveled him with the most determined look she could manage, considering her bones had turned to mush. "Don't touch me like that again," she told him.

And then she whirled around and fled.

She had taken four broad steps across the beach when hands clamped over her bare shoulders. They were large hands, callused, with strong, massaging fingers. They kneaded at the tightness in Adrienne's neck.

The moment he touched her, she tensed, yet the pleasure was exquisitely unbearable. "I said, don't touch me."

"Huh-uh," he murmured in her ear. "You said, 'Don't touch me like that again.' I'm not touching you like that again. I'm helping you work the kinks out of your shoulders. Relax, darlin'. I'm not about to hurt you."

For some stupid reason she believed him. Maybe because she wanted to. She closed her eyes and gave in to the tingling sensations that swept over her body. Over her shoulders, her breasts. Beneath the thin cotton of her halter top, she felt her nipples hardening and the heat spiraling toward her abdomen.

She had to make him stop touching her. "Nick," she managed to murmur, "don't—"

"Shh." His soft-spoken command whispered across her shoulders and tickled her ears. "I'm going to make you feel good. That's all."

In her whole life only one man had massaged her neck—Foster, and never like this.

She'd never wanted to lean into the strength of his hands. To let her head loll back until his lips brushed her forehead and whispered sweet endearments. Now she wanted all this . . . from Nick.

His hands worked a leisurely path over her shoulders. With a final, gentle squeeze, he crossed his arms over her chest and drew her against him. Flesh met flesh. Flesh that was hot and moist from the day's heat, or was it from wanting?

Wanting? Adrienne's eyes flew open. Not *this* man.

Lifting his arms over her head, she ducked from his embrace and backed across the beach. "I . . . I'll see you tomorrow."

Nick smiled at her knowingly, letting his gaze drift for a moment to the front of her halter top. "You still want to help me put together my bungalow?"

She wanted a lot of things. At the moment, helping him build his hut was not one of them. But the sooner he finished, the sooner she could focus on what she was supposed to be doing on that island. She gulped and answered a meek, "Yes."

"Ten in the morning too soon?"

"Huh-uh." She hauled in a bracing breath of the humid air. Her head was still as light as a balloon and about as full of substance. She searched madly for something, anything to put their relationship back on an even keel.

Her report. Of course. "About that proposition, Nick?"

"Yes?"

"I only told you half of it."

He shot her a hot glance. "Well, I'm waiting."

"I'll help you build your hut. In exchange, you'll take me scuba diving as soon as we're through."

# Chapter Four

That night Nick scrubbed the deck of his sailboat and polished the porthole windows. He mended a tear in the seam of his mainsail, cleaned his fishing gear, and stared a hole in Adrienne's bungalow.

If she wanted him to take her scuba diving, she could go to hell. With his luck, on her first dive, she'd find a pearl-bearing oyster.

The next day she treated him with cool indifference while they worked to sink more poles for his hut's outer wall. She made no further mention of scuba diving during the week he managed to use to fritter away sinking the rest of the poles.

The morning after they completed the circular outer wall, Adrienne emerged from her bungalow while Nick was sharpening his machete on a flint stone.

"Good morning," she yelled across the water.

Nick glanced up and missed slicing off his thumb by the breadth of a hair. Adrienne wore an emerald green tank suit that clung to the generous curves of her body like a second skin. The front V of the suit dipped low enough to reveal well-toned, ample cleavage. Her legs, by now bronzed from exposure to the tropical sun, went on forever.

Nick swallowed over a brick in his throat and smiled thinly.

"Hi," she greeted him. "What's on the schedule for today?"

He snuck a glance down her cleavage and slipped the machete in its leather sheath. "Nothing you can do in that suit."

"What's the knife for?"

"Lots of things."

"Okay, let me put it another way," she said, rolling her eyes. "Why are you sharpening it today?"

"So it will cut bamboo."

"Ah, so that's what's next."

It was, but what he wished he could do was beg off. Working days on the hut and stealing away at night to work on his project with the natives was wearing on him.

He needed the day off for another, more important reason than sleeping. This morning Murphy was ferrying over the two experts in oyster harvesting that Nick had hired.

When Nick had contracted with the Australians, he'd promised to meet them on their arrival. Knowing he dare not leave Adrienne to snoop around the island in his absence, though, he'd made other arrangements last night.

He'd waited until Adrienne's light went off. Then he had sailed around the island and met with Koli, the tribal chief. Koli had promised to personally greet the Aussies for Nick and take them to his village. If there was any problem, the chief would have one of the young boys leave a purple orchid on Adrienne's windowsill. Koli also promised to discipline whoever it was who'd left Adrienne the hibiscus.

"I might cut bamboo," he told Adrienne. "I might not. It all depends."

"On what?"

He slanted her a sly grin. "On what better offer I get."

With a toss of her head, she laughed, her dark brown eyes dancing. Her hair cascaded to the middle of her back in silky waves. Nick thought of burying his face in the softness. Of grabbing great handfuls of it. Of capturing her full, glistening lips with the kiss that had burned in his gut since he'd massaged her satiny shoulders.

She turned to glance over the lagoon. "The water looks heavenly. I think I'd like to go for a swim."

"As long as you don't go out too far. There's a drop-off out there where I anchor my boat."

"Why don't you come with me, and we'll swim off your boat?"

Nick racked his brains for a plausible excuse. He hadn't planned on Adrienne coming aboard again so soon. This morning he'd left pictures spread about the cabin she absolutely couldn't see. Pictures he'd taken in Australia to help teach the natives the tricky task of nucleating the oysters so they would produce cultured pearls.

There was also the problem of his shipboard radio. If the wrong message came across while Adrienne was on board, he'd have a hell of a time explaining the call.

Besides, he needed to be closer to Adrienne's bungalow, in case a purple orchid showed up on her windowsill.

"Tell you what," he said. "I'm beat. Why don't you swim? I'll just lie here and watch."

"Well, okay," she said, her smile fading.

She draped her towel over the hut's frame, then strolled into the lagoon. Nick reclined on the beach and watched her progress. Her fingertips trailed in the water. The water lapped at her thighs. One step farther, and the thin fabric that covered the heart of her womanhood absorbed the lagoon's wetness.

Moaning, Nick closed his hands around handfuls of wet sand. Adrienne turned, smiling, and waved at him. Then, lifting her arms over her head, she arched into the air and cut the water with barely a splash.

With a quick kick, Adrienne propelled herself from the water onto the dock and scanned the beach for Nick.

He wasn't where she'd last seen him. He wasn't in the water. And there was his dinghy, still tied up.

"Now where did he get off to?"

In her peripheral vision she caught a movement. Over there, by her bungalow.

She leaned out over the water for a better look and spotted Nick standing by her window. She yelled to him and waved. He waved back and whipped his other hand behind his back. But not before Adrienne saw the exquisite purple orchid in his hand and a sheepish, got-caught expression on his dear face.

She hurried down the dock and threw her arms around his neck. "Oh, Nick, how sweet!"

He didn't move. He just stood there like a wooden soldier with muscles. "Uh, hi, Adrienne."

She reached behind his back and pulled his hand around. The orchid he'd brought her was the biggest, the most exquisite one she had ever seen. Her heart was running pitty pat circles in her chest. She pressed a hand over the fluttering and exhaled a grateful breath. "How did you know?"

"Know what?" he asked, wiping his palms on the seat of his faded cutoffs.

"About the orchids, and my grandmother. Foster told you, didn't he?"

Nick frowned. "I don't know what you're talking about."

"Then it's a coincidence." She took the delicate flower and turned it this way and that. Her eyes misted over. "I like that just as well."

"Look, Adrienne, I've got to be going. I've got to—"

"Oh, no, you don't." She grabbed his hand and dragged him into the bungalow. "First I'm going to put this gorgeous flower in water. Then I'm going to cook you a fabulous lunch."

She took the hand-thrown pot from her nightstand and moved to the sink to fill it with water. "I knew it was you."

"Excuse me?"

She slid the orchid onto the surface of the water and shot him a knowing glance. "I knew it was you all along who left me the hibiscus. Where did you find this?"

"Uh—here," he answered as if in a daze.

"Here?"

"I mean, out there." He pointed through the window at the dense jungle growth not ten feet from her bungalow.

She moved to the window, putting the pot carefully in the center of the windowsill. "Show me where."

"Uh, I can't, Adrienne. I . . . I've got to be going. I've got to get out to the boat. I've got to—"

"No, you don't!" She shoved him in the direction of her chair. "Sit down. Give me the chance to properly express my appreciation. It isn't every day a woman receives an orchid from a man."

Sinking into the chair, Nick heaved a huge sigh.

Adrienne dug around in her freezer for something exotic to cook. "You shouldn't act so embarrassed. Being tender and thoughtful and sensitive isn't a sign of weakness in a man, any more than it is in a woman. Will you stack some charcoal briquettes in the hibachi and light them? I've got a couple of pieces of mahimahi here that should be absolutely delicious. Where did I see that clove of garlic?"

"Adrienne?"

"Hmm?"

"I'm not hungry."

"Of course you are. It's lunchtime and—" she turned around and caught him sneaking out the door. She waved a spatula in his face. "You're staying."

"Adrienne—"

"Please, Nick? Surely whatever it is you have to do can wait an hour."

"Just an hour?"

"For Pete's sake, you'd think you had a

81

schedule to meet." She unwrapped the fish and grinned at him. "And we both know you wouldn't be caught dead doing that."

Nick choked down the last piece of his mahimahi.

Not that it wasn't good. Adrienne was a wonderful cook. She'd marinated the tender fish in garlic and teriyaki sauce and onions. But a whole hour had crept by since he'd found the orchid on her windowsill. He had to get the hell out of there and make that call to the chief.

What could have gone wrong?

Adrienne refilled his tea glass and whisked the plates off the nightstand they'd used for a table. Nick dabbed at his mouth with a paper napkin. He was almost out of his chair when she plunked a platter of mangos and papayas in front of him.

Damn. He forked a piece of fruit into his mouth and gulped it down.

From now on he'd have to keep his wits about him. If he hadn't had his eyes glued to Adrienne while she snorkeled in the lagoon, he would have spotted the boy who delivered the orchid. Then he could have made an excuse to hop in his dinghy and hurry out to the boat so he could radio the chief.

He rose from his chair and rubbed a hand

over his full belly. "That was delicious, Adrienne. Thanks a whole bunch."

With a smile and the flat of her hand she pushed him back into his chair. "Where do you think you're going?"

"I . . . uh . . . need to get out to the boat to check in with Murphy. He was going to drop off some . . . uh . . . food for you today."

"I still have plenty left in my freezer."

"Well, then, I'll tell him to take it back."

"Don't do that. I'll manage to find a place for everything." She turned back to her refrigerator, one of those nifty jobs with the freezer on the bottom Murphy had scrounged up for Nick in Nouméa. Bending at the waist, she shifted the packages around. "Besides, I don't want you to leave yet."

She was still wearing her swimsuit. When she bent over, the fabric crept up her hips, revealing a wide strip of skin that hadn't been exposed to the sun.

Lord, her hips were great. Full enough at the bottom to fill his hands and sleek as a porpoise where they tapered up to her waist. Earlier, while she lay facedown in the water, watching the tropical fish through her snorkel mask, he'd sat there and memorized every curve.

He was close enough now to reach over and touch her. To satisfy his curiosity. Was her skin as smooth as it looked?

Apparently satisfied she'd reorganized her freezer, Adrienne came to sit on the bed. Leaning back on her elbows, she tossed her head, flipping her hair back over her shoulders.

Nick swallowed hard. "I've really got to be going."

"I can't tell you how much the orchid means to me," she said and smiled so softly he felt like a heel.

"It was nothing," he told her, which was the absolute truth.

She angled her head and narrowed her gaze. "The Arizona Biltmore golf course in Phoenix?"

"What?"

"I thought maybe that's where I'd seen you. Foster has golf privileges there. Before my grandmother got sick, I used to take clients golfing there now and then."

Time to get the hell out of Dodge. "I've never been there," he replied and shot a frantic glance at the door.

Adrienne must have read his intentions. She reached over and squeezed his hand. And she didn't let go.

"How did you wind up way down here? Until Foster told me about this place, I'd never heard of it."

"Just lucky, I guess," he answered and forced a wan smile. But as long as he was stuck there for a few minutes, he decided he might as well ask a few questions of his own. Maybe Adrienne would trip up and say something to tell him once and for all who the hell she really was.

"What about you? What's the real reason you need a rest?" His glaze flicked to the bare ring finger on her left hand. "Divorce?"

She bit her lip, then glanced away. "No. I've never been married."

"What? A beautiful woman like you?"

She turned back, her eyes smiling and grateful. "Thank you. That's sweet of you to say."

He gave her hand a light squeeze. "I meant it, Adrienne."

Damned if that didn't wipe the smile right off her face. She looked like she was going to cry.

She probably needed to talk. He was the only candidate for listener. He'd already screwed up by not calling the chief right away. Might as well screw up good.

He might learn something in the process.

He pushed out of his chair and hitched a hip on the bed. "You want to talk, Adrienne? You know, feelings, that kind of thing. I'm a good listener."

She offered a weak smile. "That's really nice of you, but there isn't much to say."

He shrugged. "You don't have any women friends around to talk to. And heck, I

85

wouldn't tell anybody, not that there's anybody around here to tell."

Her eyes misted over. Her lower lip trembled. "It's just that the orchid you gave me reminds me of my grandmother."

"The one who died."

"Yes, her name was Grace Summers. Her friends called her Gracie."

"I take it you were close."

Biting her lip, she nodded. "I lived with her for six years after my mother and father were killed. They died two weeks after I graduated from college."

And he thought he'd been dealt a tough hand.

Plucking at a string on the bedspread, she smiled softly. "I don't know what I would have done without my grandmother."

Nick said nothing, only waited for her to continue. But for the first time he had the feeling Adrienne wasn't Mitch and Morgan's snoop. This was no act staged for his benefit. Adrienne was hurting. She needed to talk out her feelings.

By the angle of the sun slanting through her window, he gauged the time at close to three. He knew he should make some excuse and leave, but he couldn't run out on Adrienne now. Remembering how lonely he'd been when he'd arrived on the island, he sat there and listened.

"Grandma would have loved it here. Growing orchids was her hobby. She had her own greenhouse. Her orchids weren't nearly as big or as lovely as the one you gave me. But she won a few prizes in flower shows."

"How old was she when she died?"

"Eighty-five."

"Not young."

"The women on my mother's side live well into their nineties."

"How did she die?"

"How?" She gave a brittle laugh and sat up, board straight, on the bed. Her eyes, until now soft, warm brown, and melancholic, grew cold and resentful. "I'll tell you how. She was killed."

Good God! "Murdered?"

"No one pointed a gun at her and pulled the trigger, but she was killed."

"How?"

"The worst way possible. They killed her spirit."

"They?"

"Some dirty, no-good, scum-of-the-earth con artists who stole her life's savings and her pride. Living way out here in the middle of nowhere, you probably never heard about it. There was a big scandal a few years ago. It made all the newspapers back home. Hundreds of people, maybe thousands—older men and women mostly—got suckered into investing in a private health-care plan."

Nick's heart lurched to a screeching halt. He couldn't breathe. His palms grew cold and clammy. He let go of Adrienne's hand.

He couldn't bear it if her grandmother had been one of the ones.

The mahimahi soured in his stomach. If he didn't get out of there, fast, he knew he'd throw up on her bed.

"I'm . . . uh . . . sorry, Adrienne. But I really need to get going." He tried to stand, but Adrienne wasn't through yet. She took his hand and sat there, eyes focused vaguely forward, yet seeing only the past.

"There were three men from Atlanta who flew around the country, giving what they called retirement seminars. At these slick meetings, they played on retirees' fears. They said Medicare would be bankrupt before they knew it. All the money they had invested in the federal program was going to be paid out before they needed it. Their only hope for security was to invest in private health care. And wouldn't you know these three jerks just happened to have their own company. Before they got caught, they'd sold several million shares in their dummy corporation. Eternity Health Care. They took care of health, all right—the health of their own bank accounts!"

Adrienne laughed coarsely. "Two of those jerks had their due. They're rotting in a jail

88

somewhere. But one got off scot-free. Can you believe it? Scot-free! My grandmother lost everything. Her savings. Her house. Even the little greenhouse where she grew orchids."

Nick broke out in a cold sweat. "I'm not feeling so well. I . . . I think I'll be going now."

But Adrienne wouldn't stop.

"She got sick. Really sick. It was her heart. She didn't have insurance coverage. She didn't have the four hundred dollars the doctor wanted for a physical. She was too humiliated to ask me for the money, so she simply didn't go. By the time I found out how sick she was, it was too late. I moved her in with me and took care of her, but . . ." She shook her head, the tears spilling over her lids to course down her cheeks. "It was too late."

"How long did you take care of her?"

"Two years."

Two years out of Adrienne's life, and he was as much to blame for her sacrifice as anybody. He shouldn't have believed Mitch and Morgan. He should have asked more questions, gotten more answers. Damn! "No wonder you need a rest," he mumbled.

"I didn't mind helping Grandma. She'd done so much for me. And I couldn't stand to see them put her in that rundown nursing home."

"How did you support her and yourself those two years?"

She smiled softly. "Foster's a dear man. I found out after my folks died that he had been in love with my mother, but she married his friend instead." Her smile faded. "My father. Over the years he kept in touch. Helped my father get a job once and took me on part time at the travel agency when I was in high school. When Grandma got sick, I was working full time for him. In fact, he was about to move me to Tucson to head up his new satellite agency."

She gave a little shrug. "Of course, I couldn't take the job. I told Foster I'd have to quit so I could take care of Grandma. He said he couldn't let me quit. He needed me. He had a computer and phone line installed in my apartment, and he kept me on the payroll. The agreement was I would work as many hours as I could manage. I don't think he really needed me. I think he just kept me on so Grandma's bills would be covered under his group health insurance. Now you can see why I got all bent out of shape when you implied I was his mistress. Foster's like a second father to me."

"I apologize for jumping to conclusions."

"Well, you've made up for it, I guess."

"So," he continued, to get the conversation back on track, "you went back to work for Foster after your grandmother died?"

She nodded. "I wasn't worth much, though. Foster found me staring at a screen one day. I was totally spaced out. He decided I needed a vacation."

"So he sent you here." That explained the duration of Adrienne's stay. She didn't need six weeks to write her report but to rest up and recover from her grandmother's death.

Adrienne's eyes were red. Tears clung to her eyelids. Nick felt lower than a snake's belly in a wagon rut.

"Now you see why I've got to do my best for Foster. I've got to explore this island and meet the natives and taste the food. I've got to sail and scuba dive—all of it. You've got to help me, Nick."

He would. All he could. He took her head in his hands and gently thumbed away the tears. "I'll do my best, Adrienne."

"I know you will." She turned her lips into his hand and kissed his palm. The gesture almost broke Nick's undeserving heart. "You're as sweet as Foster. He did well when he chose you to be my guide. I wish Grandma could have met you before she died."

If Nick had felt any lower, he would have crawled through a board in the floor and buried himself in the sand. He had to get out of there. Find time to sort out his thoughts. Decide what he was going to tell Adrienne. Think!

He kissed her forehead, telling himself he had no right to take her in his arms. But she didn't know that. She leaned into his chest and sighed. He wrapped his arms around her and stroked her long, dark hair with all the tenderness he had ever known.

"You're a tough cookie," he told her. "A lot of people wouldn't have held up under the strain." Look at him. When he couldn't bear the unrelenting phone calls, the jeers, the ugly looks, the *shame,* he'd fled the country.

She propped her chin on his chest and glanced up. "I only did what had to be done."

"Still . . ."

Hands on his chest, she pulled back and stared across the room, as if transfixed on some future point in time. "I learned a lesson from all this, though, besides watch who you trust and what you do with your money."

Nick flinched. "What lesson is that?"

Determination fired in her eyes. "To take care of myself so no one else will have to. I don't know how I'm going to do it. But I'm going to squirrel money away until I have a big, fat nest egg. I won't let anyone flim-flam me. I'll put my money in something safe, like certificates of deposit. If anybody tries to do to me what they did to my grandmother—" she sliced an imaginary knife across her neck "—they'll be dead meat."

"Fate has a way of dealing with people like that," he told her. How well he knew! "You'd best let it go."

"That's what my doctor says. Still, I swear, if I ever find that one jerk who's roaming around spending my grandmother's money, I'll scratch his eyes out!"

## Chapter Five

Feeling like the dregs of society, Nick took the dinghy out to the *Lorelei*.

In a way he wished he'd admitted to Adrienne that he'd been the loathsome partner she'd spoken of.

Four years ago his photo had accompanied front page news stories in every major daily in the States. It was only a matter of time before Adrienne figured out where she had seen his face.

She would never believe he'd been a victim, like her grandmother. Although he hadn't lost his life, there were times he wished he had. He'd lost everything else — his wife, his job, his career, and his self-respect.

Finally, though, he had figured out what he could do to redeem himself. To make up, in some small way, for not asking his partners the right questions. For not pursuing his nagging doubts about Eternity Health Care's financial dealings.

Nick couldn't do anything now to save Adrienne's grandmother. But he could damn well make sure no developers ripped off Ile de Fleur's inhabitants as those poor older folks had been ripped off in the States. He wouldn't let anything or anyone interfere with his project.

Not even Adrienne.

If a miracle occurred, and she didn't recognize him before she left, he would contact her someday. Tell her the truth about himself. He couldn't afford the luxury of such a confession now, though. Not until he'd secured the natives' legal rights to pearl farming on the island.

Someday, somehow he would find a way to make up for the pain he'd caused Adrienne. But one thing he couldn't do. He could never give her back her grandmother.

Right now he had other things to worry about. Ducking his head, he descended the stairs into the cabin and headed straight for the radio. He had to find out why the tribal chief had ordered the orchid left on Adrienne's windowsill as a distress signal.

The conversation with Koli was weirdly unsettling. The Aussies had arrived as planned. They were endearing themselves to the natives with opals for the women and high-alcohol content Australian beer for the men. Koli hadn't ordered anyone to leave the orchid at

Adrienne's bungalow. Furthermore, none of the natives had delivered the hibiscus earlier.

Who the hell was playing Romeo? Nick wondered, slamming down the handset. And then he chuckled. Of course. Murphy! The old seaman had a healthy appreciation for the ladies and a reputation for charming the tourists. Lately he'd been complaining about the lack of women in his life. Murphy had a sturdy dinghy. He could anchor his ferry offshore and dart in and out of the cove.

Nick radioed the ferry captain. Murph had just docked at Nouméa after an excursion to the neighboring resort of Ile de Pines.

"It's good to be hearing from you, son," Murphy chirped over the airwaves. "I suppose you're having yourself a time showing the lady around the island."

"I'm having a time, all right," Nick said, and frustration had his hand raking his hair. "You didn't by any chance pay her a visit this afternoon after you dropped off the Aussies, did you?"

"No, I didn't, which is not to say I haven't thought about it."

Damn! If Murphy wasn't the one, who was? "You haven't dropped off any other passengers in the past few days, have you? Or seen any strangers in the area?"

"No to both questions. Now tell me, son. Why would you be asking?"

"Some jerk's leaving flowers on the window-sill of Adrienne's bungalow when we aren't looking, and it isn't one of the locals."

"So it's *we* now, is it?" Murph's robust laughter crackled across the airwaves. "Not that I blame you. You're a young, healthy lad. And she's a fine-looking woman, that one."

"Murph, go soak your head. I'll talk to you later."

"Nicholas, hold on a minute. I have a letter for you. What would you want me to do with it?"

"A letter?" Nick had already received his mother's bi-weekly missive. "Who's it from?" he asked guardedly.

"Wait a minute. Here it 'tis. It's from . . . the people you've been corresponding with in Los Angeles, California. Lauderhill and Beacham."

Hot dog! Lauderhill & Beacham was the most prestigious law firm in Los Angeles. Lauderhill himself had represented Nick during the trial. Nick had hired him to wade through the legal mumbo jumbo for Ile de Fleur's natives. To execute the legal documents that would provide them with rights to pearl culturing in the island's waters. But Nick couldn't trust anybody, not even Murph, with the nature of his business with the law firm. "How soon can you get it to me, Murph?"

"I'll be dropping off the groceries you ordered the day after tomorrow. If that isn't soon enough, I could make a special trip."

Nick had two options. He could risk leaving Adrienne during the day so he could sail over to Nouméa to pick up the letter. Or he could wait the two days. "Two days will have to do," he said, slanting a look at Adrienne's bungalow. "I'm kinda tied up here at the moment."

"Oh, would you be?"

As Nick hung up the handset, he could still hear Murphy's merry laughter.

Nick prowled the deck of his sailboat, waiting for Adrienne's light to blink out so he could pull anchor and set sail for the native village.

He should have been the one to greet the two Aussies. To introduce them to the chief and the tribal elders. Nick didn't want anything to go wrong before the skilled Australians taught the natives to retrieve the huge South Seas oysters from the ocean floor.

But the Aussies weren't on his mind while the minutes crawled by, nor were the pearls.

Adrienne had his undivided attention. Leaning back in his deck chair, he trained his eyes on her open window. Was it a man or a woman who had left the flowers for her?

It damned well better not have been a man! At the thought of another guy gawking at Adrienne's lovely breasts, at her rosy nipples, her long, naked legs, a red-hot rage seized him. If he ever caught the guy, he'd bash his head in. Tell him to leave Adrienne the hell alone.

Adrienne moved to the window. Nick's chair fell forward onto all four legs with a dull thud. If he had his damned binoculars, he might be able to tell what she was wearing. If anything. As it was, he couldn't see a blamed thing. She was backlighted and appeared only as a silhouette.

For all he knew she could be returning his gaze. He started to light his lantern and swing it in a wide arc to signal hello. He thought better of it. He didn't want her to know he was watching her.

But watch her he did. He couldn't tear his eyes from her open window. Every time she flitted by, he tensed, and the muscles in his jaw flexed. Lord, now she was sitting on the bed, her back to him. She shook her head and fluffed her hair with her hands. She picked up something, a brush he thought. Yes, she was pulling it through her long, silken hair.

He counted the strokes. One. Two. Three. Perspiration beaded on his forehead. At twenty strokes he went below, filled a glass with water, and poured it over his head.

About midnight, the light in Adrienne's bungalow finally clicked off. Nick sat there on the deck for another thirty minutes. Finally satisfied she was asleep, he stole away in the moonlight, fighting to stay awake. If he didn't show up in the village to participate in the nocturnal welcome feast for the Australians, the islanders would be insulted.

Nick sailed back into the lagoon early the next morning, red-eyed and slightly hung over. The minute he caught sight of Adrienne, he cursed. She was pacing the dock like a caged cat. She probably had his day all mapped out.

Just what he needed! His stomach was queasy from too much beer and not enough food. Some merciless gremlin was pounding a drum in his head with jarring regularity. And he was as irritable as the flea-bitten hound dog he'd rescued from the Atlanta pound as a kid.

Last night he'd questioned the natives on his own. His conclusion: the chief had been right. Adrienne's admirer wasn't one of the tribal members. The only answer he could come up with to explain the flowers was that Adrienne had put them on her windowsill herself to drive him nuts. That didn't make sense, even in his fatigued state.

Worst of all, he'd spent a good bit of the night commiserating over his part in the death of Adrienne's grandmother. He needed time alone to sort it all out, to decide what to tell her and when.

And he desperately needed sleep.

Adrienne waved her hands high over her head, as if his gaze didn't lock on her the moment he sailed into the lagoon. Her bright, cheerful voice echoed over the water. "Hi, Nick! Good morning."

He winced. Was she yelling, or was it just him?

She was wearing white again—a halter top and too-short shorts. Her firm cheeks were barely covered. Miraculously, considering his weakened condition, Nick's libido dumped a load of hormones into his bloodstream. He lowered his sunglasses to get a better look.

The rays of the sun bounced off the lagoon and hit Adrienne's shorts. The white screamed at his eyes. He slammed his shades back over his eyes and groaned. And then he saw it. Her damned camera dangling from a strap around her neck.

He gunned his dinghy's motor, shut off the engine, and glided up to the dock. Smiling, Adrienne reached for the small boat.

Nick pitched her the line. "Thanks."

She took one look at him, and her face clouded over. "You look like hell."

He felt like it, too, which somehow satisfied him. He deserved to feel like hell, but he didn't need any editorial comments from her. What he needed was a whole lot of leaving alone. "Drop it, Adrienne."

"My, aren't we pleasant this morning."

He grabbed a towel and hauled himself up onto the dock. "It was a long night."

"Fishing good again?"

Not as good as last time! "Fishing? Yeah. Real good. Great. Best I've had all month."

"Did you catch any more big ones?"

Oh, Adrienne. Leave it alone. "Unfortunately, no."

"Well, I guess the little ones add up," she chirped as he ambled down the dock for the beach. "Did you bring me some?"

"No. I, uh, sold them."

"At night? You sold your fish at night? That's strange."

"Down here people don't keep nine-to-five schedules, thank God."

"Who did you sell them to?"

Boy, was she nosy! "Uh, the natives."

"Don't they catch enough on their own?"

"They're getting ready for a bougna."

"What's a bougna?"

She had the inquisitive mind of a five-year-old. Fortunately, she didn't have the body of one. "A bougna is a native feast. They take fruits and vegetables and pigs and fish and

102

wrap them in banana leaves. Then they bake them on hot stones covered with sand."

"You mean like a luau?"

"Something like that."

She scrambled after him, her tennis shoes padding softly on the weathered boards. "Oh, Nick! Can we go?"

"No."

He negotiated the three steps to the beach and found a shady stretch of unspoiled sand. Damned if Adrienne didn't follow him. He lay back on his towel, closed his eyes, and began his descent into blessed oblivion. "An hour. That's all I ask, Adrienne. One hour of sleep, and I'll do anything you want."

"I want to go to that feast."

How simple it would be if he just told her who he was and what the hell he was really doing on that island. Then he wouldn't have to play games and deceive her. "Well, you can't go."

"Why not?"

"Because . . . you're not one of them," he improvised, squinting up at her. "And it's sort of a . . . secret ceremony."

"Oh, darn! Foster would have loved that for my report."

"You're not working for *National Geographic,*" he groused and shaded his eyes with his arm. "You don't have to know everything that goes on around here, do you?"

That went over like a catch of dead fish. She plopped down beside him, pouting. At least she quit badgering him.

Or so he thought. Actually, she merely changed gears.

"What *else* did you do last night?" she asked. "Crawl in a bottle and drink your way out?"

"That," he said, "is none of your business."

"Well, excuuuse me, Mr. Helton."

She shot up from the beach and stalked toward her bungalow, her long, willowy legs practically marching. Hell, he hadn't meant to irritate her. He just needed sleep and time alone.

But she didn't deserve to be talked to so curtly. And where was she going now?

"Hey, Adrienne," he yelled after her.

She stopped, but she didn't turn around. "Yes?"

"Where are you going?"

She gestured to the thick undergrowth behind her bungalow. "In there, for a walk. I want to take pictures of the flowers."

*A walk? Uh-oh.* Nick sat up abruptly. A sharp pain pierced his skull. He winced. "By yourself?"

Over her shoulder she drilled him with a scathing look. "*You're* obviously in no condition to go."

"This isn't a city park. You can't walk

around by yourself. It isn't safe."

She shrugged one bare, silky shoulder. "I'm not afraid."

She was not going to take a step out of that lagoon without him. By the time Nick caught up with her, she was pondering how to penetrate the thick jungle wall. He leaned against the bungalow and, whistling, pretended to examine his fingernails. "Adrienne?"

She slanted him an irritated glance. "What?"

"If you're dead set on that walk, you'd better take my rifle."

"What do I need that for?"

Again, he improvised. "Wild pigs. And . . . snakes."

"Snakes?" She fingered the strap of her camera and swallowed visibly. "Are they poisonous?"

"Just the ones with the red bands around their heads and yellow spots on their sides."

Something in the brush rustled. Adrienne jumped back and blanched. It was all Nick could do to stifle a grin. "I'll go get my rifle," he told her and pretended he was heading for his dinghy.

"Uh, Nick?"

Feigning impatience, he turned around. "Yes, Adrienne. What is it now?"

"I'm not very good with guns." She tilted her head and gave him a smile that could inspire a man to fight heathen hordes. "I don't suppose I could talk you into going with me, could I?"

Aw, hell! "If you say please, darlin'."

She screwed up her nose. "Please, darlin'."

He chuckled in spite of himself. "In all those clothes you brought, do you have any jeans?"

"I sure do."

"Better change then. If you wear shorts, you'll scratch your pretty legs. As soon as you're ready, we'll leave."

Nick zipped out to his sailboat for the rifle. He'd been bamboozled, but he didn't care. He had the scent of Adrienne in his nostrils now. He couldn't sleep if he wanted to. He yanked on threadbare jeans and returned to the beach.

And waited. To pass the time, he checked the poles they'd sunk for his hut.

A few minutes later, he heard Adrienne calling his name. He turned, took one look at her and froze.

Holy Moses!

She had either spray painted her jeans on or had zipped into them with pliers. How she could walk in them was a mystery to the laws of physics.

A quickening in Nick's jeans played havoc with his attempts to stroll toward her nonchalantly.

"Nick?" she called out again.

He picked up his pace, his gaze glued to her denim-covered thighs. "Yeah, Adrienne?" His reply came out croaky, like a frog.

"If you're not careful, you'll—"

Whack!

"—run into that piece of coral."

Pain exploded in Nick's big toe. Grabbing his foot, he hopped around in the sand. It's just a toe, he told himself. But the damned toe was spurting blood like a stuck pig. Damn, it hurt!

He plunked down in the sand. He grabbed his foot and cradled it in his lap. Adrienne reached him there, concern clouding her face.

She knelt beside him on the beach. Her jeans strained across her thighs. Hell, what was wrong with him? If he hadn't been gawking at her, he wouldn't be sitting there spurting blood all over the sand.

"Oh, my!" she cried. "Look at your toe! Does it hurt?"

Hurt? Hell, yes, it hurt. And he'd be lucky if he hadn't broken a damned bone. Rocking back and forth so he could stand the throbbing pain, he answered through clenched teeth. "It's a bit . . . uncomfortable."

"That's a nasty cut. You need to see a doctor."

"There isn't one. Just get me a rag. If I can stop the bleeding, we'll go on that walk."

"We'll do no such thing." She leaned over and kissed him, a quick peck on his lips that penetrated the haze of pain. She patted his cheek. "A person has to build a fire under you to get you to move, but you are truly a sweet man. Last night you let me pour out my heart to you. Today we're going to stay right here so you can prop up that toe." She beamed. "And I'll take care of you."

He didn't deserve to be taken care of. What he deserved was the pain shooting up his leg. "It's only a toe, Adrienne. I don't need to be pampered."

"Let me be the judge of that. You forget I'm a pretty good nurse. Stay right here until I get back."

Why did everything she did remind him of the agony he'd caused her?

Adrienne took off for her bungalow at a dead run, denim hips and thighs and calves pumping. Nick moaned. Despite the pain, his neglected libido was soaring.

She returned with a first-aid kit and cleansed his wound with a disinfectant. While he clenched his teeth in pain, her long, slender fingers gently probed his throbbing toe. He imagined what magic her fingers could work stroking somewhere else. That somewhere else did some throbbing of its own.

She slipped her shoulder under his arm. "Here, let me help you up. Take it easy now."

She beamed up at him. "That's good."

Her breast pressed against his chest. To hell with his toe. He wanted to fall back in the sand and pull her with him.

Instead he hobbled to her bungalow, where she proceeded to fuss over him.

"Adrienne?"

"Hmmm?"

"I'm sorry I ruined your plans."

"Don't you worry. We'll go later."

She glanced into the thick, tropical growth bordering the beach. As if on cue, an eerie screech emanated from the growth and echoed across the lagoon.

Adrienne shuddered. "I wouldn't want to go in there without you. If I ran into a wild pig . . . and snakes . . ." She rubbed her hands up and down her arms. "They don't like the beach, do they?"

Adrienne dragged her chair and ottoman outside so Nick could sit in the shade with his foot propped up. For lunch she served him fresh fruit and shrimp salad sandwiches.

Until last night she hadn't realized her deeply held resentment had been draining her energy. Since Nick had helped her talk out her feelings, she felt like the old Adrienne. Taking care of him was her way of repaying him for his kindness.

She may have been feeling better, but Nick

was in a snit. Every time she tried to do something for him, he either snapped at her or sat there glowering.

Late in the afternoon, Nick's spirits seemed to improve, strangely at the same time he got the chills and his body temperature began to rise. When she questioned him about his condition, he explained that some coral could do nasty things to a body. He would just have to ride out the fever and discomfort.

Adrienne found an old bucket under the sink and filled it with water and ice cubes. Every ten minutes or so she dipped a folded washcloth in the cool liquid and placed it over Nick's feverish forehead.

"I'm sorry I've been such a grouch," he finally said, slipping his arm around her waist and pulling her close.

Nick's fingers grazed the bare skin of her midriff. Adrienne's pulse tripped. She tried not to show how much his touch had affected her. Still her voice betrayed her when she squeaked, "You haven't been feeling well. I understand."

He grinned up at her. "I have to admit I could get used to this royal treatment."

"You haven't had anybody pamper you for a long time, have you?"

"No, I haven't, darlin'." He hauled her onto his lap sideways. Adrienne's breath caught. "And it feels good." He angled his head and stole a quick, unprotested kiss. "Real good."

Adrienne frowned. Nick's lips were practically on fire. She pressed her palm against his cheek. Her patient's temperature was rising.

"You're not supposed to frown when I kiss you."

"But you feel hot."

The laughter rumbled up from his chest. "You noticed."

"No, I mean it." She moved her hand to his forehead. "You're running a fever."

"Yeah, darlin', and you're causing it as much as the coral."

Adrienne shifted on his lap, and something hard pressed against her thigh. Her throat tightened. Her heart did cartwheels and shot a spiraling arrow of heat to her lower abdomen. She felt the primal urge to press against the male hardness of Nick. She swallowed over the flash-hot reaction and moved to push off his lap.

"I'd, uh, better get that cold rag on your forehead."

"Huh-uh." He hooked both arms around her and captured her with a brilliant blue stare. "You've been taking care of me all day. Time for you to relax. You're going to stay right here."

"But I think you're getting sick."

"If so, it'll be one hell of an illness, darlin'."

"Nick!" She closed her eyes and laughed. She enjoyed this Nick—playful, joking, *tactile*.

Before her laughter faded, he claimed her lips. No shy man, this Nick. He bound himself to her in a bold, open-mouthed kiss that sent her pulse soaring.

Instinct had her hand on his chest, pushing him away, murmuring a faint protest into his hot, open mouth.

Desire had her relenting. She quit pushing him away, then relaxed and smoothed her hand over the hard muscles of his chest.

His chest was magnificent, as much to touch as to admire with her eyes. The moment she skimmed his hardened nipples with her fingertips, he groaned and deepened the kiss. His tongue found hers and prompted her to give and take pleasure in return.

Sitting up straighter on his lap, she looped both arms around his neck and nibbled at the lobe of his ear.

He gripped her waist in a possessive hold. "Ah, Adrienne." He murmured her name into her ear as if she was some exotic island goddess. The way he was touching her, she felt every bit the part. "I've thought about doing that ever since you got here." Standing, a bit wobbly, he scooped her into his arms and turned for the door to her bungalow.

"Nick—"

"Hush, darlin'. I won't do anything you

don't want me to do."

"But it's just that—"

He swallowed her words with a kiss, another hot, long, tongue-tangling kiss that left her weak and starved for more.

She wanted to shut out everything but the demands of her body.

She wanted to make up, in one day, for two years of deprivation.

She wanted to warn Nick about the bucket.

# Chapter Six

Adrienne lifted the bandage from Nick's knee and grimaced at the angry, red abrasion. "I sure hope I got all the sand out. Does it hurt?"

"Not enough to worry over," Nick grumbled and shifted in the deck chair.

"And your toe? Has the throbbing stopped?"

He shot her a go-to-hell look, then ducked behind the magazine she'd given him to pass the time. "My knee is fine. My toe is fine. Don't you have something to do?"

She felt along the firmness of his forearm, then pressed the back of her hand to his forehead. "Fever gone?"

He yanked down the magazine. "Adrienne, please quit treating me like I'm sick."

"I'm enjoying taking care of you," she admitted, which came as a surprise. She had gladly nursed her grandmother for two years.

After Gracie's death, though, Adrienne had been drained. If someone had asked her to plump another pillow or deliver another bedside meal, she would have fainted.

Of course, caring for Nick was a different form of labor. It gave her an excuse to satisfy the overwhelming urge to touch him.

"Besides," she said, smoothing the hair off his forehead, "it isn't every woman who can say a tall, good-looking guide fell for her."

"That does it!" He scowled at her, a flush of crimson creeping over his bronzed cheeks. "Leave me the hell alone."

"Nick, Nick," she cooed, clearly enjoying her advantage. "It isn't a sign of weakness to let someone take care of you when you're hurt."

"And that's another thing. I've lived here four years and haven't suffered so much as a hangnail. You arrive, and already I've busted a toe and banged up my knee. You're pretty, darlin', but you are super bad luck."

"Thank you. I think. Wait a minute. Did you say you've only lived here on the island four years?"

"Ah, yeah."

"Gee, I thought you'd been around here a lot longer, like ten or fifteen years." She handed him a fresh ice pack for his swollen toe. "What did you do before?"

"Before what?"

"Before you became a recluse."

"I'm not a recluse."

"Yeah, right."

"That's a woman for you. A man takes time off for himself, and she calls him a recluse."

"Four years is a little more than 'time off.' You're running away from something, Nick Helton, whether you want to admit it or not."

Adrienne got the impression if Nick could, he'd bolt out of his chair and run like hell. What was he hiding from? A wife? Bill collectors? It suddenly struck her she had almost gone to bed with a man she knew little about.

"You're quiet," he said, cutting into her thoughts.

"And you're complaining?"

"Yeah. I must be sick."

"I was just wondering."

"I know I may regret this, but what were you wondering about?"

"How old you are, for one thing."

"I'm thirty-five. What else?"

Not one to poke into a man's personal life, she swallowed her reluctance. "Have you ever been married?"

Nick's eyes turned as cold as the ice cubes on his toe. "Yes, I have." Lifting his stubborn chin, he glanced over the water, but not before Adrienne saw the hurt in his eyes. "Her name was Patrice."

Adrienne hated to invade his privacy, but

she had to know if he was still married. She was enjoying this man too much, the touch of his hands, his lips. "And?" she pressed him.

"I'm divorced. Is that what you're trying to find out?"

Only part of it. Knowing she was venturing into touchy territory, she lightly said, "I suppose she's back in the States."

"Yeah, she's back there, all right."

"Is that why you came here?"

"No."

"Did she remarry?"

"I haven't a clue." He tapped the arms of the chair with tightly coiled fists. "Look, the bottom line is, times got bad. She split. Now, if you'll do me the courtesy, I'd like to be alone."

Adrienne guessed she deserved his curt dismissal. She ducked inside her bungalow and drifted to her window. A gentle breeze fluttered her orchid's delicate leaves and scooted the blossom across the surface of the water.

Now she knew what was behind Nick's cocky arrogance and macho veneer. Hurt, at the hands of a woman. That explained why he'd given Adrienne the flowers anonymously. So he wouldn't have to risk rejection again.

" 'Times got bad,' " she murmured, and her imagination ran wild. "I wonder what that means."

* * *

Adrienne was hopping mad, but Nick insisted on sleeping nights on his sailboat while his wounds healed. No way was he letting any woman give up her bed for him just because his toe throbbed and his knee burned.

For three eternally long days, though, she met his dinghy in the morning, helped him down the dock, and doted on him all day. She refused to let him lift a finger. Every time she changed his bandage or abraded the cut on his knee, he thought about her grandmother. The more Adrienne nursed him, the more he felt like pond scum.

He did convince her they had to sail around the island to meet Murphy's launch for the groceries. On the way back to the lagoon, Nick left Adrienne at the wheel for a moment and hobbled down below. He tore into the envelope from his attorney, and his heart sank. Lauderhill told him he'd run into a snag legalizing the pearl farm.

So Nick would have to continue his damned charade and postpone telling Adrienne about his secret project.

On day four the cut on his toe had healed enough so he could wear some old, roomy hiking boots. His toe still throbbed, but his self-respect demanded he put a stop to Adrienne's caretaking.

He tied up his dinghy and, ignoring the

118

pain, strode down the dock to greet her. "Hi, darlin'."

She slid easily into his arms and grinned up at him. "It looks like my patient's off the disabled list."

And ready to pick up where he'd left off—with Adrienne, that is. For four days he'd endured the soft touch of her hands, the occasional brush of her legs while she ministered to his wounds. His friend south of his personal Mason-Dixon Line was in a state of ready alert. The mounting tension was almost more than he could bear.

Now here she was, cuddling up against him, soft, pliant, and smelling shower fresh. He considered scooping her into his arms and heading straight for her bed. But he wouldn't let himself. She might want him, too, but if she ever found out who she'd gone to bed with, she would feel like she'd been defiled.

"Change clothes," he told her. "Let's go on that hike you wanted."

She ran one finger down the curve of his chin. His resolve to keep his hands to himself slipped a notch. "I have a better idea," she said, in that understanding manner that had driven him nuts since he'd told her about Patrice.

"What is it?"

"I'd like to help you finish your hut, like I promised."

He kissed the tip of her finger, then looped his arm around her shoulder in a brotherly manner and headed down the dock. Trouble was, with Adrienne, nothing felt brotherly. "Forget your promise. I can finish the job myself."

"No way. You've been so sweet to me, and I—"

"I have not been sweet to you," he broke in. Why the hell did she have to think he was some benign god? "I've only been doing my job. Your boss paid me a lot to do what you asked. Remember?"

A flicker of hurt flashed in her eyes. Her smile faded. Damn, he couldn't win for losing.

"Then I'm asking you to show me how to finish the hut," she said, pride lifting her chin. "For my report."

"Right. Foster will definitely be interested."

"He would. His clients aren't the kind to sit around and do nothing. Mainly they need a break from their everyday pressures. They might like to do the island thing."

Nick thought back to his busy days with Eternity Health Care. "I can relate to that."

"Oh? How is that?"

Him and his big mouth! "I was in business back in the States," he replied.

"What kind of business?"

Oh, boy! How was he going to weasel out

120

of this topic? "The wrong sort," he told her. "And I'd rather not talk about it."

"Okay," she said and squeezed his hand reassuringly. "But if you ever do, I'm right here with a sympathetic ear."

He didn't want her sympathetic ear. He didn't want her compassion. When she found out who he was, she would regret every kindness she'd ever extended to him.

"So what we do first?" she asked.

"About what?"

"Nick, where is your mind? I'm talking about the hut."

"Oh, that. We need to cut bamboo. There's a thicket about an hour's walk from here. So we can kill two birds with one stone — cut bamboo and take that hike you wanted."

"Will you need your rifle?" she inquired innocently.

He felt like a creep. The only wildness the island's pigs showed these days was when the natives chased them in their pens to butcher them. There were a few snakes, but no poisonous ones. But to keep Adrienne from wandering around the island by herself, he'd keep up the charade. "Yeah, I'll just run back to my boat and get it."


Adrienne followed Nick as they wound through the lush fern forest.

The triple canopy growth reminded her of the area she'd ventured into on the windward side of the island. At times the vegetation was so thick, only the tops of the fern leaves reflected the sparse sunlight filtering through.

The smell of verdant growth was overpowering.

Adrienne dabbed at the perspiration that trickled between her breasts. She tried not to jump every time something in the underbrush moved or the screeching sound sliced the humid, jungle air.

Nick drew the menacing machete from the leather sheath he wore tied to his leg and hacked at vegetation that choked the path. Always he whistled. The sound grated on Adrienne's ears more than the eerie screeching.

She didn't think such a walk would top Foster's clients' list of ten favorite things to do. Still, she savored the freedom to study the tight, flexing muscles of Nick's tight bottom from her vantage point behind him.

She did work — some. She scribbled notes on a pad and shot pictures of everything. Nick's buttocks. His shoulders. The flowers. Their sweet nectar scented the air as if the entire island were a giant florist's display case.

They had been walking thirty minutes or so when Adrienne heard the loud snapping of a twig, the rustling of leaves. She froze. Her throat went dry. Who or what was in the bush? "Nick?"

"Yeah, I heard it."

She swallowed hard and scurried to stand close to him. "Could it be a wild pig?"

A bark sounded. Nick grinned. He pointed at a creature with gray plumes that darted across the forest floor as fast as a roadrunner.

"What was that?" she asked, letting out the breath she'd been holding in.

"A cagou."

"Well, that explains it," she said, waving her hand in annoyance.

"It's a rare, flightless bird. The French used to export them, but they became endangered, so the government prohibits it now."

Adrienne shook off the remnants of panic and made note of the cagou for her report. Wishing she had been able to take a picture of the fleet-footed bird, she followed Nick as he resumed his trek.

It wasn't long before she heard the sound of water rushing over what she presumed was a stream bed. Presently, the rush grew to a roar. A few more minutes, and Nick pulled Adrienne out of the forest onto a cliff. The sight of a waterfall coursing down one wall of a limestone grotto took Adrienne's breath away.

While she snapped pictures, Nick explained the pool at the base of the falls was connected to underground caverns. Once he'd taken a tank of oxygen and dived there. He'd been sucked through a tunnel and spit out into the ocean at a depth of one hundred feet.

They ducked back into the forest, which eventually yielded to the direct rays of the sun. Across a clearing stood a dense thicket of bamboo. The smooth, jointed stems shot upwards of fifty feet in the air.

Nick worked deftly with his machete. He cut culms an inch thick and explained that these would serve as the supports for his hut's steeply pitched roof. When he finished, he bundled the canes with two leather straps.

Adrienne followed him while he dragged the bamboo along a shorter path through the forest back to the beach.

Twice during the trek, the skin on the back of Adrienne's neck prickled. She whipped around but saw nothing. Only a brazen parrot with red plumage that stared at her with head cocked.

Back in the lagoon, Nick dumped the bamboo on the beach, pulled his T-shirt over his head, and bent to unlace his boots. Weary from the hike, Adrienne found a spot in the shade and watched Nick. His well-defined triceps were bulging. Sweat glistened on his chest like hot oil.

She couldn't shake the distinct impression

they weren't alone. She swept the beach with her gaze.

"What's wrong, darlin'?"

"Oh, it's probably just my imagination."

Nick stood and thumbed open his jeans, one brass button at a time, then pushed the tight denim over his hips.

Adrienne's mind went blank. She stopped breathing. She swallowed hard and tried not to stare at Nick's indecently narrow purple swimsuit.

He grinned down at her, his straight, even teeth gleaming in the sunlight. He took her hands and, pulling her from the sand, pressed her palms to his chest. His skin was hot and wet, his nipples hard and erect.

"Now will you tell me what's bothering you?" he said in a husky voice.

Oh, Lord! "Well," she squeaked, "while we were shacking—I mean hacking—our way through the forest, I got the feeling we were being followed."

He shot a furtive glance over her shoulder and scanned the dense wall of growth behind them. Apparently seeing nothing to explain her uneasy feeling, he curled one hand behind her neck and smiled at her. With his thumb he tilted her chin until his lips were a breath away from hers. "There were only two people back there, you and me. Just like now."

The ocean murmured in the distance. A

frigate bird's shriek pierced the air. The musky scent of Nick drugged Adrienne. She closed her eyes and sighed against his lips. Still, a slight tremor shook her shoulders. She snuggled close to his chest and willed the eerie feeling to bug off and leave her alone.

"Thanks for not making fun of me. I guess I'm still a bit jumpy."

He nibbled at the corners of her mouth. Adrienne's knees turned to rubber.

"I won't let anything happen to you, darlin'. Promise."

"You are so sweet to me," she murmured and pressed her lips to Nick's bare chest.

Nick drew back abruptly as if she'd singed him with her touch. She looked to his eyes for an explanation. In the crystalline blue she detected a strange emotion, considering what she'd just said. Misery. Yes, that was it. Whatever she had said had made him feel miserable.

"Get this straight, Adrienne. I am not being sweet to you. I'm doing a job." A muscle in his jaw clenched and he shook his head. "Ah, hell. Who's kidding who?" He crushed her to his chest. "You're more than a job to me, and you know it. The hell of it is, you deserve a lot of things. Good things. But you don't deserve me."

So, the misery had been a kind of self-loathing. Adrienne wanted to banish any mis-

126

placed guilt of Nick's once and for all. "Why don't you tell me why it is I don't deserve you?"

He hugged her so tight against his chest, she was afraid she couldn't breathe. He released her suddenly with such ferocious emotion, she stumbled back. Frightened by the intensity of his feelings, she nonetheless stood her ground. She lifted her chin resolutely and waited until his troubled gaze met her face.

"Darlin'," he said, his expression haunted, "don't you think it's eating me alive because I can't tell you?"

Adrienne wanted to assure Nick she would listen to what he said and not be judgmental. But before she had a chance to say anything, he wheeled around and plunged into the lagoon.

He swam all the way to the *Lorelei* in strong, angry strokes. What was eating him alive? What was so horrible he couldn't tell her about it?

Her skin tingled and her body ached for what he'd started between them. She stayed glued to her spot on the beach, waiting for his return.

When he didn't come back in an hour, she headed for her bungalow and stripped off her clothes. She was going to take the shower of her life.

She used up all the hot water and gallons

127

of cold. When she emerged, wrapped in her towel, Nick was waiting for her, scowling.

"Well, hi, stranger," she said, trying to effect a lightness in her voice.

He glared at her. "What do you have on under that towel?"

She lifted her chin. Her nipples tightened into hard buds under the scrutiny of his gaze. "Nothing."

"Damnit, Adrienne, you can't do that."

"I have on more than you did when you went for your swim."

"That's different."

"Because you're a man."

"Because you're a woman, and *women* are different. What if you were right? What if somebody *was* standing around, gawking at you. Maybe somebody Murphy dropped off without my knowing it." He lowered his voice to a husky rumble. "Somebody with binoculars maybe."

That would explain the uneasy feeling she'd had earlier. "I hadn't thought about that." She scanned the horizon but saw nothing.

"Then think about it. And tell me if you see anything strange."

Nick was as clinical as a statistician as, later that day, he showed Adrienne how to lash the end of each cane to the hut's circular frame.

Figuring two could play that game, she worked without smiling, snapping a picture of him each time he demonstrated a new step in the process.

The more he scowled, the more she studied him. She was sure she'd seen that face before. Where?

At nightfall, Nick packed up his tools and left for his boat, without so much as a good-bye. Adrienne felt like throwing her camera at him. Why couldn't he open up and confide in her instead of clamming up like a stubborn male?

The next morning, she heard him cursing on the beach. She also found a bird of paradise on her windowsill.

"Oh, Nick," she murmured, quickly slipping into her swimsuit. "You crazy fool. Couldn't you just say, 'I'm sorry'?"

Apparently not, for he was still scowling at her when she walked over to meet him.

He was sitting in front of the doorway to his unfinished hut, sans shirt, as usual. He was wearing his faded cutoffs, his long, muscular legs crossed. Adrienne refused to get breathless at the sight of his barely clothed body. That was her brain talking. Her pulse skimmed over her nerve endings and made a liar out of her.

With a Swiss Army knife, he was slicing off thin strips of bamboo to use for lashing.

"Good morning," she said, as if she were addressing a friend and not the man who made her body tingle. "Where do we start today?"

"With you on my shoulders."

Her pulse staggered. "I beg your pardon?"

"You remember how to tie this stuff?" he asked, thrusting a handful of lashing at her.

"Yes."

"Then turn around."

"But I—"

"Adrienne, if we're going to finish this thing by tomorrow, we can't stand around talking. Turn around."

She turned around, but not before she caught his gaze sweeping up her bare thighs. He grabbed her by the waist with his hands and said, "On the count of three, jump."

She jumped. He lifted. She landed astride his shoulders. He clamped his hands over the long muscles of her thighs. As his fingers touched her sensitive skin, she wobbled. She grabbed his head for support.

"For Pete's sake, hold still, Adrienne." Her breasts brushed the back of his head. "You're, uh, going to break my back."

"You could have spelled out what you were going to do a little more clearly."

"Well, I'm sorry."

"You'd better be."

"For that and for last night."

Smiling, she leaned forward and kissed his forehead. "I forgive you. And thank you for the flower."

He glanced up, frowning. "What flower?"

"When will you stop playing games with me? The bird of paradise you left me this morning."

His hands tightened on her thighs. "Adrienne, I didn't leave you a flower."

She heaved a sigh. "Still playing games."

"I mean it. I did not. Did N-O-T, not leave you a flower this morning."

"Then who did?"

"I have no idea. Maybe that explains the watched feeling you had yesterday on our way back. I'd like you to make sure you drop your window blinds when you undress. And maybe you'd better—"

"Wear more than a towel when I shower." She frowned into the thick, tropical growth. Was someone watching her, even then? Or watching *them?*

"I'll do some checking later," he offered. "But just to make sure you're safe, I'll move into my hut tonight so I can keep a closer eye on you."

"Then we'd better get to work," Adrienne said, glad she wouldn't be alone. "Tell me what I'm doing up here."

"For one thing, giving me an excuse to touch your incredible legs."

131

She boxed his head. "Get serious."

He chuckled. She welcomed the return of his light-hearted side. "See that pole in the middle of my hut? The one with the notches at the top?"

"Yes. You've been busy this morning, haven't you."

"Darlin', for once, I was up and at 'em before you lifted your pretty head off your pillow." He gave her thighs a light squeeze. Goose bumps popped out over her legs.

Lucky for the progress of the hut, Nick ignored his effect on her and issued his instructions. "You're going to take each one of those canes we secured to the sidewall yesterday, bend it toward the center pole, and lash it. When you're through, the roof should look like the top of an ice cream cone."

"And what are you going to do?"

He lifted his gaze and met hers. "I've got the fun part. I'm going to stand right here and enjoy myself."


Nick was trying—boy, was he trying—to keep the atmosphere light between him and Adrienne.

Which called for nothing short of a miracle. Her silky legs were draped over his shoulders. Every time she moved, her breasts jiggled against the back of his head. He

132

wanted to tell her, the hell with the hut, let's make love.

But he couldn't do that to Adrienne. He couldn't take any more liberties with her. Not until she knew who he was. Then and only then could she decide for herself if she wanted to scratch his eyes out—or give in to the heat building between them.

The following day they collected palm fronds and lashed them to the hut to ward off the rain and the sun. That night they celebrated the hut's completion by toasting each other with Chardonnay and draining the bottle. Later they grilled shrimp on the beach.

Reclining on the sand, Nick groaned. "I'm stuffed."

Adrienne lay beside him and uttered a soft, kittenlike sound. "Me, too."

Nick took her hand and squeezed it. "What do you want, Adrienne?"

"From what? Or should I say whom?"

"Life."

"That's a pretty general question."

"Okay, how about this? What are your goals, other than completing that report for Foster?"

"Goals? Let's see. You remember I told you about that satellite agency Foster wanted me to manage in Tucson?"

Nick nodded. Because of Foster and his

trusting nature, she hadn't been able to take that job.

"Part of the compensation package was profit sharing. Anyway, the manager Foster hired is getting married in August and moving to Idaho. Foster hasn't come right out and asked me, especially since I got spacy on him not long after I came back to work. But I'm pretty sure he's going to offer me the position again. I'd like to take it. I'd like to work hard. I'd like to get filthy rich."

"So money's motivating you," he remarked, unable to mask the disappointment in his voice.

"Sure. What's wrong with money?"

*Be careful. Don't say too much.* "It isn't the money so much." He scratched his head and chose his words carefully. "Let's just say I've seen more than one life corrupted by the pursuit of money."

"I've never had enough to corrupt me," she said with a half laugh. "Heck, all I want is security. A big, fat nest egg. For retirement mostly."

"How old are you, Adrienne?" he asked, amazed he didn't know that simple fact.

"Thirty-one."

He'd been thirty-one when he, Mitch, and Morgan had launched their health-care venture. Three college buddies bound by trust and ambition. If only Nick could take back

the three reckless years they had worked together.

"What's the matter? Thirty-one isn't good?"
Adrienne poked a teasing finger into his ribs
and flashed a brilliant smile. "Suddenly I'm
old and decrepit?"

. That smile could charm the socks off a
snake. It certainly lifted Nick's spirits. "What
you are is a very lovely—" he rolled to his
side and traced the curve of her chin with his
finger "—and very desirable woman. I like
you, Adrienne. I like you a lot. And I wish I
could make up for the two years you nearly
killed yourself taking care of your grandmother."

"Silly, it wasn't your fault. But how sweet
of you to think that way."

She lay there, smiling, her eyes all warm
with undeserved trust and admiration.

Nick tapped her chin. "Don't make me out
to be a prince, Adrienne. I've done a lot of
things in my life I'm not proud of. Someday,
I'll tell you about them."

She kissed him lightly on the lips. Her
thighs were brushing against his. He wanted
to roll her over and bury himself in her goodness.

"Why not tell me now?" she asked softly.

He almost did it. He nearly told her right
then and there who he was, and what he was
doing on the island. But he simply couldn't

make the confession, nor risk what Adrienne might do if she found out everything.

"It's getting late." He stood and offered her his hand. Pulling her up from the sand, he said, "What do you want to do tomorrow? Sunbathe? Swim? Sail?"

"No."

"Read?"

"Nope." She threw her arms around his waist, propped her chin on his chest and grinned up at him. "Guess again."

"I give up," he said, crossing his arms over her back. "Tell me."

"I think it's time," she replied on a sigh, "to go scuba diving."

# Chapter Seven

"Scuba diving?" Sirens screamed in Nick's ears.

Adrienne lay her cheek against his chest and gazed out over the water. "That reef's been calling to me ever since I got here."

"Well, we can't."

She looked up at him, frowning. "Why not?"

Okay, smart guy, think of an answer fast. The breeze off the ocean picked up. "It, uh, feels like it's going to rain."

Brilliant.

"Then we'll wait until it stops."

"I haven't checked out the equipment in a long time."

"I'll help you while it rains," she chirped, then eyed him suspiciously. "What's the matter? Afraid I'll show you up?"

"Diving in the ocean's a lot different than a training pool or a fresh water lake, Adrienne."

"Number one, we won't dive in the ocean. We'll stay in the lagoon. And number two, I'll have you know I'm experienced. I've dived off the Keys and Cozumel."

Nick swallowed hard and strode back and forth on the wet sand. The lagoon was where he'd found the pearls. In the oyster beds. Surely there were more waiting to be discovered. If Adrienne found one—hell! What was he going to do?

"I brought along an underwater camera."

Wonderful!

"Pictures of the tropical fish would make an exotic addition to my report." She paused. "Nick?"

"Yeah, Adrienne."

"You're pacing."

"So?"

"I've never seen you pace."

"There are a lot of things you've never seen me do."

"You act like someone asked you to baby-sit two-year-old triplets. You do like to scuba dive, don't you?"

"Well . . ."

"Great!" She gave him a resounding kiss on his cheek and backed across the beach toward her bungalow. "I'll meet you on the dock at seven, barring rain. And Nick?"

"Yeah, Adrienne."

"Get a good night's sleep."

\* \* \*

When Adrienne awoke the next morning, not a cloud marred the brilliant blue sky.

Humming, she slapped together peanut butter sandwiches and stuck them in a cooler. That, along with bananas and a Thermos of fresh water, would hold them while they were out on the boat.

If the dive went as planned, she'd cook oysters on the beach. She might even break open that bottle of champagne Foster had given her as a going-away present.

At seven, she grabbed her dive knife, her mesh bag, and underwater camera and hurried out to the dock.

And waited. Nick had apparently overslept. And just when she was beginning to think he wasn't such a lazy soul after all.

She jogged over to his hut and peeked in.

Lord, there he was. Sleeping on his stomach like a baby. A thin, white sheet barely covered his tightly muscled buttocks.

Adrienne lifted her hand to knock and stopped, enjoying the opportunity to observe Nick in an unguarded moment.

His sun-streaked blond hair was tousled in delightful disarray. One leg was hiked at a sharp angle. One arm dangled over the side of the bed. A thick book lay on the plank floor.

What books appealed to this outdoorsman, with his laid-back attitude? Men's action adventure? Spy thrillers? Westerns?

She tiptoed in and stooped to pick up the volume. *A Summary of the 1992 Tax Law,* by an expert in the field whose name she recognized.

Tax law? Who would have thought? Well, maybe that's what put Nick into such a sound sleep.

Glancing around his hut, she realized he'd worked late the night before. He'd already transferred a surprising number of items from his boat. The place looked homey, in a crude, masculine way.

He didn't have all the conveniences of her bungalow. His furnishings were few. For a bed, he'd stuck two mattresses from his sailboat side by side to accommodate his large frame. He'd brought in his ice chest, a wooden trunk, and a small, beat-up desk.

He'd stacked some personal belongings on his desk. More books. A walnut picture frame, containing—she tiptoed over—the likeness of a man and woman who looked to be in their fifties. The man was a dead ringer for Nick, except his generous head of hair was gray, not blond.

The likeness gnawed at her. Maybe it was Nick's father she'd seen before. There was something about the eyes and the mouth. Oh, well, someday it would come to her.

She turned around to give Nick a waking shake, but her eyes caught on an envelope jutting out from the stack of books. Feeling shamefully nosy, she angled her head to read the return address. "Lauderhill & Beacham, Attorneys-at-Law, Los Angeles, California."

California, huh? Maybe her mystery man truly was a beach boy from the land of surfers and sun worshippers.

Whoever he was, wherever he was from, it was time he woke up. "Nick?"

Nothing.

This reminded her of the day she arrived.

Venturing close to the bed, she cupped her hand over the curve of his shoulder and gave him a gentle shake. "Nick."

A muffled moan, more like the sound of an injured bull moose, answered her.

"It's Adrienne."

He flipped over. Grabbing the sheet in the nick of time, he squinted open bleary eyes and creased his face with a slow, easy smile. " 'Lo, darlin'."

"You," she said, stepping back a judicious step, "are late."

"For what?"

"Scuba diving. You promised to take me this morning."

"You said to get a good night's sleep."

"I said to meet me on the dock at seven."

"What time is it?"

"Seven-thirty."

He groaned and, flipping onto his other

side, slung an arm over his face. "Wake me at ten."

"I guess I could."

"Good girl."

"Or I could pour water over your head."

Nick looked up at Adrienne. In her hand was the glass of water he'd left by his bed the night before. A wicked, determined gleam shone in her eyes. By golly, she'd do it. Complaining about a lady slave driver, he tucked the sheet around his bare body and dragged himself from bed.

He could only delay the dive so long. And if Adrienne stood there any longer, mere inches away, Nick was afraid he'd haul her into bed with him and make love to her.

In retrospect, he decided he was a fool not to follow his manly urges. By noon she had hustled him out to the *Lorelei* and helped him check out his gear.

He killed an hour sailing in the open sea, another showing her how to fish for rock cod and dorado, then dropped anchor on the lagoon side of the reef. Adrienne was sitting on the starboard, grinning like an anxious child, about to launch herself into the water. Damned if he could do anything but keep her near the reef, away from the oyster beds.

Nick pulled on his rubber boots, his fins, and his gloves and hit the switch on his buoyancy compensator. "All set?"

She shot him the thumbs-up signal.

He mentally crossed his fingers. "Let's go then."

Over the next hour Adrienne fell in love.

With the lagoon, with the incomparably clear water, with the most exquisite array of tropical fish and brightly colored sponges she'd ever seen.

Nick swam beside her, making sure she didn't miss the unique creatures in neon colors that darted in and out of the bountiful castle of coral. There were elegant angelfish and orange clownfish banded in white that took shelter in anemone. The reef itself, with its deep purples and blues, contributed to the breathtaking kaleidoscope.

Nick and Adrienne concocted their own rating system, flashing one to five fingers every time they spotted a new kind of fish or other sea creature.

Nick was quite the comedian, making faces through his mask and performing clownlike antics with his magnificently toned body. And then he was beside her, taking her in his arms, dancing in the silence of the cool, deep water.

The thought of leaving all this, of leaving Nick, had Adrienne counting the precious few days she had left. In three weeks she would board Murphy's ferry. She wanted more.

143

She wanted to stay, to soak up the natural beauty, to swim, dive, sail. And she wanted more of Nick Helton.

After an hour, Nick pointed at his stomach and then at the boat. Suddenly ravenous, Adrienne nodded. She hadn't gathered those oysters for dinner yet. But they could go down again later.

Nick began his ascent. Reluctantly, Adrienne prepared to follow him.

She had her hand on the valve to her buoyancy compensator when something in her peripheral vision snagged her attention. The flash of metal. Something dark. Narrow. And long. Undulating in the water like a ribbon.

Her curiosity played with her. Every diver dreamed of finding treasures in the sea.

She wanted to check out the mysterious something. Yet, she thought, with a chill of apprehension, that brown ribbon fluttering from the virgin reef could be a treacherous eel.

She would always wonder if she didn't take a closer look.

Careful not to swim too near the sharp coral, she gathered up her courage and eased closer.

The brown wasn't an eel. She closed her eyes and uttered silent thanks. The object looked like a strap to something.

That old devil, curiosity, kicked in again. Where had the strap come from? Australia maybe? Could something possibly be attached to it?

She pulled her diver's knife from the sheath she wore at her ankle. The cutting was tricky, but she managed to free the wide strap of fabric from its mooring. When at last she pulled her find free, she felt a pull, a heaviness. A pair of binoculars drifted into view.

Binoculars? Putting some judicious distance between herself and the reef, she turned the binoculars over in her hands. She could be wrong, but darned if they didn't look like Nick's.

She hit the valve on her buoyancy compensator and began her ascent to the surface.

She could hardly wait to show Nick what she'd found.


Nick's red face and bellowing voice greeted Adrienne as she climbed the ladder up the side of his sailboat.

"Where in the hell have you been?" He practically yanked her arm off handing her over the side and onto the deck. "I got to the boat and turned around, and no Adrienne. I thought God, she's got herself cut up on the coral. Or worse, attacked by an eel. I was just getting ready to come after you."

"As a matter of fact, I thought I saw an eel." Grinning, Adrienne unstrapped her diving gear. "But it was this." She handed Nick her mesh bag.

Nick tossed the red sack onto a bench seat without so much as a glance. Veins popped out on his forehead. His eyes bored into her. "Nothing you found could justify what you did. The first rule on my boat is you don't dive alone. You can't follow the rules, you don't dive."

"I'll be a good girl next time," she promised, wishing he'd quit lecturing her and look at the contents of her bag. He would be so pleased.

"It isn't funny, Adrienne." He hauled her to his chest and gave her dripping body a fierce hug. "I was worried about you."

She took a moment to savor the feel of his arms, the concern in his voice. But she could hardly contain her enthusiasm. Still, she tried to look dutifully contrite. After all, she had taken a chance. "I won't do it again. Am I forgiven?"

"Well . . ."

"Good." She reached over, grabbed the bag, and thrust it into his hands. "Then look."

Still scowling, he glanced down. The binoculars were clearly visible through the red mesh of her bag. He took one look at them and lifted a sheepish gaze. "You, uh, found them, huh?"

"Then they are yours?"

He turned them over, and Adrienne saw his

146

initials engraved in the casing.

"Looks like they're mine, all right."

"The strap was hung up on the reef. I had to cut it. But I figured, what the heck? You could get another strap." She took the binoculars and looked through them. They were filled with saltwater, but the corrosion didn't look too bad. "Do you think you can recondition them?"

"Probably." He set the binoculars back on the bench seat and hooked an arm around her shoulders. "Why don't we eat and sail back?"

It wasn't that Adrienne was expecting a big thank-you. But Nick's lack of enthusiasm over the binoculars took the joy out of her find.

"I want to go down again," she told him. "I saw something else that interested me."

"But — "

"You don't have any pressing business, do you?"

"I guess not," he answered as if, for once, he wished he did.

"Good. Then we'll eat, lie around awhile, and go down once more before we go back."

After lunch Adrienne dug around in Nick's supply cabinet and found a can of lubricating oil. In no time at all, she had the binoculars disassembled, cleaned, and put back together again.

147

Nick cringed when, proud as punch, she lifted them to her eyes and scanned the shore of the lagoon.

"I can't believe our luck. These are as good as new. And to think they've been in the salt-water for—when did you say you lost them?"

"A couple of weeks ago," Nick answered evasively. "Do you want to go down again now?"

Still focusing on the shoreline, she fluttered her hand. "In a minute." Then she brought the binoculars down with a puzzled frown. "I remember when you lost them. It was the day I got here. No, the night." She slanted him a suspicious look.

Uh-oh. Pieces of the puzzle were falling into place in her quick mind. Nick reached for his diving gear. "We'd better hurry up and go down."

"You said," she continued, "that you lost them while you were fishing . . . on the other side of the island. If that's true, how did they wind up way over here?"

"The current?" he offered with an innocent shrug.

"No way."

And then it dawned on her. It hit her in the face like a big, fat fish. She lifted the binoculars to her eyes and refocused on the central portion of the beach. Here it comes, Nick thought. *I'm a dead duck.*

148

Sure enough, she yanked the binoculars down, her cheeks blazing. "I remember that night. You told me I had absolute privacy. I took a shower. I . . ." She nailed him with a venomous stare. "Did you drop anchor out here and spy on me that night through these things?"

Nick gave a nervous laugh. "Now why would I do that?"

"You did!"

"Adrienne, I didn't mean—"

"Well, we'll fix that, won't we?" She hauled off and sent his binoculars sailing.

The last Nick saw of his two-hundred-dollar binoculars, they were slipping below the surface. He groaned at the pop of escaping air bubbles.

If Nick thought the day's worst was over, he had another think coming.

Adrienne wouldn't speak to him. She went below and locked the cabin door behind her. While she was gone, he kept an eye on the lagoon's beach. This might be a good time to catch Adrienne's secret admirer leaving her another flower. He figured wrong.

When she emerged an hour later, her eyes were still blazing. She strapped on her diving gear and waited while he followed suit.

Once in the water, she swam behind him to

the entrance of the lagoon, her anger evident in her jerky movements. She took one look at the small craft the French had sunk during World War II and gestured so what? with her hands.

Nick tried to get her to explore the rusting wreckage, but instead she whirled around and took off for shallower water. She swam to the one place he'd hoped to avoid.

The damned oyster bed.

# Chapter Eight

Poised on the edge of the horizon, the sun blazed a crimson path across the ocean as Adrienne climbed out of the dinghy.

She didn't help Nick tie up. She didn't help him unload. She didn't give a fig if he starved to death.

She stalked down the deck without a backward glance and headed for the shower.

She hadn't spoken a word to Nick since the second dive. Every time she looked at him, she pictured him leering at her nude body through his binoculars and her blood boiled.

He had lied to her. He had deceived her. For two cents she would have dumped the oysters over his miserable head and left him to stew.

How dare he set her up to be ogled at! Her first night on the island had been the only time in her life she had risked walking outside without a stitch of clothes.

The humid island air, almost intoxicating in

its fragrance, had caressed her bare, beleaguered body like the hands of a lover. What a fool she'd been to buy Nick's story about her having complete privacy there on the lagoon!

When she emerged from the shower, Nick was lounging in her chair on the dock, his face bathed in the pink glow of sunset. Beside him lay her dive bag containing two dozen huge South Seas oysters she'd retrieved from the lagoon.

Anyone without a prevalent lazy streak would have already shucked half the oysters. But, oh, no. Not Nick. He'd left the work for her.

She marched over, picked up her bag and shot him a haughty glance. "How do you like them? Raw or cooked?"

He shrugged. "Cooked, I guess."

"Good." She sat cross-legged on the dock and picked up her dive knife. "We'll have them raw."

"Adrienne, I didn't mean to—"

"Do what? Invade my privacy?" She stuck the tip of a knife in the seam of the ragged, encrusted shell and tried to pry it open. The darned thing wouldn't budge. "Then exactly what did you intend to do while you were leering at me behind those binoculars? Count my freckles?"

"You don't have any freckles."

"And wouldn't you know!"

152

"I'll admit I was looking at you." His gaze drifted lazily to her breasts.

She felt like socking him, but she didn't. All she did was sit there, furious that her cheeks were burning and her nipples were forming into hard little knots.

"I swear, Adrienne, I didn't expect to see . . ."

She shot him a murderous look.

"Aw, hell, what's the use? You won't believe me anyway." He pushed out of the chair and crossed to the dock's edge.

He was right. She probably wouldn't believe a thing he told her right then.

"Why don't you forget about fixing dinner?" he said, his back to her. "I'm not that fond of oysters anyway."

"Well, I am!" She wiped her forearm across her forehead, tired of wrestling with stubborn mollusks and an impossible male. "How do you get these darned things open?"

"It's really not hard."

Barely containing her temper, she laid her knife on the dock's weathered boards and crossed her arms over her chest. "Then maybe you'd like to do it."

A smart man would have seized the opportunity to make amends. Not Nick. He just stood there, staring out over the lagoon, ignoring the work that had to be done.

She was too familiar with that dreamy-eyed

posture. She'd seen it often enough in her father while she and her mother grabbed any job they could get to pay the bills.

"What I'd like to do, Adrienne," he replied in a quiet voice, "is sit and talk."

"Fine. We'll sit and talk while we open these stubborn things."

"There's something I need to tell you."

She shrugged, not caring what he had to say. If he wanted to do anything, he could help her shuck the stinking oysters. Lord, she already smelled like a sewer. "These are impossible to open! Could you give me a hand here?"

The lazy bum still didn't budge. If he wouldn't give her a hand, she'd find a way to pry the darned things open. "Do you have a crow bar?"

"On the boat. Why?"

"Guess. I'll be right back." She grabbed a towel and took off down the dock for his dinghy.

"Adrienne?" he called after her resignedly.

Rolling her eyes, she yelled back, "What, Nick?"

"Come on back. I'll shuck them for you."


Nick sat on the dock and grimly regarded the pile of oysters. He was utterly and completely at the mercy of nature's whimsy. As

154

they said in the comic books of his youth, if he found a pearl in that mess of crustaceans, the jig was up.

With a childish brand of desperation, he willed Tarzan to swing over the lagoon on a sturdy jungle vine and rescue him. But the only thing swinging in the lagoon was Adrienne's slender foot. She sat in her chair cross-legged and jerked her bare foot up and down while she waited for him to begin.

"Well?" she prodded him, the sharp edge of irritation in her voice.

Resigned to the inevitability of the task, Nick began.

"First, always hold the oyster in a towel to protect your hand. Then, slip the tip of the knife into the seam of the oyster, like this, and wait. The oyster senses an invasion, so it tightens its adductor muscle. But if you wait a minute or two, it will think the danger's past and relax. Then—" he jammed the knife deeper into the seam; with a twist of the blade he popped open the shell and prayed "—you catch it by surprise."

"Well, I'll be darned." Frowning, she hunched forward in her chair. "Do another."

Careful not to appear too obvious, Nick gave the slimy grayish meat inside the shell a quick glance before setting it on a tray.

No pearl! One down and twenty-three to go. He breathed a sigh of relief, selected another oyster, and repeated the process. By the fourth, he'd about decided lady luck just might be riding on his shoulder, for once.

Especially when Adrienne apparently got bored with the routine and disappeared into her bungalow without a word.

His spirits lifted. With her out of sight, if he found a pearl, he could sneak it into the pocket of his cutoffs. She'd never know.

Then click, whine. She was back with that blasted camera. Instinctively, Nick ducked his head.

If he had half a brain, he'd take a lesson from her. He'd fling her damned, offending camera into the lagoon and with it all her exposed film.

But suddenly his brains weren't in charge. Adrienne knelt on the dock beside him, the smoothness of her thigh brushing up against his. His thoughts fractured along several disjointed paths. One had him wondering if Adrienne had ever been made love to on a dock. Another had him figuring his goose was cooked if she found out who he was. Yet another had him wondering what the hell he would say and do if they found a pearl. Pretend it wasn't any big deal? Then break her shortwave radio to make sure no one else found out what potential the lagoon had?

"I think I'm ready to try it now." Rising to her knees, she reached for the biggest oyster.

As she did, her breast brushed against Nick's arm. Then Adrienne picked up the knife.

He swallowed hard and waited while she mimicked his demonstration.

Snap. The shell yielded. She grinned. "I did it!" The joy of discovery brightened her face. She thrust the open shell halves into his hands and chose the sixth oyster from the pile.

Nick quickly studied the meat. Phew! No pearl. Not even a tiny one.

By the time she'd opened ten more oysters, Nick was breathing easier. Only six more lay on the dock, ready to play havoc with his plans.

He was not foolish enough to test lady luck. He took the knife from Adrienne and handed her a clean towel. "That ought to be more than enough for dinner. I'll just pitch these back in. Why don't you go inside and make a salad? I'll clean up this mess."

"No way. I'm just getting the hang of it." She retrieved the knife. "Hand me that big one over there, will you?"

Nick decided a bit of horseplay could serve as a diversion. He plucked the mollusk from the pile and offered it to her. When she reached for it, he moved it behind his back. "I didn't hear you say please."

"This from a man who's in the doghouse big time?"

Keeping the oyster out of reach, he leaned over and stole a quick kiss.

She shoved him in the chest, but not before he'd tasted the sweetness of her lips.

"You have a lot of nerve!"

Grinning, he spread his arms wide. "So string me up. Shoot me. Feed me to the sharks."

"I wouldn't want to give them indigestion."

He pretended to be injured by her comment. "Would you forgive me if I said I'm sorry?"

"That depends on what you're sorry for."

He grinned and tried not to laugh, but the chuckle rumbled in his chest. "I'm sorry," he said, "that you looked so luscious strolling across the beach that I couldn't help myself."

"Have you forgotten I'm holding a knife?" she screamed.

"You wouldn't use it," he returned, playfully fending her off with his hands.

"Don't push me, Nick Helton."

"Darlin'," he said, daring to steal another kiss, "the last thing in this world I'd do is push you away from me."

Eyes blazing, Adrienne dropped the knife and doubled up her fist. "If you try that again, I swear I'll slug you."

"Then take your best shot, sweetheart, because I am going to do it again. You taste too damned good to leave alone."

He moved fast, capturing her fist, then her

lips. She squirmed in his arms and protested into his mouth. The more she thrashed, the more driven he was to subdue her. Something had been building in him since she'd arrived. It erupted with a driving intensity to prove to her she felt it, too.

She had her weapons. He had his. Arms that crushed her to his chest. A tongue that teased and taunted. Hands that ranged her body, giving pleasure.

The protests she uttered into his mouth gradually changed to whimpers of sweet ecstasy. Nick deepened the kiss. If Adrienne wanted to slug him when he broke away, he'd take it like a man.

When their lips parted, she didn't slug him. Eyes closed, she pressed her cheek against his chest and let out a ragged sigh. "I'm sorry."

She was sorry? Holding her close to his thudding chest, he stroked her silky hair and kissed the top of her head. "For what?"

"For throwing your binoculars back into the water. For being tired and irritable and smelly and . . ."

He took her face in his hands and ran his thumbs over the exquisite smoothness of her cheeks. "You know what, darlin'?"

She wet her lips with her tongue, leaving them moist and glistening in the moonlight. With great restraint Nick refrained from taking that silky bit of heaven into his mouth.

When she spoke, the word came out ragged. "What?"

He grinned. "You smell almost as good after a shower as you look."

She socked him in the chest. "You're impossible!"

"At least I got you smiling again. Boy, can you hold a grudge!"

"You ain't seen the half of it, buster." She pushed him away and picked up the knife and an oyster.

"Oh, I don't know, I think I saw at least half of everything."

She hauled off and pitched the oyster at him. He ducked. It sailed into the lagoon with a splash.

Only five more to go.

If he'd thought he could tease his way out of the other oysters, he was mistaken. Adrienne gave up the battle and tackled the last few. By now experienced at shucking, she popped open another. The big one. She started to pass it to him, then her eyes grew as big as saucers.

"Nick, look!"

He looked. His heart stopped. Everything he'd worked for the past four years vaporized into air.

Nestled in the mantle of the oyster was a pearl. Not just any pearl, but a perfectly round, iridescent sphere the size of a marble shooter.

"Well," he remarked, careful not to show the panic that was closing up his throat, "it looks like you're a very lucky lady."

She plucked the gem from its bed and delicately placed it in the palm of her hand. "I've never seen a pearl this big in my whole life. How much do you think it's worth?"

Nick tried to keep a steady voice, but it was difficult. "It's hard to tell. Probably anywhere from ten to fifty thousand."

"Oh, Nick." Adrienne pressed a hand over her chest, and the tears came. Big, fat tears that streamed down her cheeks. "I've never had that much money at one time in my life."

Then the inevitable happened. Clutching the pearl tightly in her hand, she said, "Let's open the rest. Maybe we'll find more."

While Adrienne watched, Nick shucked the other four oysters. When he had finished, she sat glaze-eyed on the deck. In her hands she held not one lustrous pearl, but two.

"Do you have any idea what these mean?" she marveled, rolling the pearls around in her hand.

"Yeah," he said and expelled a despondent sigh. "I sure do."

She bit her lip and choked over the tears. "This changes my whole life." She curled the pearls into a tight fist and pressed it against her chest. "I can't wait to tell Foster." She

161

snapped the fingers of her other hand. "That's right. I don't have to wait!"

She scrambled to her feet and headed for the bungalow.

Nick intercepted her at the door. "What do you think you're doing?"

"I'm going to radio Foster. If my calculations are correct, he should still be in the office." She brushed past him into the bungalow. "Do it for me, will you? My hands are shaking too hard."

Panic clawed at Nick's throat. He had to think of something fast. Beds of natural pearls were seldom found. If Foster told the wrong person about the underwater cache, within days the island would probably be swarming with treasure hunters.

The lagoon's booty of natural pearls wasn't the point. The real risk was that someone would put two and two together. Figure out that the lagoon, with its rich nutrients and calm waters, was the ideal place to culture pearls. Fortune seekers would have no compunction about laying claim to island waters for that lucrative purpose.

Nick was too close to reserving those rights for the natives. He wouldn't see his plans wrecked by a call to Foster Trent. Until the papers were signed and the farm was operational, he couldn't let another soul know what Adrienne now knew.

He needed time. Damned if he wasn't going to get it.

"Sit down, Adrienne."

"Yes, maybe I'd better." She backed up to her bed and eased onto the mattress, her gaze still glued to the pearls. "His number in Phoenix is area code 602-555-9637. How long do you think it will take to patch through the call?"

"I'm not going to call your boss, Adrienne. And neither are you."

She looked up, somewhat dazed. "Why not?"

He prayed for divine inspiration, then told part of the truth. "I'm fond of the natives around here. I'm trying to watch out for their interests."

"What do their interests have to do with calling Foster?"

"If people hear you found pearls in the lagoon's oysters, the treasure hunters will be so thick around here, you'll have to swat them like flies. It'll be like the gold rush in Alaska. Ile de Fleur won't be this peaceful, unspoiled island anymore."

Still clutching her pearls, Adrienne rose from the bed and proceeded to pace. It only took her a minute to digest what he'd said.

"Number one, Foster can be discreet. Number two, if my report's positive—and it looks like it will be—he'll build his resort here. His clients will spend weeks here, like me, only in more lavish surroundings. Many will scuba dive. Surely one of them, at least, will be as lucky as me and find pearls. Then it's only a matter of time before what you fear will happen will happen anyway."

Nick should have known Adrienne was too quick to accept what little he'd told her. He ran a frustrated hand through his hair. "Aw, hell, Adrienne." He plunked down on the bed and pulled her to stand between his legs.

He was so weary of the charade. He wanted to tell her, the hell with the pearls. The hell with Foster. The hell with weeks of deception and lies. Let's think about you and me and make love. But he'd long ago quit putting stock in dreams, and he'd learned the hard way the people a guy trusted most could betray him.

"I guess I'd better tell you the truth," he began.

"Maybe you should."

Did he know the truth anymore? In order to protect the natives, he'd told so many versions of it since Adrienne had arrived, he'd almost lost count. The worst part was, he cared for Adrienne. A whole lot. She wasn't just the beautiful travel agent with incredible legs he was being paid to show around the island. She was a friend.

Who was he kidding? Adrienne was more

than a friend. She was the woman who tortured him at night in his dreams with fantasies of hot, exquisite lovemaking. Yet she was more than potential good sex and mindless passion. She had spunk and a quick wit. She was generous, gentle, and caring. He didn't want her to walk out of his life in three weeks. If his relationship with her had a prayer of surviving, there could be no dishonesty or betrayal between them.

He wanted to confide in her. Trust her with the truth. All of it. But he'd seen that avaricious gleam in her eye. It was the same gleam that had corrupted Mitch and Morgan. He had to think of the natives.

"I found my first pearl two years ago," he began. "It was about the size of those in your hand. I knew it was worth a lot of money. You see, my father's a jeweler."

"A jeweler," she repeated. "Oh."

"Money, though, didn't mean flip to me. The islanders had been terrific. They helped me over a particularly difficult time in my life. I thought, what the heck? The pearl, by all rights, belonged to them. So I took it to the chief."

"What did he say?"

"He gave it right back to me."

"Why?"

"The people here are unique. They haven't been corrupted by the outside world. Trust is

valued. Friendship is treasured. Gems, like that
pearl, are simple adornments. The chief said
they had plenty. I could keep that one. All in
all, I've found about a dozen."

"Wow! If they're this big, that means you're
sitting on anywhere from a hundred and
twenty thousand dollars to—"

"Six hundred thousand," he supplied.

"No wonder you don't have to worry about
earning a living."

"I didn't sell them," he said, discounting the
one he'd sold to pay for his trip to Australia.

"Because you didn't want anybody to question where you'd found them?"

"At the time, I simply didn't need or want
the money. To tell you the truth, I stuck the
pearls in an old sock and forgot about them.
Then I heard the French were opening up the
island to foreign investors. Murph told me
what had happened on other islands when our
so-called modern civilization arrived. The natives ended up losing the land they'd lived on
for centuries. I knew once the developers and
the tourists arrived here, the treasure in these
waters—the pearls—would be scooped up by
outsiders. It didn't seem right to me. I decided
I *had* to do something."

"So what did you do?"

"The natives had been good to me. I wanted
to show them my gratitude. I've been working
like a dog on a project for the past six

months. Right now I'm trying to tie up the legalities. When I'm finished, all the pearls extracted from Ile de Fleur's waters will belong to Koli's tribe."

"You are a dear man," Adrienne murmured and kissed him softly, sweetly on his lips. Then her smooth brow knitted into frown lines. "But if the natives don't want the pearls, what good will it do?"

"They can sell the pearls and buy things they need, like a medical facility. Schools where they can learn languages and more sophisticated living skills so they can negotiate with outsiders and not get ripped off."

Adrienne opened her palm and stared at the two pearls wistfully. A heavy load lifted off Nick's chest. At least part of the truth was out.

The relief was short-lived. Nick wasn't telling Adrienne everything. That meant he was still lying. Also, in protecting the natives he was depriving her of that nest egg she had her heart set on. A rotten spot ate at his insides.

And then it came to him. Maybe he could convince her she could keep the pearls. He could arrange for his contact in Nouméa to buy them. She'd have that nest egg!

"Well, there's only one thing to do then," she said on a sigh of resignation.

"What's that?"

One corner of her mouth lifted, then

dropped. She rolled the pearls around in her palm, then slowly closed her fingers over them. "I have to give these to their rightful owners. Bright and early tomorrow, before the natives go to their fields, I want you to take me to the chief."

Nick almost choked. What could he say now? "Why don't you, uh, sleep in. I'll be happy to talk to him for you."

"No, I want to be the one. Besides, I've been anxious to meet him anyway. If I'm lucky, he'll show me around the village. I'll need you to interpret for me, of course."

Oh, boy! Nick had talked himself into a corner. He couldn't take Adrienne to the village. There were too many cages to hide. Cages where the oysters would live in the lagoon while they spun the lustrous nacre around the implanted nuclei and made cultured pearls.

Even if the natives were able to hide all the cages and the two Australians who'd been teaching them, Adrienne would quickly smell a rat. Some of the locals spoke enough English to converse. She'd ask questions. She'd learn Nick hadn't told her the whole truth. Then she'd never believe he was acting on behalf of the natives.

He needed time to come up with a plausible reason for not taking her to the village. "I'll radio the chief in the morning and make sure it's convenient for him." He stood and feigned

168

a yawn. "Right now, I think I'll hit the sack. I'm beat."

She looped her arms around his neck and pressed her forehead to his. He closed his eyes and inhaled the scent of heaven. "But we haven't eaten," she complained.

"I'm not hungry anymore, except for you."

Smiling, she tilted his face and kissed him reverently on the lips. He had to get out of there. His resolve to do the honorable thing was fading fast. The center of this thinking was slipping below his belt line.

"Nick?"

"Hmm?"

"I can't tell you how much I admire you. Not many people would be as selfless as you are."

It took some doing, but Adrienne persuaded Nick he needed nourishment before he retired for the night.

As a sign she'd forgiven him for the binoculars incident, she opened a bottle of dry white wine and toasted their find. She sautéed the oysters in a few ounces, then split the rest with him.

After dinner, she made Nick lie on her bed. Straddling his hips, she moistened her hands with coconut oil and gave him a long, leisurely massage. By the time she'd worked her way to the base of his spine, desire was flowing through her veins like hot honey. She bent over and kissed his back, wanting to make love to him, wanting to give this fine man the best of her.

The moment her lips touched his skin, he tensed. Before she could ask him what she'd done wrong, he pushed himself off the bed and crossed to the doorway.

Her cheeks flamed with embarrassment. Her stomach coiled into knots. She choked back the disappointment at learning Nick had deceived her. After the teasing words and suggestive comments, he didn't want her after all.

Unsmiling, Nick lifted a finger to his forehead in a mock salute. "See you in the morning, Adrienne."

She crossed her arms over the ache of wanting that tore at her chest. "Don't forget to make that call."

# Chapter Nine

After flip-flopping on her narrow bed for two hours, Adrienne finally gave up trying to sleep.

She glanced out her window and saw light spilling from Nick's doorway onto the beach.

So he couldn't sleep either.

"Serves him right," she grumbled and plugged the cord of her notebook computer into the bungalow's power source. One minute he was crushing her to his chest in a bone-melting kiss. The next he was pushing her away.

Which led her to believe there must be someone back home he couldn't forget. Someone who drove him to the island four years ago. His ex-wife maybe, even though he'd told her otherwise. Or someone on Grand Terre or another neighboring island.

Her cheeks flamed hot with embarrassment. If Nick were romantically involved, why had he let her think he was attracted to her?

Thoughts, visions, feelings nagged at her while she summarized the day's dive for her report. Too many things about Nick didn't add up. Twice she caught herself staring at the monitor, seeing his face. The feeling she'd met him before was overwhelming. But where? When? If she knew, perhaps she'd have the explanation to his inconsistent behavior.

Maybe, she thought, slipping a thin cotton sleep shirt over her head, she should have her film developed and send a picture of Nick to Foster. She and Foster had been friends so long, there was every chance he might have met Nick, too.

She awoke at daybreak to the sound of a husky, male voice. "Time to, uh, wake up, sleepyhead."

Her eyes popped open. Nick was standing over her bed, his eyes doing a thorough job of appraising her. As his gaze lingered on her breasts, her nipples tingled and hardened into tight peaks.

Adrienne's first impulse was to pull the sheet up over her breasts. She knew Nick could see the evidence of her arousal through the batiste nightshirt. But why bother being modest? He had seen everything already. And a part of her didn't want to hide from him. Rather it wanted to strip off the nightshirt and pull him into bed with her.

"What are you doing here?" she asked, wondering if her eyes revealed as much as Nick's.

"I'm here to take you sailing." He whirled around, walked to the refrigerator and yanked open the door.

Adrienne contemplated sneaking up behind him and letting her breasts casually graze his back. But she still stung from his rejection the night before. She watched while he poured the remaining orange juice into a glass and set it on her nightstand. He backed up two steps and crammed his hands into his pockets. "You've got twenty minutes to get dressed."

"Why the rush?"

"If we leave now, we can be back tonight."

"Back from where?"

"Nouméa."

"What a marvelous idea!" She scrambled to her knees, grabbed her brush from the nightstand, and pulled it through her sleep-tousled hair. "I'd like to do some shopping. And Foster said the food there is delicious. Why don't we take our time and stay overnight?"

He cleared his throat and glanced away. "I can't, Adrienne."

"Why not?"

She waited for him to explain why he couldn't stay overnight in Nouméa, but no explanation was forthcoming. He probably didn't want to spend the night in a hotel with her. She tried to hide her embarrassment with a casual shrug. "You could always leave me there.

I could get a ride back on Murphy's ferry."

"Huh-uh. I promised your boss I'd watch out for you. Where you go, I go."

"If it's Foster you're worried about, you needn't bother. I'm old enough to take care of myself," she said hotly.

"It's nothing like that. I'll explain later."

Well, good. Then maybe she'd understand what the heck was going on.

He paused in the doorway. "By the way, I talked to the chief."

"Great! When can we see him?"

"We can't."

"But you said—"

"I said I'd speak with him, and I did, on the radio." The hint of a smile curved his lips. "That's why we're going to Nouméa. See you in fifteen."

Adrienne darted outside after him. "Wait a minute. You're going too fast. Why can't we see the chief, and what does your talking with him have to do with us going to Nouméa?"

His gaze drifted down over her body. Now that she was outside in the direct rays of the sun, her nightshirt hid nothing. Certainly not her response to Nick.

She wasn't ashamed of how she felt. Lifting her chin, she flipped her hair over her shoulders. Until she knew for sure there was another woman in his life, she wasn't going to hide or ignore how Nick made her feel.

"The, uh, chief's, uh, busy," he muttered, wiping a palm across his mouth.

She smiled, taking pleasure in his discomfort. "Doing what?"

"Doing—huh?"

"What is he doing, Nick? Why is it he can't see us?"

"Hell, Adrienne, I don't know!" Beads of sweat were popping out on his forehead. "He's a busy man. Besides, you don't need to see him."

"Why not?"

"Because he's giving you the pearls."

"He's what?" she shrieked, launching herself into his arms. "Say that again."

His Adam's apple bobbed up, then down. The muscles in his jaws flexed.

He took her arms and set her back from him. "I said the chief's giving you the pearls. As a . . . a reward for your honesty."

"I can't believe it!" She twirled around. "I just can't believe it."

"I thought that would make your day. I'll meet you at the dinghy in fifteen minutes. I've arranged for you to sell the pearls in Nouméa."

"I'll be ready in ten," she said, ducking back inside to pull white slacks and a cotton sweater from her dresser.

"Good, because by tonight, you're going to be a pretty wealthy lady."

\* \* \*

The sleepy island was just awakening when Nick and Adrienne set sail. As they crossed the reef, the morning sun turned the blue of the ocean into a glittering sea of gold.

"I was so excited, I forgot to ask," Adrienne said. "Who's going to buy my pearls?"

"A discreet business friend," Nick answered and raised the jib.

Discreet business friend sounded rather seedy to Adrienne. "Is he on the level? I mean, can we trust him?"

"He's fair with his prices, and he won't reveal the source of the pearls to anyone."

Something was wrong again. For one thing, why hadn't Nick let Adrienne offer the pearls to the chief herself? Nick was hiding something. What? "How do you know this man?" she inquired suspiciously.

"I met him through my father."

She could believe that. Nick had said his father was a jeweler somewhere back in the States.

"He's a trusted family friend," Nick continued. "His specialty is buying gems for private collectors who wish to remain anonymous."

That didn't sound up-front either. "Why would collectors want to remain anonymous?"

"To keep jewel thieves at bay."

Jewel thieves? Adrienne toyed with the idea

176

of telling Nick to forget his discreet business friend. She would keep the pearls and sell them to a reputable jeweler back in the States.

Yet selling them in Nouméa would enable her to get out from under the burden of her grandmother's twenty-five-thousand-dollar debt sooner and save Adrienne some interest. She could even sock away a bundle in a retirement fund and earn interest instead of paying it.

If there was any money left, then what? She closed her eyes and lifted her face to the ocean breeze. In her entire life she'd never possessed discretionary funds—money after the bills. Every time she thought she was getting ahead and dared to dream, fate had intervened. Usually in the form of her father. She had learned it was easier not to dream than to live with the disappointment.

But darned if she wasn't dreaming now, of splurging for once. Of shopping. She hadn't purchased any new items for her wardrobe in two years. Except what little she'd picked up at the Nouméa airport on her way to Ile de Fleur.

She relented. She would sell her pearls through Nick's friend.

Nick spoke little the rest of the trip, maintaining his post at the wheel. He navigated deftly around the shoals and coral banks that littered the thirty-five-mile strait between Ile de Fleur and the baton-shaped island of Grand Terre.

Soon the craggy mountains that formed the island's spine loomed in the distance. Adrienne hoped she could talk Nick into delaying their return to Ile de Fleur. She wanted to rent a car after conducting their business. Then they could drive over the winding roads to the east coast, where the deeply eroded mountains rose out of the sea.

At mid-morning, Nick sailed through a slit in the barrier reef that circled the island six miles off the coast.

The ocean rollers broke against the coral into foamy plumes, then calmly joined the sheltered waters of Nouméa harbor. Tankers, freighters, barges, outriggers, and other sailboats glided in and out of the busy port facilities.

Nick tied up at the yacht club pier. Nearby, luxury hotels dotted the beach, which yielded to a hilly peninsula on Grand Terre's southwestern tip. Beyond lay the business district, their destination.

Nick crammed a floppy-brimmed hat on his head. He led Adrienne along a zigzag path of back streets, past boutiques, sidewalk cafés, and old houses with gingerbread iron grillwork. The sight of hand-painted fabrics, carvings made from pandanus bark, and necklaces of mother-of-pearl sharpened Adrienne's shopping urge. The aroma of fresh pastries and Gallic cooking had her stomach growling.

Seeing crusty loaves of French bread in a deli window, she tugged on Nick's arm. "Let's stop here. I'm famished."

"If we don't hurry, we'll miss Pierre," he said, not breaking stride. "At eleven, everyone breaks three hours for lunch." He looked both ways for traffic before crossing the street. "And I really would like to get back tonight."

"Oh, Nick, let's stay, just one night." She patted her purse, where she'd carefully stored the two pearls and a dozen rolls of film that needed developing. "We'll have enough money."

"We'll see," Nick allowed.

Adrienne's heart fluttered. Maybe lack of funds was the cause for his earlier reluctance to remain in the cosmopolitan city overnight.

Pierre, a courtly gentleman Adrienne judged to be in his sixties, greeted Nick with a warm embrace. One look at his kindly eyes, and Adrienne's misgivings about him vanished. He smiled over Nick's shoulder and winked at her.

"You did not tell me that Mademoiselle Laurel was so lovely." Sweeping Adrienne with an admiring gaze, he kissed the back of her hand. "My friend here has been taking good care of you during your visit? *Oui?*"

"Most of the time," she responded truthfully, liking the way her name rolled off Pierre's tongue with a heavy French accent.

Nick shot her a shuttered glance.

"You must call me if you need anything. If

179

Nick will not respond, I certainly will."

"Flattery will not get you her pearls any cheaper," Nick said dryly.

Adrienne got the distinct and pleasurable impression Nick was a bit jealous of his worldly friend.

Pierre and Adrienne shared a laugh while he locked the shop's door behind them. Finally Pierre led them through a curtain to the back room, then down a flight of stairs to a basement. At the end of a corridor they entered what Adrienne assumed was a private showing room.

Pierre ushered them to a long, narrow table covered in black velvet. He helped Adrienne into her chair beside Nick's, then took the third behind the table. "Our friend . . . Nick . . . tells me you have been lucky."

Adrienne blew out an anxious breath. "I hope so."

Pierre laughed. "Nick has a good eye for pearls as well as women."

"I wouldn't know about the latter," she replied stiffly and wondered what kind of women Nick saw on his excursions to Grand Terre.

"Forgive me, mademoiselle. I meant that as a compliment. I was referring to you, not to the others."

"Pierre, old boy, you're doing a good job of putting your foot in your mouth."

"Then perhaps we should proceed," the jeweler said, his eyes now hungry. "You brought the pearls?"

Adrienne removed the gems from her purse and placed the two lustrous spheres on the soft fabric. With not a little hesitation, she drew her hands into her lap. Some woman would wear the gems proudly one day. Adrienne wished she could be that woman. But she needed the money the pearls would bring much more than their decorative qualities.

"Ah, they are grand ones, are they not?" Pierre murmured, devoting his full attention to the pearls. He squinted around an eyepiece and examined them.

Hardly able to wait for the jeweler's appraisal, Adrienne lifted her gaze to Nick's face. The way he was looking at her made her feel warm and fuzzy all over. Even if he was wearing that stupid hat.

He dipped deep into his pants pocket and pulled out a wad of something white. "Here," he said, pitching it onto the table in front of Pierre.

"A sock?" Adrienne queried.

"Take a closer look."

She worked the tight knot loose, then emptied the contents of the sock onto the table. Three more exquisite pearls, as large as hers, but with paler pink shading, rolled onto the black velvet.

"I didn't think you were going to sell yours."

"I'm not." The corners of his mouth lifted in a smile, and his eyes sparkled. "You are."

"But how can I?"

He closed his hand over hers and gave it a light squeeze. "They're my present to you, Adrienne. No strings attached."

"You're giving these to me?" she asked, thinking surely she had misunderstood what he'd said.

He merely shrugged, as if he'd given her a bag of gum drops, nothing more. "They've been lying around in a drawer on the boat. I figured you could make better use of them than I could."

Adrienne's heart filled to bursting. Smiling at Nick bleary-eyed, she leaned across the table and gave him a tender kiss. She wished she could find the words to tell him how much his gift to her meant, but she had a hunch he knew.

She regretted every shameful thought she'd ever had about him and his character. He was honorable and trustworthy. And on top of all that, he was generous.

Pierre excused himself to make a phone call. When he returned, he took his seat and smiled broadly. "Mademoiselle, I have a buyer for your pearls. This is the sum I am prepared to offer."

He slid a piece of paper before Adrienne's

eyes. Her gaze fell to the number handwritten neatly on the page. She took one look, and her empty stomach did a giant flip-flop. She read it twice to make certain she wasn't dreaming. "One hundred and sixty thousand dollars?" Feeling faint, she pressed a hand to her chest and tried to calm her scampering heart.

"For the finest of pearls, *oui*. The gentlemen buyer has asked that I design a brooch and matching earrings for his . . . lady friend. The price is agreeable with you?"

"Oh, yes," she squeaked, and they all laughed.

"Then, as they say in your country, let us shake on it." He extended his hand across the table and took Adrienne's trembling fingers.

"One hundred and sixty thousand dollars. I can hardly believe it!"

Pierre placed each pearl in a black satin pouch of its own, clearly pleased with the deal he had struck.

Nick winked at Adrienne and pushed back his chair. "While we're near a phone, I'd like to call my folks back in the States. Do you mind?"

"No, go ahead," she told him, still dazed by the sum of money Pierre had offered her.

"You may use the phone upstairs in the showroom, by the cash register," Pierre instructed Nick and watched him leave. "And now, mademoiselle, I must know. In what form do you wish your compensation?"

Adrienne had to take two deep breaths before she could find her voice again. "If at all possible, I'd like ten thousand dollars cash—half in francs, half in U.S. dollars—and three cashier's checks."

The jeweler drew a gleaming, black Mont Blanc pen from his breast pocket and jotted down her instructions. She dictated the name of the executor of her grandmother's estate, to whom she would send a twenty-five-thousand-dollar check to cover Gracie's debts. The second check, for one hundred thousand dollars, was to be made out to the Fifth National Bank of Phoenix, as a direct deposit to Adrienne's savings account.

When she returned she would consult Foster for his advice on investments. She wouldn't consider anything the least bit shaky, though. She'd probably opt for a long-term certificate of deposit she'd roll over until her retirement. She tried to calculate how much one hundred thousand dollars would be in thirty-five years at the current interest rate. But her head was still swimming too much to compute the answer.

Pierre's voice broke through her reverie. "That leaves twenty-five thousand."

"Make the third check out to me, for that amount, Pierre," she said with a broad grin.

She had definite plans for that check. Very definite plans indeed.

Being rich made Adrienne even more ravenous. Pierre had given her an immediate two thousand dollars in francs. He promised to have his bank courier over the balance of the cash, plus the three cashier's checks, by closing time.

In the meantime, Adrienne figured she and Nick could buy a decent meal.

"Come on," she said, dragging him to the front door. "Lunch is on me, and—" she lowered her voice to a whisper "—after that I want to check into a wickedly extravagant hotel."

Her voice must have carried, for she heard Pierre give a lusty laugh. *"Bon appetit,"* he bid them, as they left. "And, do not hurry, Mack. The checks will be here after you and Mademoiselle Laurel . . . dine."

*Mack?*

Cramming on his sunglasses, Nick pulled Adrienne into the street and around a corner.

"He called you Mack," she said, trying to keep up with his long-legged pace.

"He gets me mixed up with a friend of his. What are you hungry for?"

What she craved wasn't on any restaurant menu, but she wasn't about to say that to

Nick. Not yet anyway. "Anything but fish."

"How about Italian?"

"Sounds good to me."

He ducked down another side street and gestured to a sign above a hole-in-the-wall restaurant. "How about there?"

"Nick," she replied, drawing out his name in complaint, "I want to eat someplace nice."

"The food's good here. You'll like it."

Adrienne peeked through the window and grimaced at the hackneyed Italian décor. Red-and-white checkered tablecloths and Chianti bottles dripping with candle wax. "I had something a little classier in mind." She turned, draped her wrists over his shoulders and nibbled at his lower lip. "Let's check into the Grand Nouméa. I'll treat you to lunch there. Oh, Nick. I can't tell you how happy you've made me."

He glanced over her head, then pulled her arms from his shoulders, as if he didn't want to be seen being intimate with her. "Hotel food isn't always the best."

"Foster said the Grand Nouméa has a five-star restaurant." She took a quick look behind her and saw little. Only a man with a camera slung around his neck who appeared to be window-shopping. What had Nick seen, and why was he acting so suspicious?

"If I didn't know better, I'd say you were avoiding checking into a hotel with me." She shot him a coy grin. "I won't take advantage of you. Promise."

"Tell you what," he said, disregarding the teasing nature of her comment, "why don't we ask Pierre if we can borrow his car? We'll go for a drive around the island. Take in the scenery and the local color. You want to try the native dishes, don't you?"

"Well, yes," she replied over her disappointment, "but I hate to prevail upon Pierre. We could rent a car."

"Pierre wouldn't hear of it, I'm sure. Come on, let's catch him before he leaves for lunch."

Adrienne didn't want to argue with Nick, especially after his unbelievably generous gesture. For the price of the three pearls he'd given her, she could forego spoiling herself in the hotel for the afternoon. They could always check in later.

Nick drove Pierre's late-model convertible north, then headed east over the winding, mountainous passes. Adrienne pulled out her camera and captured for Foster, and for memories, the breathtaking waterfalls and lush fern forests.

In villages they encountered along the way women and children smiled shyly but gladly let her take their pictures. Nick explained the natives were still ruled by chiefs. Most of the men worked in the nickel strip mines that scarred the mountains like open sores.

Nick and Adrienne lingered in one village, sampled several dishes prepared from the staple, yams, then went on their way.

Late that evening they met Pierre at his shop. He presented Adrienne with her three cashier's checks and the balance of cash due her. With no small amount of pleading, she persuaded Nick to stay one night at the Grand Nouméa.

She was still running her fingers over the numbers on the checks when their cab pulled into the circle drive in front of the posh hotel.

"You're sure you want to do this?" Nick asked, his hand on the door. "We could save two or three hundred bucks by sleeping on the boat, then sailing back in the morning."

"Why do you think I asked Pierre for some cash?" Adrienne slipped the checks into her purse and zipped it shut. "I'll tell you why. Because I'm going to spend some of it, and I'm not going to feel guilty. I want to have my hair and my nails done. I want to get a massage and buy some new clothes. Heck, we could stay two days. What do you feel like doing?"

"Taking a shower and going to sleep."

Was Nick really that tired or was something else bothering him? Whatever his problem, Adrienne wished he would get into the spirit of the occasion. She pulled some francs from her

188

purse and handed them to the cab driver.

"It's okay. I'll take care of it," Nick told her and motioned for the doorman to help her from the cab. "Go ahead and check in. I'll meet you later. I want to stop by the boat and grab some clean clothes."

"You could buy new ones," she offered brightly.

"That won't be necessary. I won't be gone long." He reached through the open window to pull her face level to his for a much-too-platonic kiss. "when I get back, we'll celebrate."

"Oh, Nick?" she said as he was about to walk away.

"Yeah, Adrienne. What is it?"

She pulled a small plastic bag from her purse and handed it to him. "Would you be a dear and drop these off at that all-night photo service I saw when we turned the corner?"

"Sure," he said, and took the bag.

"If they want extra for one-day service, that's okay."


Nick almost dropped Adrienne's film in the trash but changed his mind. She would need her pictures for her report to Foster Trent. Nick would simply toss the prints that showed his face clearly. That way she couldn't study his face to help her figure out where she had seen him. And she couldn't take a good likeness of him back to the States where it might fall into the wrong hands and resurrect the old, sensational story.

He dropped off the film, then walked the half mile to his sailboat.

He hopped on board the *Lorelei* and ducked into his cabin. He sat there, in the dark, sipping a beer and grumbling to his miserable self. How in the Sam Hill had he thought he could bring Adrienne to Nouméa and be himself?

Every time he walked into a room or turned a corner, he imagined someone had spotted him and was doing a double take. Someone who tried to figure out, like Adrienne, where he'd seen Nick. The apprehension had him acting like a damned spook.

It had, after all, been four years since his face had been plastered over every newspaper and television station back home. And then he'd had a mustache and worn his hair in a short, conservative cut. But people had a way of remembering his eyes—piercing they called them. And the color—almost aqua blue like the lagoon—made them all the more memorable. Wearing dark sunglasses during the day might seem natural, but at night? That alone might have people turning their heads to stare at him.

He would feel like the lowest form of life if Adrienne found out who he was before he told her himself.

Pierre had almost spilled the beans. He'd called him Mack loud enough for Adrienne to hear. Nick hoped Adrienne had bought his hasty explanation for Pierre's slip. But then, why wouldn't she? She trusted Nick as no one had in four years.

The fact she invested that much faith in him ate at his stomach like a burning ulcer. He had to reveal his identity before she discovered it by accident. Before he lost all respect for himself.

"Aw, hell, what's the use!" he grumbled and picked up the hand set on the radio. He had to check on things back on Ile de Fleur.

The chief was not in one of his better moods. The natives apparently weren't natural divers. Tanks or no tanks, they couldn't stay down long enough to harvest the oysters needed for the implanting process.

Nick told the chief not to worry. He'd bring some experienced Polynesians to the island. They were particularly adept at diving.

About as adept as Nick had become at lying.

*Tell you what, fella. You don't like it? Do something about it.*

Right. Just walk right in and say, "Hey, Adrienne. I'm the louse who killed your grandmother."

Cursing at himself, he pulled on his best clothes—jeans and a white linen shirt with billowy sleeves his mom had sent him. By the time he'd stuffed his toothbrush and a change for the next day into a paper sack, he had formed a plan.

Tonight he'd talk Adrienne into ordering room service. After dinner and a glass or two of wine, he'd bolster his courage. He'd tell her who he was and wait for her to scratch his eyes out.

Adrienne took a sip of wine and studied Nick over the fresh flowers delivered to their second-floor suite.

While she'd been at the hotel grooming herself from head to toe, Nick had apparently been working himself into a blue funk. Storm clouds had nothing on the scowl ingrained in his face. He hadn't uttered half a dozen words since they'd sat down to dinner. And darned if he wasn't poking at the tender chateaubriand as if it were a charred hamburger.

She supposed she should be irritated by his dark mood, but she couldn't bring herself to be angry. Not with Nick. Not with the man who had freed her from financial worry for the first time in her life. Not with the man who had walked into the hotel room with a shirt open almost to his waist. His glorious chest had her pulse pounding.

"I, uh, like your shirt." She let her gaze drift down the open placket. With very little encouragement she'd say to heck with dinner, but she got the distinct impression Nick didn't share her ardor.

"Thanks. My mother sent it to me."

"Where do they live—your mom and dad?"

Nick's hand froze on his wine glass. He seemed to think for a moment, then took a deep breath and expelled it. "In Atlanta."

"So that's the hint of Southern accent in your voice."

"I haven't lived there for a long time."

"Oh?" she responded casually, aware he was discussing a matter he'd avoided since she'd met him. She took another sip of wine and continued her questioning. "Where did you live before you came here?"

"California."

"San Francisco?"

He stared at his plate for a moment, then lifted his gaze. "Huh-uh. Los Angeles."

Los Angeles. Hmm. She remembered seeing the return address on the envelope in his hut, that of a law firm in Los Angeles. His divorce lawyer maybe?

Something twitched in her memory. "Los Angeles. I accompanied a tour to the 1988 Summer Olympics there. Maybe that's where I saw you."

"I'm afraid I missed those Games," Nick commented.

"Oh, well." She took a chance and forged on. Apparently if she wanted to learn more

193

about Nick's personal life and how it affected her, she would have to pry it out of him. "Tell me, what brought you all the way down here? You said it wasn't to get away from your wife, but I can't help wondering."

Focusing on his fork, he turned the piece of silverware over and over on his plate. Then he sat back in his chair and folded his arms over his chest. "To tell you the truth, she was part of it." He glanced up, his eyes reflecting some emotion. Misery? Resentment?

Nick could have told her that his marriage was none of her business. He could have said she was butting in where she had no business, but he didn't. He merely met her gaze, openly and honestly and said, "Patrice and I were married six years. And to answer the question you haven't come right out and asked, I don't love her. I don't miss her. It was over a long time ago. We never had children, so there's no reason to keep in touch."

"Forgive me for being nosy."

"It's okay, Adrienne. I don't mind if you ask questions. Maybe it would be better that way."

"What do you mean, 'Maybe it would be better that way'?"

"I mean," he said, and lifted his gaze to stare straight into her eyes, "there's a lot about me you don't know."

She gave a nervous laugh. "You are an enigma."

He cocked his head. "Come to think of it, I don't know a whole lot about you."

"Like what?"

"Where you grew up, what it was like, that sort of thing."

She dabbed at the corners of her mouth with her napkin, not sure how much she wanted to talk about her growing up years. Still, if Nick cared for her, he would be as curious about what made her tick as she was about him.

"I've lived in Phoenix all my life. I'm an only child. My family wasn't exactly what you'd call rich."

"Money isn't all that important in the scheme of things, Adrienne."

"It is when you don't have enough to pay the bills."

"Oh. Well, you have a point there," he said, and she hoped she hadn't made him uncomfortable by her statement.

"I didn't tell you that for sympathy. I just wanted you to know why the pearl money means so much to me."

She gazed out the window. The lights of another luxury hotel farther on down the beach winked in the distance. "My mother wouldn't believe it if she knew I was staying in a hotel as fancy as this. You see," she continued, and drew her attention back to Nick, "my father was a dreamer. He never kept a job longer than a month. Mom and I supported the family."

"What did your mother do?" Nick asked in a soft, understanding voice.

"She only had a high school education, so she didn't qualify for much. She worked on the production line at a tire manufacturing plant, and she checked groceries."

Nick reached across the table and ran his finger over the knuckles of Adrienne's hand. "And you?"

"I had a paper route from the time I was ten, and I baby-sat. When I was sixteen I went to work for Foster afternoons and Saturdays."

"Doesn't sound like you had much of a chance to be a kid."

She shrugged. "I survived. With Foster's help."

"You said he's been like a second father to you."

"He and my mother and father were close friends in high school. I told you Foster and my mom were once in love. She wanted to get married when they graduated. Foster decided he was too young for such a commitment. He wanted to live a little first."

"That's understandable. Eighteen's awfully young to settle down."

"Foster enlisted in the army and developed a taste for travel. My mother was crushed. She turned to my dad. They married a year later.

196

It wasn't until my parents died that I found out from my grandmother that Foster had never stopped loving my mother. He never told Mom, of course. But he was always there when any of us needed help. And he was my biggest booster."

"My grandmother has been that for me. It's really nice to have someone like that, especially when things don't work out the way you plan."

"I know what you mean. When I was the editor of my high school newspaper, I dreamed of editing a women's magazine one day. There were times when I thought I should be more practical, but Foster told me to never give up the dream. He even helped me get a full scholarship to Stanford."

"Stanford?" Nick whistled. "That's a high-powered school. I'm impressed. But I thought you said you lived all your life in Phoenix, and what happened to the journalism career?"

"I had to turn down the scholarship, and, well, in college I decided journalism wasn't for me after all."

"You turned down a full scholarship to Stanford?" Nick asked incredulously.

Adrienne folded her napkin neatly in her lap. "Dad lost his job again. They needed me at home. It was okay, though. I went to night school in Phoenix and got my degree in marketing."

"How old were you when your parents died?"

"Twenty-five. I was supposed to move to Washington, D.C. I canceled my plans for a number of reasons. Debt, for one."

"God, Adrienne," he said and picked up her hand. "Your life hasn't been a bed of roses, has it?"

"No, but things are looking up now." She squeezed his hand. "Thanks to you. I wish my grandmother could have met you."

The smile in Nick's eyes faded. He released her hand and took a long swallow of wine.

"Where did you go to college?" she asked, thinking it was her turn to learn more about Nick.

He cleared his throat. "Yale."

"Talk about a high-powered school!"

"Dad was a Yale man. From the time I was a kid that's where I wanted to go. I had it a lot easier than you. There wasn't a shortage of money."

"Did you like it there?"

"It was a great place to get an education. And to learn how to sail."

"Which came in handy when you got here," she added brightly.

"Right."

She wondered what had made this Yale man abandon his life in the States. Then she let her gaze drift from Nick's face to the open placket of his shirt, and her curiosity faded. All those fantasies she'd been having while she prepared herself for the evening came back to her.

Adrienne didn't want to ask questions anymore. She didn't want to talk. She wanted to be close to Nick. To put her arms around his waist, to breathe in his scent and soak up his goodness.

But Nick hadn't given her one clue he shared those feelings. Not since he'd walked into the hotel suite anyway. And how could she forget how much his rejection of her that afternoon had hurt?

"The dress new?"

Well, good, the man wasn't dead! "You like it?" She stood and twirled in front of him in a froth of aqua chiffon. The strapless designer dress in the hotel boutique had been indecently expensive. For once she'd said, hang the expense. She'd paid for the outfit with cash.

"It's . . . nice." His gaze lifted from her shoes to her hair. Adrienne got the impression his eyes weren't really seeing. "Really nice," he tacked on in a flat voice.

She'd gotten more reaction from men when she'd worn sweatpants. She looped her arms around his neck and scooted onto his lap sideways. "This isn't exactly the ambiance I'd hoped for this evening."

"I'm sorry if I've ruined it for you."

"You haven't, but I do get the feeling something's bothering you. If so, I wish you'd tell me." She kissed him lightly on the lips. "I'm a good listener."

One corner of his mouth lifted, then dipped back into its moody repose. One of his hands found her waist; the other rested on her thigh. But the fingers of that hand were making stroking movements that drove Adrienne straight through the ceiling.

She nuzzled his ear and tugged on his earlobe with her teeth.

"Adrienne, stop it." He untangled himself from her arms and set her standing. "I think I'll take a walk."

There was one catch to the iceberg treatment Nick was dishing out. While sitting on his lap for a too-brief moment, she could tell he was experiencing an intense physical reaction to her. Whatever was eating at him, it wasn't her.

She kicked off her heels. "That sounds like fun. I'll go with you."

"Aw, Adrienne, don't you know I need to be alone?"

"I know what you need." She snuggled up against him, flicking the bare skin of his chest with her tongue. "And it isn't being alone."

He dug his hand into the thick mass of her freshly shampooed hair. "You're wrong."

"Nick Helton, you're not a very good liar."

"That," he said, in a gruff voice, "is what you think."

* * *

Like a pesky child, Adrienne followed Nick down the balcony stairs and onto the now-deserted beach.

He took off at a brisk pace, hoping to put distance between them. From the restaurant's open-air night club, the clink of crystal and the plaintive notes of a French love song wafted over the beach. In the distance a ship's horn sounded over the crashing of the breakers. Adrienne said nothing, only padded along beside Nick, her slender feet bare in the wet sand.

If Adrienne would leave him alone for a half hour, he'd find the words to tell her. To elaborate on what she'd just learned about him and his years in the States. Instead, she strolled beside him, the soft fabric of her dress clinging to her long, slender legs in the humid night air.

Was she wearing anything underneath that dress? He drew in a deep breath. Yeah, she was. Perfume. Something hot and spicy. A scent that made him want to grab her and make love to her there on the beach.

She slipped her arm around his waist and regarded him with trusting eyes and full, moist lips. "Do you ever think you'll get tired of living on the island?"

So she was going to ask him questions after

all. He would be honest. Soon the ruse would be over. "I doubt it. I like the easy pace. Everything I want is on that island." *At least until you leave, it is.* "If the fish hold out, I'm set for life. Best of all, I like the natives. They're generous and trustworthy, and . . ." Hell! Why had he said trustworthy?

"What if you get sick and need someone to care for you?"

"I'll cross that bridge when I come to it."

"Do you ever think about going back to the States?"

"No."

"Not even for a visit?"

"Huh-uh."

Apparently undaunted by his cryptic answers, Adrienne continued. "What did you do before you came here?"

"I was an accountant. A CPA."

"You're kidding!"

"Why does that surprise you?"

"You don't exactly fit the CPA mold, although that explains the tax manual I saw you reading."

"What mold is that?"

"Every accountant I've met had his finances organized on a ten-year spread sheet. And you don't even want to think about the future, much less plan for it."

"Maybe you don't know me as well as you think you do," he warned her and tried to ig-

202

nore how he was responding to the nearness of her.

"Maybe," she admitted on a sigh. "But I like what I know."

She whirled around in front of him and walked backward across the sand. "You are the most generous man I've ever known."

"Just because I gave you three pearls?"

"You've given me much more than that." She halted, smoothing her hands over his chest and gazing up at him with so much admiration he wanted to scream, "Get away from me! I'm a fraud. I don't deserve you."

"I don't know what I did to deserve you," she said.

"Aw, Adrienne." He pulled her close, tangling his hand in the mass of silky hair that smelled of gardenias. "Stop. Please. I'm not worthy of your admiration."

"But surely after what I told you about my background, you can understand my gratitude. You've given me the one thing I've never had. Security. If I'm smart and invest the money from the pearls wisely, I'll never have to worry about being a burden to anyone. I only hope somehow my grandmother knows. She was so worried about me there at the last."

"Adrienne?" he said and tasted her lips one last time before he launched into his confession. "I have something to tell you."

She flung her head back and gazed up at

him, the desire in her eyes as clear as the bay's water. She nipped at his chin, pressing her breasts against his chest. "And I have something to tell you." She took his hand and tugged in the direction of the hotel. "Let's go back to the room."

"No!" he answered, pulling away. "You go back."

She stood there, watching him back off down the beach. Her dark eyes brimmed with tears. He wished he could tell her to get lost, to forget she'd ever met him. But all he could think at that moment was that he loved her. That as soon as he overcame the yellow stripe down his back and confessed everything, she would tell him to get the hell out of her life.

"I'll be back later," he called out. "Don't wait up for me."

## Chapter Ten

Adrienne plumped her pillow and turned her back to the balcony and the stairway that descended to the beach.

For two hours she'd lain there, with the door wide open. Even the distant roar of the ocean couldn't lull her to sleep. Every time she heard a strange sound, she tensed, thinking Nick had returned to apologize for his rudeness.

But he hadn't come back. She glanced at the clock. Two a.m. He was still out there, on the beach somewhere, or maybe off with the woman she'd conjured up in her mind.

His rejection still stung like the slap of a hand. Her stomach muscles ached from the tensing. She was wearing the hot pink satin teddy she'd purchased in the hotel boutique. She had thought Nick's eyes would light up when he saw her in it. When he stripped it from her willing body. That had been the wishful thinking of a foolish woman.

Maybe Nick was smarter than she was.

Maybe he'd accepted what she kept pushing to the back of her mind. That she could no more live with a man of his languid nature than she could swim back to Phoenix.

She wanted a man with ambition who didn't mind working hard and reveled in the pleasure of achievement. A man who could earn a living and support his wife in the child-bearing years. Who wouldn't leave her and her children to carry the load, as Adrienne's father had. Nick was as laid-back as they came and could not care less if he earned a buck.

And yet, she kept going back to what he'd told her tonight. He'd been an accountant, a CPA. One didn't earn that certification without working like a dog. Too, he had shown signs of industry when they'd built his hut.

*Admit it. You'll rationalize away your fears because you love him, don't you?*

She was considering that particularly aggravating question when she heard the grating of feet on sand on the balcony stairs. She pretended to be asleep, even when the bed at her side sagged beneath Nick's weight.

"Adrienne."

She fluttered her eyelids and tried to look like he'd awakened her.

His hair was wind-tousled. His bare chest gleamed with the sheen of perspiration. He smelled musky and wild, like a stormy sea. He had her pulse clamoring. "Hmm?"

"I'm sorry to wake you, but I've got to tell you something."

His tone of voice was ominous. What did he have to tell her? Good-bye? Panic seized her, erasing the signs of pretended, lingering sleep. She didn't want to hear farewells. She wanted him to tell her he loved her. Then she wanted him to show her how much, with his large, long-fingered hands and his glorious mouth.

He traced circles on the back of her hand. "You, uh, shouldn't let your feelings for me get too serious," he began.

Ready to fight for what was slipping through her fingers, Adrienne grabbed fistfuls of his shirt. The backs of her fingers brushed the hot, slick swells of his chest. Her stomach tied itself into a huge knot. "You should have warned me about that weeks ago."

Closing his eyes, he lolled back his head. "Adrienne, Adrienne. You don't really know me."

"Are you wanted by the police anywhere?"

"No."

"Are you married?"

Outrage flickered in the stark blue of his eyes. "I wouldn't be in a hotel room with another woman if I were."

"Are you involved with anyone else?"

He gave a lopsided grin. "I haven't been with anyone in so long, I was thinking about applying for sainthood."

207

"That's all I need to know." Releasing the folds of wrinkled linen, she pushed his shirt aside and smoothed her palms over his chest. His nipples turned into hard peaks beneath her caressing fingers.

A shudder ripped his shoulders. He opened his mouth to speak, but Adrienne lifted herself from her pillow and swallowed his words. She would make him forget the hurts in his past, she would make him give in to the feelings that had his blood racing even now beneath her touch.

She broke the kiss and, tugging the sheet from beneath his weight, threw it aside. The refrigerated air sent goose bumps flying over her hot skin.

"God, Adrienne, what are you wearing?"

"Something I bought for you." She lifted his hand and placed it on the triangle of hot pink satin covering her abdomen. His touch was electric, his gaze searing. She moistened her lips to ready herself for him. "I like the feel of satin next to my skin."

She placed his other hand on the inside of her thigh. Her pulse shot through the ceiling. "But I like the feel of you better. Nick," she said, curling her fingers around his neck to urge him closer, "make love to me."

Nick tried to resist Adrienne. He really tried. But the need burned in her eyes like hot coals, and not just physical need. But Lord, that alone had her all aquiver. Her teeth captured the fullness of Nick's lower lip. Her breasts, spilling over that scrap of hot pink satin, heaved in and out, as if she couldn't get enough air or enough of Nick. A muscle in her inner thigh ticked beneath his hand.

He might burn in the hell of Adrienne's outraged mind someday, but he couldn't refuse her tonight. Nor could he silence the thundering rush of blood in his head.

She rubbed his hand over the silky skin between her thighs. The last thread of Nick's restraint snapped.

So did Adrienne's patience. While he plundered her mouth, four hands worked feverishly to undo the last two buttons of his shirt, to yank it over his back, to work his jeans over his hips.

The denim had just hit the floor when her moist, eager tongue found his chest. He dug his hands into the silken mass of chestnut waves and moaned, "Darlin', wait."

She drew back and, propping her chin on his chest, regarded him with sultry eyes. "Why?"

"It's been so long. I'm already about to explode."

She shot him a wicked grin and wriggled in his arms. "If you do, I doubt you'll qualify for sainthood."

"Somehow," he mumbled, sliding the black

lace straps of her teddy off her shoulder, "I don't think I'll mind the sacrifice."

Adrienne shut her eyes as Nick's lips closed over her breast. He suckled one taut nipple, then the other until she dug her hands into his shoulders and cried out from the sheer, exquisite pleasure. Her hands moved across his back and found their way to his hips. Rock-solid hips that flexed tightly when she smoothed her hands over the fullness of him. Hips that eased up so she could close her hand around that pulsing part of him she hungered to feel inside her.

"Oh, darlin', yes. Do that. Yes!"

What a heady feeling it was to give him such pleasure. Just when she thought her heart would burst from the look of ecstasy on his face, he did some pleasuring of his own. He peeled the teddy from her body, kissing her skin as he bared it. When he reached the apex of her legs, he flicked his tongue over the tender flesh of her inner thighs.

Adrienne's eyes flew open. She gasped, then found enough air in her lungs to cry out, "Oh, Nick."

"You like that, darlin'?"

All she could do was nod and whimper.

"And this?" He eased his fingers into the moist heat of her, and she cried out anew.

A glorious trembling began in her abdomen.

A burning hot path that spiraled to her breasts and to her limbs like quicksilver.

Instinctively, she parted her legs for him. He knelt in the V. She felt him pressing against her wet entrance. She lifted her hips, unable to feel him inside her soon enough.

"Darlin'," he said, pressing a kiss on each eyelid, "open your eyes."

Somehow she managed to do as he bid her. Through passion-glazed eyes, she found him hovering over her, his weight braced on his elbows.

"Are you sure you want me?" he implored her.

She not only wanted him. She needed him. Her body ached for him. Tears stung the corners of her eyes. Her breath was so short, she could hardly speak. "Yes," she uttered on a shuddering sigh. "Oh, yes, Nick."

Nick slid a hand beneath Adrienne's hips and lifted her as he entered the tight moistness of her. An oven of sweet heat that tightened around him and trembled. Once he was inside her, he was lost. Lost in the heat and the driving need to pour himself into her and consume her goodness.

The climax came swiftly, for Adrienne, as well as for Nick. His last coherent thought was that, for the first time in his life, God had granted him a small piece of heaven. Her name was Adrienne.

He loved her. And he'd committed the unpardonable sin by making love to her.


Adrienne awoke the next morning, knowing her life would never be the same. She loved Nick without reservation. She had given herself to him. Whatever barriers he had erected between them, she would scale.

She was aware of a tenderness between her legs, a soreness in her lower abdomen. Thinking of the many ways he had made love to her, she chuckled. Maybe just one more time, she thought, and rolled over to her side.

But Nick was gone.

She found him sitting on the beach, staring off into the ocean, his arms propped on bent knees. He wore his cutoffs. Nothing more. A light breeze lifted the blond hair off his shoulders. Adrienne eased down beside him and pressed her cheek to his arm. He smelled like the musky scent of their lovemaking. "Hi."

He didn't move. His only acknowledgement that he knew she was there was his one-word response. "Hi."

"You left before I could give this to you." She pulled a decorative gift bag from behind her back and placed it between his legs on the sand.

"What is it?"

"A present."

212

"Aw, Adrienne, I wish you hadn't."

"It gave me a lot of pleasure. I found it—them—when I was shopping. Open it."

He lifted the square package in his hands and slowly stripped off the paper. He lifted the top off the box and folded back the white tissue. His mouth slanted in a half smile as he glanced at the binoculars. "Does this mean I'm forgiven?"

"It means I'm not worried about you leering at me any longer. I'd hoped, when I bought them, that what happened between us last night would happen." Turning her cheek, she pressed a kiss against his arm. Her devil tongue darted out for a quick taste of him. "I figured since you can see me—really see me—anytime you want, you'll put these to legitimate use."

"I guess you don't understand the male libido," he joked with a wry grin and put the binoculars in the box. "Thanks. I can use these, in more ways than you think." And he quickly glanced away.

He hadn't even tried out her present. He just sat there, staring off into nowhere. What was eating at him? What had driven him from the room last night? Surely he wasn't sorry for what had transpired between them.

"Nick, about last night—"

"I want you to forget last night."

She stumbled to her knees and glared at

213

him. "Well, it just isn't that easy. Not for me. In case you haven't figured it out by now, I love you."

She expected him to smile or pull her into an embrace, or tell her where she could go with her love. Anything but the reaction she got. None whatsoever. He sat there, looking like he wished she'd drop dead.

If he didn't love her, she needed to know now. "And you?" she inquired with a warrior's boldness. "How do you feel about me?"

He didn't answer her. Not right away. He picked up a small seashell and traced her initials in the sand first. "Sometimes there are more important things than love."

"Yeah, right. Name one."

"A man's honor. His self-respect."

"Would you care to expand on that?"

"Not now. It's too late."

"You wish last night had never happened, don't you?" she asked, panic squeezing the breath from her chest.

He looked at her with a sad, wistful expression. "Darlin', I don't. But you may regret it one day soon."


Several days later, Adrienne replayed that conversation in her head, wondering what Nick had been trying to tell her.

Did he love her or didn't he? And what was

214

this crazy talk about a man's honor and self-respect?

On the trip home he had spoken only a few words, and then as succinct answers to her questions. Back on the island he had avoided her for four whole days. He disappeared for hours at a time, sometimes walking, sometimes sailing.

Why the quiet treatment? And did it have anything to do with what he wanted to tell her when they had made love?

"Men!" she grumbled, and flipped the power switch on her notebook computer so she could summarize her trip to Nouméa for Foster.

During the next two hours, she managed to write only one coherent paragraph. So she switched to sequencing the prints Nick had picked up for her from the photo service in Nouméa while she checked out of the hotel. She wished more shots of Nick had turned out. And she'd have to remember to ask him to remove his sunglasses whenever she took his picture again. None of the prints showed his gorgeous eyes.

While sorting through the pictures, she dwelled on the irony of her situation. For years she had thought if she only had enough money, she could solve her problems. She could pay her family's bills. She could give her grandmother the finest in medical care. She could bury Gracie with dignity, instead of only

215

being able to afford a simple graveside ceremony.

Now Adrienne had more money than she'd ever dreamed of, and the problems that plagued her were worse than ever.

In two weeks, she was scheduled to fly back to Phoenix. If she couldn't get Nick to tell her what was troubling him, she might never see him again.

And, Lord help her, she loved that big, blond lug so much her heart would break if she couldn't make him admit he loved her — and soon.

She debated ripping her airline tickets into pieces and tossing them into the lagoon. She knew, though, if she wasn't on her scheduled flight back to Phoenix, Foster would radio her. Then he'd be on the next plane to New Caledonia.

She'd never been one to let things happen. She hit the save key, then pulled up a blank screen and marshalled her creative resources. She began a list. A list of ways she could get Nick's attention.


It was strange how things worked out. While his personal life was in the toilet, Nick's project with the natives was moving at breakneck speed.

Through Murphy he'd located a half-dozen discreet Polynesian divers who ferried over to the island. The Australians organized dive teams, utilizing the Melanesians as boatmen and record keepers. Two of Koli's tribesmen had already shown excellent leadership capabilities. They were being trained as team captains.

Soon they would harvest the island's eastern waters where the stronger currents yielded huge South Seas oysters. Next the oysters would be opened a crack for the delicate implanting process. Tiny round beads cut from mussel shells would be inserted in the oysters' flesh. Hopefully they would react to the implant irritation by secreting nacre around the beads.

Once implanted, the oysters would be placed in the bamboo cages and lowered into the quiet lagoons on the island's western shore. I₂ the natives were skilled, vigilant, and lucky, in two or three years, 10 percent of the oysters would yield marketable pearls.

The only problem was, every time Nick thought pearls or said pearls, Adrienne's face popped into his mind. That meant she was constantly in his thoughts. Adrienne in that hot-pink teddy. Adrienne crying out in ecstasy, then lying limp and sated against his sweat-slickened chest. Adrienne's face aglow when she mailed money back home that would provide a secure future for her. Adrienne's joy at giving him the binoculars. Her disappointment when she looked through her prints and discovered some shots of Nick hadn't turned out.

Someday when he confessed everything, he'd mail her the pictures and explain why he didn't want her to have them at the time. Because he wanted to keep his location a secret until the pearl farm was the legal property of the natives. If the wrong people back home found out what he was doing, they'd have a field day in the newspapers with it. Then there would be no telling who would show up on the island with what intentions.

He was driving himself to exhaustion. When his body ached from fatigue, he couldn't quite shut out that inner voice that told him he was a fool. That he loved Adrienne. That he should give serious thought to following her back to the States.

When such inane thoughts crossed his mind, he immediately dismissed them. Back home someone would recognize him. Heck, lots of people would. If Adrienne didn't find out who he was before she left Ile de Fleur, she sure as hell would in the States. Then she wouldn't speak to him, much less listen to him propose marriage.

He also had his parents to consider. God, how he missed them! But he loved them too much to cause them the renewed embarrassment and shame his presence in the States would prompt.

Then there were his responsibilities to the islanders.

Murphy, whom Nick had finally entrusted with his pearl plans, had offered a solution. The Irishman had encouraged Nick to hire an overseer for the pearl culturing farm. That would open up a fresh option for him: he could move elsewhere, to Europe perhaps, and take Adrienne with him.

Murph's suggestion had as many holes as a net dive bag. Besides the obvious problem of his true identity, Nick wouldn't have the money to hire an overseer for an extended period of time. Not after he sold more pearls to pay the Polynesian divers and his attorney. And he wouldn't let the trusting natives down by leaving them stranded.

On the sixth night of his return from Nouméa, Nick met Murphy's ferry. Murphy loaded him down with supplies, including an extra shortwave for his hut, and stuck a bulging envelope inside one of the boxes.

"Who's it from?" Nick asked.

"Your attorney in the States."

"Keep your fingers crossed," Nick said with a grin and turned to load the supplies into the *Lorelei*.

"Hold up. I almost forgot. Here's a couple of packages for your lady friend."

"Adrienne?"

"Is there another?" Murphy inquired with a shuttered glance.

"You know there isn't," Nick grumbled.

"Stick them up here on top. I'll see she gets them."

"Will you now?"

"Why do you ask?"

"Oh, no reason at all."

"Have you been talking to her?"

Murphy shrugged. "Only once or twice, over the radio. Now, listen, son, and follow my directions."

"How complicated can it be to deliver two packages?" Nick groused.

"Give her this one," Murph instructed, pointing to the smaller parcel. "If it doesn't work out, give her the other one."

"Why don't I just give her both and let her choose?"

"Will you just do as I ask?" Murph complained, his Irish temper starting to flare.

"All right," Nick agreed.

"I think she'll look terrific in it. Tell her not to worry about the size."

Nick raised a puzzled brow. "The size of what?"

"None of your business. Just give her the message."

"I don't know why some people can't say what they mean," Nick mumbled and headed down the dock. To himself, he muttered, "I wonder who else she's been talking to."

He decided he'd better pay Adrienne a visit first thing when he returned to the lagoon.

The sun was setting by the time Nick delivered the supplies to the village and sailed back to his hut and Adrienne.

She was nowhere in sight. He left the smaller package on her neatly made bed, wondering if she was sleeping any better than he was. And then he heard her sweet voice drifting through the window. He peeked outside and connected with his sweat glands.

She was in the shower, singing, her eyes closed, just like the time he'd watched her through his binoculars. The sight of her bare calves and feet below the stall's thatched sides did more for him this time, though. He knew how silky those calves felt sliding up over his hips. He recalled with a surge of blood to his nether regions what heaven lay at the apex of her thighs.

He could barely see the upper curves of breasts, like before. Instinctively his palms curved to fit those exquisitely sculpted mounds.

She reached up and turned the water off. Nick ducked out of sight. If he got caught inside her bungalow, he might have more than silky limbs to encounter. He strode outside and on down the beach toward his hut.

She saw him, damnit. "Hi, Nick."

He answered without breaking stride or glancing sideways, at least not so she could tell. "Hello, Adrienne."

He almost made it past her without getting

221

close enough to breathe her freshly scrubbed skin. The door to the shower swung open. She stepped out, not five feet away. She wore only a towel, a wet towel, tucked negligently around her sweet body.

He shoved his eager hands inside the pockets of his cutoffs and conjured up visions of smelly fish parts. Anything to keep his traitorous body from reacting to the sight of her in that damned wet towel.

Adrienne merely smiled as they passed on the beach. She flipped her long, chestnut hair over her shoulder, and a few cool drops of water sprinkled his hot, bare chest.

Another couple of seconds, and she was behind Nick. Not even mental visions of dead fish could derail his thoughts now. He wondered how her cute little butt looked sashaying down the beach in that wet towel. He searched for an excuse to turn around and snapped his fingers.

"Hey, Adrienne," he called out, and backed across the beach.

"Yes, Nick?" she answered without turning.

His breath whooshed out of his lungs. His mouth went dry. The towel barely covered the curve of her butt. He could see the line separating the golden tan of her legs from her sweet cheeks. Sweat popped out on his brow. He backed right into his own damned hut and whacked the back of his thigh

222

a good one. He'd have a bruise, for sure.

Suddenly she halted and turned around, catching him with his gaze where it shouldn't have been. "Did you want something?" she called across the beach sugar sweetly.

Yeah, he longed to holler. You! But he hauled in a deep breath and said, "Murph sent you a package. It's on your, um, bed."

"How dear of him."

"He said not to worry about the size," Nick remembered to add.

"The size?" She frowned. "Oh, well."

And before Nick knew it, she and her sweet butt had disappeared into her bungalow.

Nick was so worked up, he almost forgot to open the envelope from his attorney.

At first glance, the contents were no surprise and called for a celebration. He radioed the chief and told him the good news. They had six months to get their operation going. During that time no one else could claim pearl culturing rights to the island's waters.

It was while the chief was inviting Nick to the village for a celebration the following evening that Nick found the letter's second page. The white sheet of paper contained a postscript, scrawled in ink in the lawyer's bold handwriting. Lauderhill wrote that the day before the letter was dated Mitch and Morgan had been released from prison, two years early on parole.

Nick wadded the sheet in his fist and flung it across the room. Thousands of retirees had been robbed of their investment money by those two jerks, and they got off two years early for good behavior. How much money did they have to slip in the right pockets for that to happen?

Nick wished Lauderhill had told him more about Mitch and Morgan. Their plans especially. But then Lauderhill, whose aging aunt had been ripped off in the health-care scam, had served as Nick's attorney *pro bono*. Lauderhill hadn't been paid to do the legal work, much less any sleuthing.

What if Mitch and Morgan were trying to find Nick to make good their threat for revenge? The letter was postmarked a week ago. The horses' rear ends could be on Ile de Fleur now, for all he knew. He'd have to warn Adrienne somehow to be careful, and he'd have to do a better job of watching out for her.

He told the chief not to expect him for the party but promised to drop by the next day.

Four weeks ago Nick would have liked nothing better than to get stinking drunk with the locals. Since Adrienne had arrived, he had better things to do with his time.

He planted his chair in his open doorway

and gazed across the beach to her bungalow. As he watched for a glimpse of her, the strains of a mournful country-western ballad wafted across the air. The music had him thinking about dancing with her. Hell, the song had him fantasizing about making love with her.

As he watched, occasionally Adrienne drifted by the window. He couldn't see much, the dark of her hair, a flash of tanned skin, something hot pink.

*Hot pink.* His throat tightened. He leaned forward, propping his forearms on his knees and squinting. Was she wearing that damned teddy? The thought of the scrap of satin and lace had his pulse pounding. And if she was wearing it, why?

His gaze shot to the binoculars she'd given him in Nouméa. They were sitting on his trunk. He looked back out the doorway and saw an article of clothing fly through the space encompassed by Adrienne's window.

What on earth was she doing now? Undressing? And, he wondered with a roaring in his skull, what part of her body had she just bared to the night air?

He saw something else flying. In the flash of a second, he had those binoculars in his hands and focused across the stretch of beach. His hands were trembling so badly, he wasn't sure he could see much if she did step into view.

Wrong. There she was. Oh, Lord! She wasn't

225

naked, but she wasn't wearing much. Three indecently small scraps of hot pink, two on her
jiggling breasts, and one down there. She was
dancing, swaying to the honeyed beat of the
music. Her eyes were closed, an expression of
pure ecstasy on her flushed face.

He remembered how she'd looked up at him
when he'd entered her. That same flush of heat
had colored her cheeks when she'd gifted him
with her sweet body.

The sight of this nymphlike Adrienne
scorched his skin. Sweat dripped down his face
and trickled over his bare chest. Damn, he was
thirsty!

Holding the binoculars to his eyes with one
tight fist, he reached over and lifted the lid to
his ice chest. He grabbed a beer and flicked
the tab up with his thumb. He took a long
slug, but it didn't do any good. His skin was
blazing. Nothing but burying himself in
Adrienne's body could douse the fire.


At about ten, Adrienne heard the telltale
squeak of the boards outside her bungalow. As
rehearsed, she turned her back to the open
doorway. Swaying to the soul-wrenching beat
of the tune, she lifted her arms, elbows out,
and swept her hair off her shoulders in a pro-
vocative posture.

Knowing Nick was behind her, watching her

every move, she took her dear sweet time swaying to the music. When she was sure Nick had gotten a good long look at her, she spun around and feigned surprise.

It wasn't difficult. He was wearing one of his narrow swim briefs. Purple this time. That's all. Rivulets of water streaked over his finely sculpted chest from dripping hair. She steeled herself to keep her hungry gaze on his scowling face.

"Nick," she said, letting her hair down, but giving her head a sassy shake. "How long have you been there?"

"Long enough. What the hell are you doing?"

"Celebrating. I finished my report today. I was just wishing I had someone to dance with." She held out her hand. "Want to join me?"

He wanted to join her all right, but not on the dance floor. She knew it. He knew it. He wouldn't admit it.

Yet.

"No, thank you, I don't feel like dancing tonight." His gaze dipped low on her body. "What the heck are you wearing?"

"A bikini." She twirled around. "Do you like it?"

"What there is of it." His hands knotted into tight fists. "I didn't think you wore bikinis."

"I ripped my swimsuit the other day. You

227

weren't here, and I didn't know what to do. I didn't think you would approve of me swimming naked in broad daylight . . ."

She paused for effect and had to hold back a smile. Nick's gaze was burning a blatantly hot path over her body. "I found Murphy's call letters on the radio and got lucky. He was in Nouméa and ran an errand for me."

Nick swore and raked a hand through his damp hair. "Is that what was in that package I delivered for Murph? That scrap of nothing?"

"He was a sweetheart to shop for me. The only problem is, I told him I wore a ten, and he bought me an eight. Do you think it's too tight?" She pivoted again, hoping the top stayed in place.

"Tight isn't the word. It's . . . it's indecent. Now I know what Murph meant about the second package."

"What second package?" she asked innocently.

"He gave me two packages and said to give you the second only if the first one didn't work out. He was probably worried you wouldn't want to wear that . . ." he gulped hard, ". . . that little bit of nothing you have on. Not that I can blame him. Maybe that second package contains another swimsuit with a few more inches of fabric. I'll just go get it."

"Now, Nick." Adrienne sauntered across the room and draped her wrists over his shoulders.

He smelled of soap and beer. His eyes glittered with barely contained desire. The moment her skin touched his, a pectoral muscle twitched. She let her gaze drop to his chest, smiled, then tilted her head and focused on his eyes. "Don't you like me in this one?"

His attention strayed to her cleavage for a brief moment. "Liking you in it isn't the problem."

Eyes closed, she gave her head a saucy shake so her hair shifted across her bare back. "When I needed a new swimsuit, I thought, what the heck? I'll buy a bikini. Who's to see it but you and me anyway?" She tapped the tip of his nose with one finger and moistened her lips with her tongue. "And you haven't been around enough to notice."

"Adrienne," he said, his voice husky, "I think I'd like to go for a swim. Can you keep that thing on in the water?"

"Who knows?" she returned brightly and snatched a towel from her chair. "I guess we'll see, won't we?"

## Chapter Eleven

The moonlight slanted across the lagoon in a shimmering silver ribbon. In the distance the ocean broke against the reef, outlining the entrance to the lagoon in foamy white. At high tide the waves rose and fell in a rhythmic, undulating murmur. The smell of musk and the promise of a steamy, tropical night hung in the air.

Adrienne waded in first, then broke the water in smooth, even strokes. Nick followed, expecting the water to sizzle at any moment from the heat surging through his alert body.

Ahead of him, Adrienne rolled over and lay floating on her back. Her perky breasts thrust skyward. The tight buds of her nipples poked at the hot pink fabric that slashed in narrow strips across her mounded flesh. Nick sank below the surface to cool off. He came up with a nose full of water and sputtered, no cooler for the effort.

When he saw Murph he was going to give

him hell. If Adrienne sneezed in that size eight scrap of nothing, she'd send her bikini top flying.

With a splash, she dolphin-dived and disappeared. Treading water, Nick whirled in the water. Where the hell had she gone? Didn't she know she ought to be careful doing such foolish tricks at night? She could get—ouch! What was that nipping at his calf? A turtle?

With hair?

Masses of it swirled about his legs. And oh, God, breasts—he was sure they were breasts—grazed the backs of his thighs. He reached down and, grabbing what he could, yanked Adrienne from the water.

What he yanked was her bikini top. The thin strap tied over her back resisted, then snapped.

"Ouch!" she cried out. "That hurt."

She was treading water now. Each time she kicked her feet, the upper curves of her breasts rose above the water. Nick groaned, wadding her teeny bikini top in his hand.

"I'm, uh, sorry, Adrienne. I didn't mean . . . that is, aw, hell, here!" Gulping hard, he thrust her top at her. His fingertips grazed her nipples. He snatched back his hand and knotted it into a fist beneath the water.

"A lot of good this will do me." She turned and swam six strong strokes toward the beach. In a form that would make a fielder proud, she stood up in water to mid-thigh, hauled off and threw her bikini top onto the beach. She stood

231

there, as if trying to decide what to do next, her bare back shiny wet.

Nick's throat tightened. What would she do now? With Adrienne, he couldn't guess. His thoughts were way past haywire. His body had sprung to life like a young stallion's. No way was he going to stay there, treading water, and let her irritation drive her out of the water and away from him.

He had swum within ten feet of her when she turned around. If Nick hadn't been a strong swimmer, he would have drowned. His stomach clenched into knots, and his breath caught. She stood there, her head held high, her fingers dangling in the water. The lagoon lapped at the pink triangle between her legs. Although she was almost naked, her regal posture told him she was comfortable with who she was, where she was, and whom she was with.

She could have been a sculpted statue. The part of her she'd protected from the sun with her one-piece swimsuit shone like alabaster in the moonlight. Lush breasts, the inward tuck of her narrow waist, her smooth, flat abdomen.

Nick's heart lurched. *She's giving herself to me,* he thought, in the brief moment before his brains scrambled.

Dragging leaden legs over the sandy lagoon bottom toward her, he somehow found his voice. "Adrienne . . . ?"

He had uttered her name as a question. She answered it by striding toward him, her pendulous breasts inviting the touch of his hands, his mouth. "Yes, Nick," she said with a lift of her chin and a tremulous smile. "You wanted me?"

"Want you?" He took her hand and pulled her willing, supple body into his arms. "Darlin', you've got me tied into so many knots I can't think straight."

"Good. I don't want you to think. I want you to touch me. All over." She trembled in his arms. "I want you to make this horrible, aching feeling go away. I want you to make love to me," she pleaded. Taking his head in her hands, she parted her lips in invitation.

Nick lost himself in the silkiness of her mouth, in the tangle of tongues and arms and legs. Adrienne's skin was like wet, slick satin beneath his hands and his mouth.

Adrienne shivered, shaking one coherent thought into Nick's addled brain. She was cold. He should scoop her into his arms and carry her to his hut. But, dear Lord, the things she was doing with her hands!

Thanks to her, his need was too great, too urgent. That was all too evident when Adrienne broke the kiss. With a wicked smile, she slid her breasts down the front of his body and eased the damned confining swimsuit down his legs.

Gazing up at him with hot, adoring eyes, she eased back up, sliding her breasts slowly up his thighs. Nick glanced down. "Darlin', if you don't hurry back up here, I'm going to—" and then she flicked the tip of him with her tongue.

Once. He couldn't breathe. Twice. He took her by the shoulders. Her mouth closed over him, and his heart jolted. With trembling hands, he yanked her from the water.

Her eyes were huge and wounded. "I don't know what got into me. I've never done that before. I'm sorry I, that is, I'd hoped, oh, forget it." She turned to go. "I'll see you tomorrow."

Nick's chest was heaving. He drew in a deep draught of air and shuddered before hauling her back into his arms. "You're not going anywhere. And I don't need an apology. It wasn't that I didn't like it . . ."

"Then why . . . ?"

"Tonight's for both of us, darlin', not just for me. Come here."

Grasping her waist with his hands, he lifted her from the water so he could swirl his tongue around her nipples and take the distended tips gently between his teeth. She threw back her head and moaned, then slid her legs around his waist and locked them behind his back.

"Adrienne . . ."

"Nick, please." She shifted the narrow strip of fabric between her legs, looped her arms around his neck, and positioned herself for entry. "I need you now."

And Nick needed Adrienne. He closed his eyes and joined her, right there in the lagoon.

"Do you hurt . . . anywhere?" Nick asked.

234

Adrienne chuckled and snuggled against him on his bed. In a couple of hours, the sun would sneak over the eastern horizon and seal the night in her memory. "For the first time in four days, I don't hurt."

"Not even here?" Sliding his hand between her legs, he touched her there and bent to kiss her taut belly.

Her eyes drifted shut. She moved against his probing fingers. "Does that answer your question?"

"I was just worried, with the saltwater and all." He laid his head on her abdomen and smiled up at her. In the glow of his lamp, he looked surprisingly sad, considering they had made love practically all night. "I never want to hurt you, Adrienne. No matter what happens, I want you to believe that."

She smoothed her hand over his cheek. Her heart was bursting with so much love for this man she couldn't bear to contain it. But what had prompted the pitiful look on his face, and what was this nonsense about him hurting her?

Maybe he hadn't decided yet if he could make a commitment to her. Well, there was still time. "I love you, Nick."

"I know, darlin'." He sighed over her abdomen.

She waited for him to return the endearment. He didn't. His gaze strayed from her face. He focused across the room, or maybe across the world. She had no way of knowing. She only knew she wouldn't let him slip away from her again. She would make him admit how he felt for her.

"You love me, don't you?" she asked him boldly and braced herself for his answer.

"You know I do."

It wasn't enough. "I need to hear you say it."

He sighed, as if it were an effort to tell her.

She pushed his head off her abdomen. "I'm going." Stinging from this latest rejection, she wrapped the sheet around her bare body and scrambled off the bed.

He caught her arm. "Where are you going?"

"Back to my bungalow." She pulled from his grasp and headed for the doorway. "Where I can have a pity party."

She was halfway out the door when he called after her, "Adrienne, don't leave."

She halted her retreat, but she didn't look at him. She couldn't. If he didn't tell her what she needed to hear, her empty stomach would knot up, and the tears would flow. "Why shouldn't I?"

"Because," he said, his voice cracking, "I do love you."

She hesitated, sure he was going to tack on a "but" to the endearment and turn it into another rejection. He didn't. She turned around. Nick gave her a lopsided grin and opened his arms.

The fear, the hurt melted like ice in the South Seas sun. She dropped the sheet and launched

236

herself into his arms. "Why did you make me drag it out of you?"

He pulled her tight against his chest. "There's just so much else."

She glanced up, uneasy with the doubt that had crept into his voice. "Men can be so disgustingly vague. What else?"

"The reason I'm here, on this island."

"I know why you're here. You're running away, but that's in the past." She wriggled in his arms and grinned. "What else?"

*"What* I'm doing here."

"Nick, Nick, I know *what* you're doing here." She dismissed that with a wave of her hand and pulled away. "The pearls. Wait here, and I'll be right back."

"Where are you going?" he asked.

She was already running on the beach, naked as a jaybird and relishing the rush of night air on her bare skin. She'd never felt freer or happier. She had Nick to thank for that. He loved her! "To get something," she called out.

"Don't be too long," he yelled.

"Don't worry. I wouldn't think of it."


Morning had not yet crept into the lagoon by the time Adrienne changed into the contents of Murphy's second package—a black and gold bikini in a size ten. She was about to gather the makings of a sunrise breakfast picnic when she heard a strange noise outside her window.

"Nick?"

No answer.

A strange sense of foreboding crept over her. Ducking out of sight of the window, she tiptoed through the shadows to the doorway. Then, bolstered by a deeply drawn breath, she stuck her head outside and collided with a young Melanesian boy of about six.

"Well," she said, catching him by the shoulders. "Who do we have here?"

He smiled up at her shyly. In the tradition of the native males, he was wearing only a sulu, a wrap-type skirt in a colorful, floral fabric. His teeth and the whites of his huge brown eyes gleamed from a darling, dark face. He held a white orchid. He thrust it into Adrienne's hands.

"For me?" she said, pointing to her chest.

He flashed a wide grin and nodded.

"Why, thank you. I'm honored."

So this was her anonymous admirer. Nick truly hadn't left her the other flowers. A part of her lamented that discovery. Another was won over by the charming little boy who gazed up at her pie-eyed.

She smoothed her hand over his kinky black hair and smiled at his youthful innocence. What had Nick been like as a small boy? How would he be as a father to a child such as this?

Again she pointed at her chest. "I'm Adrienne. Adrienne," she repeated.

He rolled his eyes and lifted his shoulders in a show of childish delight.

She pointed at his chest. "And you? What's your name?"

He frowned and shook his head.

She remembered Nick saying on the day she arrived that the natives didn't speak English. "That's okay," she soothed, kneeling on the dock so she could face the boy eye to eye. She took his hand and squeezed it. "I don't understand your language either. Maybe before I go, we'll both learn."

It suddenly struck her that this young child must have negotiated his way from the village to her bungalow in the dead of night. There was still at least an hour until daybreak. Whether or not he was skilled at fending off an attack by a wild animal, she couldn't permit him to go home by himself.

She put the orchid in water, then took the boy's hand and headed for Nick's hut. "We'll just wake up Nick, and he'll take you—"

The boy dug his feet into the sand and shook his head briskly.

"He won't hurt you," she assured him. "Come on now."

The boy wouldn't budge an inch. He kept tugging on Adrienne's hand and pointing at a slight opening in the lush growth that bordered the beach.

Adrienne noticed a path of small footprints leading from the opening to her bungalow's window. She figured the boy wanted to return along the same path. She could tell if she let go of his hand, he'd hightail it off by himself. If he did, she'd worry herself sick for his safety. She called out to Nick twice, but got no answer.

"He must have fallen asleep," she murmured out loud and chuckled as she realized why.

She remembered Nick talking about contacting the chief on a couple of occasions. That meant the chief had a shortwave radio. If she accompanied the boy to the village, she could get in touch with Nick when she arrived there to let him know where she was. He could sail around the island to pick her up, or she would wait while he walked the distance.

She persuaded the boy to return with her to her bungalow so she could slip into her tennis shoes and pull some jeans and a shirt on over her bikini. Then, hoping the spear she had purchased as a souvenir in Nouméa would fend off any snakes or wild pigs, she took the boy's hand and followed him outside.

"I've been wanting to see your village anyway," she said, although she knew he couldn't understand her. "I just hope Nick doesn't flip his lid when he finds out I went without him."


The path the boy took led them through the fern forest. At about daybreak they emerged on the beach of another exotic lagoon.

The wet sand was alive with hermit crabs scurrying for cover and sea gulls poking their beaks into the water for an early breakfast of spawning fish. Two large sea turtles came out of the glistening water and crawled onto a huge, flat rock.

Adrienne thought of Nick. She already missed him. Later she would relish the opportunity to curl up next to him on the beach and soak up the rays of the sun.

After an hour's trek, she and the boy rounded the curve of yet another lagoon to arrive at the village. This inlet of the sea was wide, but didn't make as deep a loop as hers and Nick's lagoon. The strip of beach, though, was wider, extending from the water at least fifty feet. The gleaming white sand yielded not to a lush fern forest but to a clearing that stretched as far as Adrienne could see.

In the clearing, open-windowed huts with conical roofs similar to Nick's were clustered around what looked like a communal area. A totem pole, into which menacing faces had been carved, served as the central spire for each hut. Besides numerous coconut palms, brilliant poinsettia plants with scarlet foliage dotted the clearing, reaching as high as sixteen feet.

The lagoon's surface was dotted with canoes apparently returning from a night of fishing. The boy called out across the water. A man turned and waved. Adrienne figured the bare-chested native who wore a necklace of exquisite shell beads must be the child's father. She briefly imagined how hostile she would feel if a stranger came walking into her neighborhood holding her son's hand.

She stuck her spear in the sand before following the boy into the village and hoped she'd be welcome.

A woman in a red-and-orange floral Mother Hubbard hurried across the clearing and took the little one's hand. Adrienne didn't have to be a linguist to figure out she was giving the youngster a well-deserved scolding.

"Hello," she said. "I'm Adrienne Laurel." She pointed over her shoulder. "I'm on Ile de Fleur visiting, back there, with Nick. Your son came to see me, and I thought it would be wise to make sure he got home safely."

When the woman heard Nick's name, she broke out in a broad grin. She took Adrienne's hand and, chattering in her own language, pulled her into the village.

Adrienne became the welcome guest of this tribe of friendly, industrious natives. The boy, whose name she learned was Santu, the son of the chief, took her on a tour of the place. She watched the islanders roasting coffee beans over a fire on a piece of ironlike metal. She observed the women hilling sweet potatoes and shredding coconut meat. She wondered what the bamboo cages that were stacked in every available space in the village were intended for.

"What," she murmured out loud, "do you plan to do with all those cages?"

A passing tribesman, who wore a necklace

similar to the chief's, paused, then turned to her. "Cages?"

She nodded. "You speak English?"

He beamed a toothy grin, obviously proud of his ability. "Cages for oysters. Make pearls."

"Pearls?" That didn't make sense. But neither did the man's ability to understand and speak English.

He pointed toward the lagoon and added, "In water."

Adrienne started to ask him what the cages had to do with making pearls when the chief rounded the hut. Adrienne wasn't sure whether the chief was upset with her or with his tribesman. But he pulled the man away, talking in sharp, scolding tones in his native tongue.

Maybe it was time to call Nick.

Adrienne got nowhere in her attempts to communicate to Santu that she needed to radio Nick. She attempted to leave, but the chief's wife wouldn't hear of it.

She made Adrienne sit on a woven mat outside her husband's hut with Santu. There she served Adrienne and her son a feast of local delicacies. Adrienne sampled a half dozen versions of yam, a bread made of corn, a kind of jelly, coconut milk, and a juicy, red fruit she couldn't identify.

Adrienne tried to make mental note of the foods for her report. The meal was filling but not what she would call gourmet fare. Judging from the leanness of the natives, though, she decided the diet must be nutritious and lacking in much fat.

She glanced across the clearing and did a double take. Two men wearing khakilike clothes were emerging from a hut. They were tall men, with the pale skin of Caucasians, albeit tanned. They took one look at her, exchanged glances, tipped their hats, then headed for the communal work hut.

Who were they? she wondered with a chill of apprehension. Nick was supposedly the only Caucasian on the island, or the only English-speaking one at least. He said the islanders hadn't intermarried, either.

A half dozen men whose skin was deep golden brown, not dark like the Melanesian natives', emerged from the same hut. Their hair was straight, not kinky. They looked like Polynesians.

"Santu?" she said, and pointed at the nonnatives. "What are those men doing here?"

A shadow crossed the mat. She looked up. It was Nick. He wasn't smiling.

"You could have left me a note."

Adrienne scrambled to her feet. "When I went to my bungalow to change and scrounge up some breakfast for us, I caught this little rascal leaving me an orchid."

"So," Nick said, scowling at the youngster, "Santu's been your secret admirer."

"And this time he delivered his flower at night." She turned to put a protective arm around the boy, but he backed away and ducked into the hut. "He was dead set on coming back to the village right away. I wanted to wake you so we could take him together, but Santu wouldn't come with me to your hut. I called out to you twice, but you didn't answer."

"I fell asleep," Nick replied and, taking her hand, ran his thumb over the tops of her fingers. "I was worried sick when I woke up and you weren't there."

"I'm sorry. I didn't think about leaving a note. I figured I could contact you when I got here, but, well, it hasn't exactly been easy to communicate with the natives."

"I only knew you were here because the chief radioed me. Come on," he said and took her elbow. "I brought the boat. We'll sail back."

"Wait. I need to say good-bye to Santu and thank his mother for her hospitality. And—" Adrienne lowered her voice to a whisper "—you might want to check out something before we leave."

"What's that?" Nick asked and raked a weary hand through his hair.

"There's something strange going on here."

"Like what?"

"There are men here I don't think you know about. Two with skin like ours, tall, tanned. And six I suspect are Polynesians. They saw me, but they didn't speak to me. And look." She pointed at the stacks and stacks of cages. "I asked one of the islanders what the cages were

245

for, and you know what? He spoke a little English. He said something about oysters and pearls and the lagoon. What if the secret's out? What if those men found out about the pearls and they're already harvesting the island waters? Nick, I'd be worried if I were you."

"Come on," he said, apparently not worried a bit about her observations. "I'll explain everything on the way back, but we've got to hurry. A storm's brewing."

Adrienne paced the deck of Nick's sailboat, unable to believe what he had just told her over the howling wind.

"So, all the time I've been here you've been working on this pearl project and lying to me about it. You lied to me about the natives speaking English. You lied to me about wild pigs and poisonous snakes so I'd be too afraid to wander around the island by myself." Her cheeks burned, even in the now chilly breeze. "I can't believe I was stupid enough to believe that one!"

"I couldn't risk telling you the truth, Adrienne. Not until I got those papers from my attorney in Los Angeles that said the pearling rights to the island's waters were legally the natives'. And I just got those yesterday."

"So why didn't you tell me last night?"

"If you'll recall, I was otherwise occupied." He shot her a hot, reminding look that jolted

246

her back to their night of lovemaking.

She shut the exquisite memories of those hours from her mind She had trusted Nick with her heart and her body, and he hadn't loved her enough to take her into his confidence.

"And there's nothing for you in this pearl culturing farm? Not a nickel?"

"Do you find that so hard to believe?"

"Yes, all of this!" she yelled and swiped at the tears of betrayal. "You said you loved me. How could you lie to someone you love?"

"Believe me, it wasn't easy, darlin'."

Adrienne's stomach turned over at his use of the familiar endearment. "How do I know you're telling me the truth when you say you love me?"

"I guess you'll just have to trust me on that one."

"Why should I?"

"Hell if I know!" Nick bellowed over the wind. "But I'll tell you what. If I had it to do over again, I wouldn't do anything differently. I learned a long time ago that the people you invest the most trust in are the ones who sometimes betray you." The boat lurched. "Watch out. Here comes a big one."

Adrienne braced herself on the cabin roof, but Nick's warning came too late. The boat's bow dipped, and the spray of a big wave drenched them both.

Adrienne wiped the stinging saltwater from her eyes and glared at Nick, feeling downright miserable. "How am I supposed to know when you're lying and when you aren't?" she shrieked.

Nick said something in return, but the wind ate up his words. Rain was pelting them now like stinging needles. Nick pointed to the hatch and mouthed the word, "Go."

Adrienne gave up on the conversation and went below, thankful they'd be back in the lagoon within minutes.

Then what? she wondered and stared out the porthole at the stormy sea. Her throat constricted. Her heart sank in her chest like an anchor. She needed time. Time to think through what Nick had told her.

Nick gave her all the time she wanted.

Days. He disappeared for hours at a time, presumably to work in the village.

While he was gone, Adrienne went over everything Nick had said and done since she'd arrived. She realized he'd told lie after lie after lie. Fuming, she waited for him to come to her and admit that lying to her was the biggest mistake in his life.

He didn't.

She decided hell would freeze over before she went to him. So she shut him from her mind and wrote an addendum to her report about her trip to the village.

At least she tried. The seven-page addition didn't make a lick of sense in its draft form, except in her assertion that the village should be off-limits to visitors. She was afraid a continuing string of ogling strangers would disrupt the islanders' simple life. There really weren't any other sights or scenery to see that they couldn't observe on Grand Terre anyway.

She radioed Foster and told him her work was done. When she heard his voice, the tears came. She tried to hide her misery, but she couldn't fool him. Weeping over the wires, she confessed to Foster that she had fallen in love with Nick and that he had lied to her.

Foster said not to make any rash decisions, as he'd done when he enlisted in the army and left her mother. Adrienne couldn't stop crying. Distraught over her emotional state, Foster offered to fly down and accompany her back to Phoenix. However, Adrienne pulled herself together and told him she could make the trip alone.

In less than a week she would leave the island. She would resume her life as a travel agent. Nick would stick around on Ile de Fleur and busy himself with the pearl culturing farm.

God help her, she still loved him. Even though he had lied to her. What was she going to do?

At dawn three days before her scheduled departure, panic set in.

Adrienne hadn't slept a wink the night before. As the lagoon came alive with the now-familiar cries of parrots and barks of cagous, Foster's advice finally penetrated her haze of anger.

She paced the interior of her bungalow, putting herself in Nick's shoes. She finally conceded that Nick might have had a reason for withholding the truth from her about the pearls. After all, he had been protecting the natives, not himself. He might have made a mistake in not trusting her, but his motives hadn't been selfish.

She thought about her conversation with Foster and his warning not to make any hasty decisions. Foster knew only too well what could happen when one did. The decisions he and Adrienne's mother had made had affected their entire lives, and those of others. They had been denied their love because they hadn't put their feelings for one another before all else.

"And you're going to make that same mistake," Adrienne chided herself, "if you don't think of something quick."

Now that she'd opened the door to her mind, all Nick's good qualities came rushing back to her. His quick wit, his boyish charm, his ability to make her relax and enjoy the simple things in life.

When she had arrived on the island, her nerves had been rubbed so raw she could hardly function. She had healed. She had Nick to thank for that. She no longer carried around that driving need to avenge the wrongs committed against her grandmother. In the place of hate and resentment was love — pure, simple, and healthy. Trust in a man with old-fashioned values. A man who had made a few mistakes, but hadn't she, too?

She smiled, thinking how she had regarded him as a lazy, good-for-nothing bum. All the while he was helping the natives, without recognition, no less. And mostly at night, after he had fulfilled his responsibilities to her and Foster.

She remembered Nick saying when times got tough, his wife had split. Which is exactly what Adrienne had done the first time a problem surfaced between them.

"Oh, Nick," she murmured, glancing out her window at his hut and berating herself for wasting days they could have been together. "I'm sorry for being such a prideful fool."

She couldn't offer her apologies quickly enough. She darted across the beach to his hut, hoping Nick was awake and would at least listen to her.

She bolstered her courage and peered inside. Her heart did joyful somersaults. Nick was sprawled on his stomach on his bed, sleeping like a baby. A very big baby.

She tiptoed over, prepared to wake him up with a kiss on his bare back. Or maybe she'd just crawl into bed with him.

Selfish woman! She had nodded off at around three in the morning, and Nick had yet to sail back into the lagoon. He couldn't have been asleep more than three hours. She could tell from his drawn face and his haggard look that he was exhausted. The poor man needed his sleep. And, she admitted selfishly, he would probably be more likely to listen to her apology if he had a good rest.

She'd just leave him a note, a few words to let him know how wrong she'd been to judge him so quickly. Later, when he awoke, they could talk. She would fix him breakfast, and then they could make love. Wrong! First they would make love, and then they'd eat. Or maybe they'd skip it altogether.

Having a difficult time refraining from giggling, Adrienne glanced around Nick's room for something to write on.

There was only one logical place to look — the table piled high with papers that served as his desk. Adrienne tried to imagine him as an accountant — organized, logical, and sequential. She almost laughed out loud. Nick Helton did not fit the mold. With an efficient secretary, maybe. But not by himself.

On top of the desk there wasn't so much as a scrap of paper she felt free to write on. Careful not to let it squeak, she eased opened the drawer. Ah, there was a pen, at least. And . . . a letter. A letter addressed to N. McKenzie Holton on stationery from that attorney in Los Angeles. The guy ought to know his secretary didn't proofread well. Nick's name wasn't Holton. It was Helton, for Pete's sake!

Hoping to find some notepaper beneath the letter, she pulled it from the drawer. The letter's salutation—Dear Mack—leapt off the page.

*Mack?* She frowned. His name wasn't Mack.

A memory crept into her confused mind. The day in Pierre's jewelry store. Pierre calling Nick "Mack" as they left. Nick dismissing the mistake as confusion on the part of his friend.

Yet his attorney addressed him as Mack. Why had Nick lied that time?

Her attention lifted to the addressee section of the letter, near the top, at the left of the page. She skimmed the name briefly and frowned. N. McKenzie Holton. N—Nick. Mc-Kenzie-Mack. Nick Holton. Mack Holton. N. McKenzie Holton.

*N. McKenzie Holton?* Adrienne grabbed the desk for support, then forced herself to breathe deeply. In, out. Calm down. She was being silly. Overreacting. Nick couldn't be the N. McKenzie Holton who had defrauded her grandmother.

The fact Nick had obviously lied about Pierre's reason for calling him Mack combined with Adrienne's feeling she'd seen Nick's face before. Could he be *the* monster N. McKenzie Holton?

Her gaze shot to Nick's sleeping hulk and back to the page. The Nick she knew, the wonderful, giving, selfless Nick couldn't be the man whose eyes she had sworn she'd scratch out if she ever met him. She loved Nick. She couldn't be quick to judge again. She had to trust him.

She sank into the chair and pressed a hand over her chest. Her heart was thumping wildly.

She had to read the letter. She had no choice. There had to be an explanation for the sameness of names. Maybe the lawyer's secretary had transposed names on two letters. Maybe . . . oh, Lord. Adrienne's hands shook so hard, she could barely read. *Please, let me be wrong.*

She knew before she read two sentences, there was no mistake in names. Nick had said he was from Atlanta. Adrienne remembered watching a cable news network with Gracie when the health-care scam had unfolded. The reporters had interviewed a retired couple in Atlanta. They still lived on the block where N. McKenzie Holton had grown up. Adrienne had pitied the poor couple. They couldn't believe the bright boy who had mowed their lawn and fed their cat when they were on vacation had squandered their life's savings. They'd invested their last penny in his company.

A company that had been incorporated in California. The trial had taken place in Los Angeles. Los Angeles, where the attorney practiced law. Where Nick had said he lived.

Adrienne was overwhelmed by a sick feeling. She rocked in the chair, her arms and legs and chest — oh, God, her chest — aching so badly she had to shake her head so she could continue reading.

The more she read, the dizzier she felt.

The letter warned Nick, or Mack, that his

partners, Mitch Calhoun and Morgan Priestly, had been released from prison. That the lawyer's suspicions had been well-founded about the attractive brunette who showed up in the attorney's offices a couple of months ago. She had, indeed, been working for Nick's former partners when she wheedled his current whereabouts from the firm's receptionist. The attorney warned Nick to be careful. He closed by saying he'd had lunch with the prosecuting attorney for his case a week ago. The latter had asked after *Mack's* welfare.

Adrienne returned the letter to the drawer and sat back, so numb she couldn't move. She did manage to turn a bitter gaze to Nick.

To Mack.

He still lay sprawled on his stomach. One arm dangled over the side of the bed. One hooked over the place on the pillow she had shared with him one whole night. She had made love with him. She had seduced him! The man who might as well have put a gun to her grandmother's ear and pulled the trigger.

The bile in her stomach jettisoned to the back of her throat. How could he have dared to touch her? How could he think of making her feel, by his lies and his deceptions, that he loved her? Even now, she couldn't believe he didn't really love her.

Think! she told herself. Listen to your mind, instead of your heart.

Squeezing her forehead in her hand, she ran

through the events of the weeks since she had arrived on Ile de Fleur. Her thoughts snagged on those damned binoculars of Nick's and the fact he'd been spying on her that first night.

Her cheeks burned with the memory. He had leered at her while she walked across the beach, practically nude. After her initial anger had faded, she had decided he was just behaving like any man who'd been stuck on a remote island for four years. Who could see, or date women only with considerable effort.

Now she wasn't so sure. Something in the attorney's letter sprang to mind. The mention of the brunette working for Nick's former partners. What was it she'd done? Oh, yes. Misrepresented herself so she could find out where Nick was living for his former partners.

A brunette, huh? She, Adrienne, was a brunette. When she had arrived, Nick had treated her with buckets of disdain. Was it just possible he suspected she was that same brunette? That she had come to the island to spy on him for his partners?

Yes! That made sense. That first day when they had been waiting for high tide, he had asked her why she'd come to the island. No, that wasn't right. He'd almost interrogated her. At the time she had thought he was merely being intentionally rude, because Foster had already explained to Nick why she was coming.

Then Nick had built a hut on the lagoon when he had a perfectly good place to live on the windward side of the island. Nick's agreement with Foster had been that he would be available via shortwave to do as Adrienne asked. At the time, it seemed rather funny to Adrienne that Nick wanted to put up a hut right there on the beach, within sight of her bungalow. But, being the trusting fool that she was, she dismissed his quirky behavior. His actions fit with his odd and capricious nature.

Maybe all this time, he'd been watching her to make sure she didn't . . . do what? Contact his partners about his whereabouts? That didn't mesh. Why had he been spying on her then? What else hadn't he confessed?

She remembered telling Nick about her grandmother. How Gracie hadn't gone to a doctor when she fell ill, because she had no insurance, nor the money to pay for a physical. Adrienne had even talked about Nick's former company, Eternity Health Care. If he had been any kind of a man, he would have revealed who he was.

Yeah, right. He was going to admit he was the man whose eyes she wanted to scratch out. If she knew that, she would have radioed Murphy and been on her way home that very day. And poor Mr. Helton, or Holton, or whatever his name was, would have had to give back the precious money Foster paid him to serve as her guide.

She remembered now, with sudden clarity, how Nick had acted strangely in Nouméa. He hadn't wanted to stay all night on the island.

He'd hidden behind sunglasses and that stupid floppy hat during the day. She was willing to bet he was afraid someone might recognize him.

She almost had! Lord, that's why his face had kept niggling at her consciousness until . . . they made love. That's when she had developed a deep, abiding trust in Nick.

Made love—Lord, she couldn't believe she had welcomed Nick inside her. A shiver ripped her shoulders. She felt dirty. Violated.

For once she prayed her grandmother didn't know what was happening to her. If she did, she would be hopping all over heaven like a riled banshee.

The hut was closing in on Adrienne. She had to get out of there, away from this poor excuse for a man.

She tiptoed to the door. In her peripheral vision she saw Nick's binoculars sitting on his trunk. She snapped them up and took them with her. When she was halfway to her bungalow, she hauled off and sent them sailing into the lagoon.

She showered quickly, in cold water. She hoped the biting spray would diminish the feelings for Nick that lingered in her stubborn heart.

The shower didn't relieve the ache in her heart. But it did one thing. It crystallized her thinking. She realized Nick's conscience had been eating at him. At least she thought that had been the reason he acted so strangely in

Nouméa. That night she sprang her hot pink teddy on him, he had told her he wanted to talk. How much would he have confessed if she'd given him the chance?

Fool! Nothing. There weren't enough words in the language to explain what he'd done back in the States. Nothing he could have told her would have diminished her antagonism for him. He'd said vaguely, "There's a lot about me you don't know." Then he had erected a stony barrier between them. Being the trusting fool she was, Adrienne had figured no secrets could alter her feelings for him. She had scaled the temporary wall he'd built around himself. Then back on the island—her face flamed at the remembrance—she'd seduced him again.

And he'd let her!

She sought solace in her bungalow. Even there, the memories of Nick tortured her. She had to get away. Today. She couldn't spend one more day on the same island with Nick.

And to think she had planned on apologizing to him! If she hadn't found that letter in his drawer, she would have. Then she would have spent her last hours with him trying to persuade him to listen to his heart.

The trouble was, the scoundrel didn't have one!

Before she left, she would give Nick the lecture of his life. She might have to tie her hands behind her back to do it, so she wouldn't haul off and hit him.

The thought of touching him again had her insides twitching.

*No, no, you're not supposed to feel that. Be strong for Gracie. Do something! Pour water in his face and tell him his subterfuge is over.*

Suddenly she thought of a better idea. One that would require the performance of her life. She grabbed a piece of yellow, lined paper and penned a note.

While Nick was still sleeping, she returned to his hut. In nothing flat, she was in and out and on her way back to her bungalow. She trembled every step of the way.

# Chapter Twelve

She was doing it again. Making him hot all over. Making his nether regions swell with a need so intense he thought he'd explode.

The intoxicating scent of Adrienne filled Nick's nostrils. Hazy fragments of his dreams had him smiling at her remembered cries of ecstasy.

Daylight crawled over his eyelids, heralding the arrival of morning. Weary from too little sleep and a slew of twenty-hour days, he groped the bed beside him for Adrienne's silky thighs and opened one eye.

He quickly squeezed it shut again. The damned bed was empty. Even though he knew in his heart Adrienne wouldn't be beside him when he woke up, he never gave up hope.

The tightening in his chest was almost unbearable. He loved Adrienne as he'd loved no other woman. Lord, how she had loved him back! But *had* was the key word. *Had,* as in past tense.

He pushed off the bed, squinting against the sun filtering through his doorway. He couldn't feel worse if he'd downed a whole barrel of the Aussies' high-alcohol-content beer.

He'd lost his taste for beer. Since Adrienne had found out he'd been lying to her, he hadn't even felt like eating.

Tomorrow she would leave, which would be no skin off her nose. She'd be glad to get away from him and the island. But she wasn't going to leave until he told her the truth about himself. All of it. Then any hope he had of salvaging what they had together would vanish like soap bubbles.

Life without her was going to be a bitch. That's what the last few days had been anyway. Morning, evening, meals, the changing hues of the ocean—none of it had any meaning without her. Koli's wife had thought Nick was sick and tried to get him to drink one of her herbal remedies.

No herbal remedy could make him forget the emptiness. Adrienne had become a part of his life as essential as breathing.

And it wasn't just the sex, though that was good. Damned good. He'd never met a woman so seductive and playful and uninhibited. More than the sex, what had him aching at the thought of losing her was her inherent goodness. That was a quality he had decided didn't exist anymore outside his simple island world. That's why he'd stayed on Ile de Fleur. Because it was easier to be alone than to go somewhere else and risk being betrayed again.

The hell of it was, he'd done to her what he couldn't bear having done to him. He had betrayed her trust. For that he would be eternally sorry.

He had promised the Aussies he'd go out on a dive for oysters today. He dragged himself off the bed, intent on pouring some melted ice over his miserable head to shake out the cobwebs.

He was halfway to the ice chest when he spotted what looked like a piece of yellow paper on the floor. He picked it up and saw his name written across the front. He ran his finger over the elegant handwriting that reminded him of Adrienne's long, willowy legs. He opened the note and read, hoping against hope.

"I came over to apologize, Nick. You were dead to the world, and I didn't want to wake you, so I'm going back to my bungalow to sleep. (I haven't been able to sleep much since our argument!) If you get up before I do, I'd really appreciate your doing me a favor.

"Santu left me another orchid last night. I'm worried about him. I wrote him the attached note. Would you be a dear and run it over to him and speak with his mother? (You'll have to translate the note, of course.) Try to impress on Santu that I appreciate his gift, but he worries me, and I'm sure his mother, too, when he goes out at night. Tell him I'll never forget him, and I'll write.

"Take your time. When you get back, if you'll listen to me, I have a lot to say. Okay?"


Attached was a note to the chief's son. In it Adrienne promised she'd send Santu prints of the pictures she'd taken of her with the boy using her camera's timer.

Nick broke out in a grin. He wanted to run over to Adrienne's bungalow and make love to her, right then. If she forgave him for lying to her about the pearls, maybe she would understand when he revealed his true identity to her. Maybe there was a chance of salvaging what he and Adrienne had together.

He glanced across the beach. He couldn't see any signs of activity in Adrienne's place yet. He thought about the errand she had asked him to run.

He didn't relish spending half the day away from her, especially since she was scheduled to leave tomorrow. He could probably radio the chief and accomplish as much. Still, the errand would give him a few hours to think. To rehearse what he was going to say to Adrienne, now that he had the chance.

He turned the page over and dashed off a

quick note telling Adrienne he'd left about eight-thirty for the village. That gave him ten minutes to shower and pull on his cutoffs. With any luck, he'd be back by twelve. He signed it "All Ears, Nick" and hoped she'd appreciate the humor.

After showering and dressing, he reached for his binoculars where he'd left them on the trunk.

That was strange. They weren't there. Nor were they anywhere else in his hut.

*Oh, well,* he thought. *I was so bone-tired when I got in last night. I probably left them on the ship.*

On the way to his dinghy, he stuck his head inside the door of Adrienne's bungalow. One look at her, and his heart melted. She was curled into a ball like a kitten. All her soft, womanly places were covered up.

He started to walk over and kiss her goodbye, then thought better of it. He didn't want to awaken her. She deserved her rest. And he wasn't ready to talk yet.

Instead he left his note where she had—in the middle of the open doorway. He weighted the note with one of her tennis shoes.

And left.


The padding of Nick's deck shoes on the dock grew fainter and fainter, then stopped. Adrienne opened her eyes but didn't move.

Nick could always change his mind and come back, God forbid.

For a moment all she could hear was the frantic thudding of her heart. And then, there it was, the sputter of a gasoline engine starting. The whine of the dinghy's motor as Nick pulled away from the dock.

Adrienne crept out of bed and hid in the shadows at the side of the door. She watched Nick haul himself up on the *Lorelei* and hoist the sails. The powerful muscles played across his back as he cranked the anchor into the boat. Adrienne's last thought as he sailed across the reef was she hoped she never set sight on his miserable face again.

Everything depended on timing. She picked up his note and read his message with stony indifference. Yet he had told her what she needed to know — how long he expected to be gone. Three and a half hours. She figured an hour in the village, which left two-and-a-half hours' sailing time. In a little over an hour, he should be in the village and busy talking to Santu. That meant the safest time for her to call Murphy without a chance of Nick listening in on his radio was in an hour and a half.

Perfect. She yanked her suitcase from beneath the bed and began stuffing her belongings inside. Everything she'd worn when she'd been remotely intimate with Nick she left in her drawer. The strapless aqua dress she had bought in Nouméa. The hot pink teddy. The bikini. By the time the hour rolled around to contact Murphy, she was packed.

Murphy had just left the Windward Islands when he answered her call.

"Good morning to you, Adrienne," he greeted her. "And what can I be doing for you this bright, beautiful morning?"

Adrienne was careful not to reveal her actual plans. Murphy was fond of her. She knew that. But his friendship with Nick predated his acquaintance with her by four years. She didn't want to put Murphy in the predicament of compromising that relationship.

Besides, there wasn't time to explain why she was attempting such a drastic measure. "I never did thank you for getting me that item I wanted," Adrienne began.

Murphy chuckled. "You wouldn't be upset with me for changing the size now, would you?"

"If I were, would it matter?"

"Only if you promised never to wear it so I could see you in it."

"That's what I thought. Listen," she continued, trying to sound enthusiastic, "I want to spring a surprise on Nick. I need your help."

"Anything for you."

"He's off to the village on an errand this morning. While he's gone, I'd like to get over to Nouméa. You wouldn't by any chance be planning to dock here this morning, would you?"

"Sorry, sweetheart. I'm afraid I'll be tied up for the remainder of the day."

Adrienne's heart sank. She'd never be able to maintain her ruse if Nick returned. He would want to kiss her. She couldn't stand the thought of him touching her again. What was she going to do? "I'm scheduled to leave tomorrow, Murph. I really need to go today."

"As luck would have it, there is another way if you can find your way to the airstrip."

"What way?" Adrienne asked, glancing at the formidable fern forest outside her window.

"There's a fellow named Winslow in Nouméa who runs an air taxi. I heard him squawking on the radio last night. Apparently he's flying into your island there about one o'clock this afternoon. You could ride into the city with him for a paltry sum, but I'm afraid the trip back this afternoon would cost you a lot of money."

"I don't care about the expense. Could you make the arrangements for me?"

"Consider it done. I'll let you know if there's a problem."

Adrienne closed her eyes and blew out a breath. Her plan was going to work after all. She tried not to sound too excited. "How far is the landing strip from here?"

"No more than an hour's walk."

Adrienne glanced out her window. "Could you give me some directions?"

"There's a fairly new path that leads out of

the north side of the lagoon. Nick has a map somewhere, but be careful, sweetheart. The path could be overgrown, and you could easily become lost. It would be better if you would wait till Nick returns. He could go with you himself."

"I realize that, but if I wait for Nick, it will ruin the surprise."

"If it would save you the trip, I'd be more than happy to shop for you," Murph offered. "I promise to behave myself when it comes to the sizes."

"Thanks for offering. This is something I really need to do myself. Promise you won't say anything to Nick if he calls you."

The horn on Murphy's launch sounded. Adrienne felt a tug of regret. She liked the old seaman. This would be the last time she'd talk with him. Her voice cracked. "You've been a real friend, Murph. If I don't see you before I leave, it's been a pleasure knowing you."

"If you think you're getting away without a proper good-bye, you're vastly mistaken, sweetheart. I've got to be going now. Have fun on the big island, and God bless you. I'll call back if there's any problem."

Adrienne clicked off the power to the radio, hating that she had to deceive Murphy. Someday, when she had her wits about her and the terrible ache in her chest had dulled, she would write him a long letter and apologize.

But now, she had a map to find.

It took every ounce of courage she could muster to walk back into Nick's hut. She tried not to look at the bed, but she couldn't help it. The sheets were still in a tangled mess. Nick's scent still lingered in the air. She remembered the morning she woke up, after their night of lovemaking, with that scent in her nostrils.

Adrienne nearly choked over the burning in her throat. She blinked back the tears and forced herself to open the drawer where she had found the damning letter.

It suddenly struck her that Nick's story about the pearling rights to the island waters could be another ruse. Suppose he was working to make sure *he* got all the pearls. The magnitude of the possibility staggered her.

By the time she found the map, more pieces of the puzzle had fallen into place. Nick had been reluctant to take her scuba diving because he was afraid she'd find pearls. That explained his strange behavior when they shucked the oysters. That was why he didn't let her give her treasures to the chief herself.

She was willing to bet the chief knew nothing about those pearls. Nick had probably been systematically harvesting them for some time with no intention of turning them over to the natives.

If so, he was doing it again—ripping off another bunch of poor, innocent people.

And she had unknowingly participated in his

scheme. She berated herself for selling the gems to Nick's discreet business friend, without speaking with the chief.

She'd been duped, like her grandmother. She could live with that. After all, Nick had probably duped the islanders in the same fashion. If he had, she would have to relinquish her nest egg to them, too. By all rights, the money would belong to them.

But the hardest thing of all to relinquish would be this stubborn feeling for Nick that persisted in her heart. Damn him! She still loved him.

# Chapter Thirteen

By the time Nick tied up his dinghy in the lagoon he had shared with Adrienne for six wonderful weeks, the sun had reached its zenith and begun its slide to the western horizon.

He hopped up onto the dock, a spring to his step.

He'd always done his best thinking when alone. This morning was no exception. He'd decided he hadn't been fair with Adrienne. He hadn't given her a chance to understand what had happened back in the States.

After she blew up and stewed for a few hours, she would probably put herself in Nick's place. She would understand that his only fault had been in trusting too much. Along with those poor retired folks, he'd been a victim of the scam, too.

Adrienne was nowhere in sight. He stuck his head in her bungalow and frowned. Something wasn't right. For one thing, her computer was missing. Apprehension seeped into his stomach. If something had happened to her while he'd been gone, he'd never forgive himself.

Swallowing hard, he took a closer look around and found other things missing. The picture of her grandmother she kept on the dresser, her makeup kit. Her suitcase!

The drawer to her dresser was open. A blur of hot pink caught his eye. Adrienne's teddy? The vision of her in that seductive scrap of satin and lace kicked up the beat of his heart.

He pulled the drawer open and took a closer look. The teddy was there, and along with it, Adrienne's sassy hot pink bikini, plus the dress she'd bought in Nouméa.

The barklike cry of a cagou pierced the air. A sense of foreboding swept over Nick. He backed away from the dresser, as if it were possessed. And then he ran like hell across the beach in hopes Adrienne was waiting for him in his hut.

Murphy's voice was squawking Nick's call letters as he walked through the doorway. Adrienne wasn't there. Nick grabbed the handset, almost crushing it in his palm.

God, what had happened to her? He had been a fool to leave her alone. If Mitch and Morgan had arrived on the island and harmed so much as a hair on Adrienne's pretty head, Nick would see they burned in hell.

"Yeah, Murph, what is it?"

"Trouble, son."

Nick's heart lurched. "Have you seen Adrienne?"

"No, but—"

"Murph, she's gone."

"I know."

"You know!"

"She called me up this morning about eight-thirty."

Eight-thirty? That was about the time Nick had left for the village on Adrienne's errand. She had been sound asleep, safe in her bungalow. "What did she want?"

"She asked if I was planning on stopping off at the island today. She said she wanted to hop over to Nouméa while you were gone."

She left willingly? Nick's world came crashing down on his shoulders. "Why?"

"Something about a surprise for you, son."

"Some surprise. She's . . ." Nick's voice cracked. "I think she's left for good, Murph."

"Surely you're mistaken. She was only talking about going shopping."

"Why would she take her suitcase and her clothes and her computer if that were the case?"

Murph hesitated. "I'm afraid I can't be the one to answer that question. At any rate, I told her I couldn't give her a lift."

"Then where is she?" Nick boomed into the mouthpiece.

"Calm down, son. There's a lot you need to hear, and there isn't much time. I told her

274

Winslow was due in there about one o'clock this afternoon, and she could ride back to Nouméa with him and do her shopping. She asked if I could make the arrangements. I told her I'd be happy to oblige. I was to call her back if there was a problem."

"She doesn't know how to find the landing strip," Nick said.

"I told her you had a map around there somewhere."

Nick's gaze shot to the drawer where he kept the crude map he'd made of the island. The drawer was partially open. He crossed the hut in two strides, yanked the drawer open and groaned. The recent letter from his attorney was also gone. If Adrienne had read that letter ... God. His head lolled back, and he moaned. Of course she'd read the letter. She knew who he was.

That's why she was gone. She'd left him, not having enough faith in him to wait and hear his side of the story. Just like Patrice.

Anger and frustration and pure fear of losing Adrienne burst through his veins.

"Nick, son, are you there?"

"Murph, I've got to go. I've got to try to stop her."

"That you do. But there's more you've got to know before you run off half cocked. When I radioed Winslow, he said, sure, he could give Adrienne a lift to Nouméa when he dropped off the two fellas on Ile de Fleur."

"What two fellas?" Nick asked guardedly.

"That's what I'm trying to tell you. Nick, are you sitting down?"

"Murph, get to the point."

"The point is, the two fellas are from the States and go by the names of Mitch and Morgan. They told Winslow they'd be wanting to fly back to Nouméa tomorrow with an extra passenger. The Aussies aren't scheduled to leave. The Polynesian divers aren't either. The natives wouldn't be caught dead in a plane. That only leaves you and Adrienne, and I thought she was leaving on the ferry with me. Neither of you has told me anything about having visitors. What with the trouble you had a few years back in the States, I got to worrying . . ."

Nick dropped the handset, grabbed his machete, and tore out of his hut. He had to intercept Adrienne before she reached the airport.

At their formal sentencing, Mitch and Morgan had sworn they'd get Nick for turning state's evidence. As if he hadn't suffered enough because of them.

Nick wasn't worried about himself. Adrienne was his concern. If she so much as mentioned his name when Mitch and Morgan disembarked from the plane, they would make an immediate connection. Nick's old partners weren't dumb. They'd seize the chance to get to him through her. After four years in jail, they wouldn't be in a mood to be pleasant. If anything happened to Adrienne, Nick would be to blame.

A couple of months ago Nick had painstakingly cut a path to the airstrip in anticipation of Adrienne's arrival. By now it was overgrown. He ran by instinct, cursing the need to stop and hack at the cloying vines and hardy tropical plants that blocked his way. Perspiration streamed down his face and onto his chest. The air was so thick he could hardly breathe. His heart was pounding so hard he was afraid it would explode in his chest.

He saw a trampled vine here, a broken fern there. How in the hell had Adrienne made her way along the path without help? A large blob of paisley in the undergrowth caught his eye. He stopped and discovered it was Adrienne's suitcase. He ran his fingers over the handle, almost able to feel her presence.

He glanced around, and his blood went cold. From the bent branches, he could tell Adrienne had ventured off the path. What if she got lost? What if she never made it to the airport? What if she fell off the steep cliff a few hundred yards to the north and tumbled into the pool that had sucked him into the ocean?

*Lord, please, don't let her get hurt.*


Adrienne stumbled into the clearing, her

277

arms and legs screaming for a rest. She'd fought through the dense fern forest, through mangroves, coconut palms, and acacias. She'd hiked up rolling hills scattered with candlenut trees and tall pines that looked like cocktail picks.

Just when she had begun to wonder if she'd taken a wrong turn, she came on a broad, grassy field baking in the midday sun. She glanced at her map. "Savannah," Nick had written in the area that encompassed the landing strip. This looked like a savannah. Maybe this was it.

She shielded her eyes from the scalding sun and took a look around. The field was flat and dry with a sea of yellow grass that shimmered at the slightest breeze. *It looks like wheat,* she thought, and squinted her eyes to see through the heat rising up in dizzying waves.

Her vision blurred. Black spots peppered her vision. She was going to faint!

Bending at the waist, she grasped her knees and took several deep breaths. She might as well have stuck her head in an oven. The dry air burned her lungs. She tried to swallow and choked.

Just when she was sure she was hallucinating, she thought she saw something in the distance. She squinted her eyes and looked again. Yes, a thatched hut. Like the one she and Nick had built. Only larger. Carved totem poles on either side. A narrow strip of black that slashed horizontally across the savannah between Adrienne and the hut.

The landing strip. She'd found it!

Renewed strength surged through her veins. She was going to get out of there. With any luck, she'd be airborne in an hour.

She shifted her computer to her other hand. Thank God she'd had the sense to pitch her suitcase into the undergrowth. When she got back to civilization, she could buy new clothes. After she cranked up the air conditioning, took a long, luxurious bubble bath, and drank water. Ice water. Pitchers of it.

She licked her lips and tasted dirt.

She trudged on, her khaki slacks and blouse clinging to her damp body. She wondered if New Caledonian puddle hoppers had stewardesses and air conditioning and ice water.

*You are hallucinating!*

The terminal, if one could call it that, was empty. Adrienne shuffled across the dirt floor and collapsed onto the narrow wooden bench that lined the round structure. Looking for something with which to fan herself, she opened her purse and saw her map.

Nick's map. She bit her lip. Now that she'd reached her destination, the emotions welled up inside her. She wanted to despise him and everything he stood for. But the feelings that had grown over the past several weeks wouldn't be denied. They kept bubbling up inside her, clouding her thinking with disbelief.

How could she have been so blind? To have ignored so many clues that Nick wasn't who or what he claimed to be? She tried to tell herself she was in love with a man who didn't exist. But the man who had laid claim to her heart was no figment of her imagination. He was blue eyes that could coax a smile from her one moment and heat her blood the next. He was a husky voice calling her "darlin' " and an expressive mouth that knew all her secret places. He was strong arms and a broad chest that made her feel secure and at peace with the world. He was the man who had given her the freedom to dream again.

He was a liar who would never tell her another lie.

She thought of him bounding down the dock and sticking his head in her bungalow to find it deserted. She wondered how long it would take him to figure out she had left for good.

A pang of conscience shot through her aching chest. Maybe she shouldn't have gone until she saw him. At the time, though, telling him what he'd told her—nothing—seemed appropriate. Truth to tell, she wasn't sure she could bear seeing him again.

Because, God help her, she still loved him, no matter what he had done. She was afraid if she listened to his excuses for deceiving her, she might be tempted to believe more lies.

Through mist-shrouded eyes, she remembered the cocky, self-confident man he had been the day she arrived. She also recalled the first hint he had a tender side. When he saw how exhausted she was, he'd put the sheets on her bed.

If only he'd possessed the strength of character to be honest with her.

She heaved a sigh and glanced at her watch. In forty minutes the plane would arrive. In another thirty, they'd land in Nouméa. She contemplated collapsing overnight in a hotel before she boarded a plane for the long trip home. But the sooner she left the exotic South Seas, the sooner the healing would begin.

She wanted to discuss a few things with Foster before she flew home. Whether or not she should consult the French authorities about Nick's conduct on the island. Who did own the pearls she had found in Ile de Fleur's waters? If the natives, the authorities should be tipped off. They should know a man with Nick's background might be involved in some nefarious scheme to rip off the islanders. In the same event, she would feel obligated to place the proceeds from the sale of her pearls in a trust fund for the islanders. And she could kiss her sweet retirement fund good-bye.

She hung her head and wept for the futility of it all. But more than the loss of the financial security that had been her obsession, she mourned the passing of her innocence. She had believed

Nick. Because of his betrayal, she wasn't sure she'd ever be able to trust a man again.

A shadow broke the sunlight slanting across the dirt floor. The shadow of a man. A very large man, his generous shoulders blocking out a wide triangle of light.

She looked up, and her heart stopped. Even though the backlighting made his face too dark to be identified, she immediately recognized this man. She had memorized the hard contours of his body. *Nick*.

Her first impulse was to go to him and let him embrace her with his long, strong arms. To tell him she was sorry for leaving so hastily. To ask him to say she was wrong.

Those were the impulses of a foolish woman. There could be no mistake about Nick's identity. She gathered up her courage, lifted her chin, and said, "Hello, Nick. Or is it Mack?"

He snorted. "Well, what do you know. The lady's speaking."

His gruff voice sent her jumping. She didn't have to see the murderous expression on his face to know what he was feeling. The force of his anger made the hair on her arms stand up and the dry, hot air crackle with electricity.

"Get your things," he ordered her. "We're getting out of here."

Goose bumps popped out on her shoulders and swept down her arms. She squared her shoulders and gave him a chilling look. "I'm getting out of here, but not with you."

"Adrienne, we don't have time to argue. Do as I say. I'll explain along the way."

"No," she replied flatly.

He strode into the hut and pulled her up by her arm. His hand was hot, his palm wet. Her heartbeat stuttered. "You can walk, or I'll carry you. Your choice."

"Let me go," she asserted, pulling against his hold on her. Yet the doubts swirled in her muddled mind.

"Adrienne, I swear, you can be so pig-headed." He bent to pick her up. She scuttled out of his grasp.

"I'll thank you to keep your hands off me, *Mack*."

He barely flinched. "What's the matter? Afraid if I touch you, you might think with your heart instead of your head?"

He'd guessed too close to the truth. Ignoring his question, she asked one of her own. "How did you find me?"

"Murph."

Why hadn't she guessed? She shrugged and looked away, but not before she sized up his appearance.

He looked terrible. His face was flushed, his hair damp. Perspiration streamed down his jaw and dripped off his chin. The bare legs beneath the frayed hem of his cutoffs bore angry, red slashes, as if someone had just whipped him with a willow switch. Adrienne's own legs still stung from the branches that clawed at her while she threaded her way through the forest. But Nick had negotiated the same path with his legs exposed. He could have saved himself the effort.

"I'm not leaving with you, and that's that."

"I'm not asking you to leave with me. I'm asking you to get out of here until the plane lands. You're in danger."

"Right." She gave a slightly hysterical laugh. "The big, bad boogey man's going to get me."

He hooked his thumbs in the front pockets of his shorts and, studying his feet, shook his head. "There's a lot you don't know."

"I know enough," she said, feeling the fire of anger spark to life again.

"You just think you do."

"I can read," she shot back.

"But not between the lines."

"What are you trying to tell me?" she asked, hoping against hope there was some logical explanation for the horrendous nightmare.

He glanced at his watch. "We have a little time. If I spell it out for you, maybe you'll do as I say."

He prowled the confines of the hut, then took a seat on the opposite side, facing her. She watched while he hunched forward, bracing his dirt-streaked forearms on his thighs.

"The plane's going to be here in about thirty minutes. I've got a lot to tell you, and that isn't much time, so I'd appreciate it if you'd just hear me out."

Adrienne couldn't look at Nick. The tears welled up inside her. She didn't want to give him the satisfaction of knowing how much she was hurting. Her throat constricted. She couldn't talk. She lifted her hand in a pitiful gesture of acquiescence and made the mistake of looking at his face.

Lord, what had he done to himself? She stifled a cry. His cheek was cut. As she watched, he swiped at the blood with his hand. She started to offer him a tissue from her purse but thought better of it. She couldn't get that close to him or she'd either hit him or hug him. She didn't want to do either.

"Save your breath, *Mack*. I know what you're going to tell me. You see this morning I came over to apologize for not understanding why you had to lie to me about the pearls. You were asleep. I knew you hadn't returned until after 3 a.m., and I figured, I'll leave him a note so he'll see it when he wakes up."

"So you went snooping through my drawer."

"I *looked* in your drawer for a piece of paper to write on," she continued. "That's when I found the letter from your attorney." She resented his caustic attitude. She'd done nothing wrong, other than leave. He was the one who had lied to her. He was the one who had taken her trust and betrayed it, a second time.

"And now you think you know everything."

"I know who you are," she said with a

haughty lift to her chin. She was almost relieved the anger was back. She could deal with that better than the pain of realizing what she and Nick had shared was a mockery.

"And who do you think that is?"

"N. McKenzie Holton. Mack Holton. The last man in the world I ever wanted to fall in love with."

He gave a dry laugh. "Don't worry, Adrienne. I hardly think you loved me. If you did, you would have given me a chance to explain what you read in that letter."

"Explain what? Do you deny you're Mack Holton?"

"No."

She shrugged. "Case closed."

He sat there for a minute, saying nothing. The chilling cry of a bird rent the silence. Perspiration trickled down the valley between Adrienne's breasts. She dabbed at the moistness between her cleavage with a tissue, praying the plane would land soon.

Nick shook his head and stared through the open doorway. "I thought when I came here I could get away from people like you."

Adrienne bristled. "What do you mean, 'people like me?' "

"People willing to believe the worst. People with closed minds."

"Well, pardon me, Nick, or Mack, or whatever your name is. But I have a particularly good reason for having what you call a 'closed mind.' Or have your forgotten my grandmother? She's dead because of you and those two miserable partners of yours."

"Did it ever cross your closed mind that I didn't go to jail along with them for a damned good reason?"

"I know why you didn't. Because you spilled your guts to save your own hide."

"Strange the prosecuting attorney didn't see it that way."

"What do you mean?"

"He never pressed charges against me."

Adrienne shrugged. "I'm sure that was just a formality."

"Tell you what. When you get back to the States, give him a call. He'll tell you I didn't do anything wrong but trust the best two friends I'd ever had in my life."

Nick stood to pace. Adrienne sat there, watching him. His hands were knotted into fists, the muscles bunched in his arms. His jaw was a square block of granite. The anger radiating from him was almost frightening.

She wished the plane would hurry up and land. But he'd managed to raise her curiosity. For some wild, crazy reason she found herself wanting to hear his story. "Spit it out, Nick. There isn't much time left."

Nick whirled on her. "All right, here it is. You can choose to believe it or not. I was innocent, damnit."

"Yeah, right."

"Okay, I take it back. I was partially responsible."

"Now we're getting somewhere."

"Once the media picked up on our private health-care plan, the money came in so fast we could hardly count it. Money we had to invest. That was Morgan's department. He had mentored under one of the most highly respected mutual fund managers in the country and had his own track record that was impressive."

"And the other guy?"

"Mitch? He was our super salesman. I had no reason to suspect anything was wrong until I worked late one night on end-of-the-month reports. The last page of Morgan's expense account was missing. I walked into his office, figuring the rest of it might be in his out basket. The phone on his private line rang. I let the answering machine get it. I recognized the voice—one of Mitch's contacts at a company we'd invested in. He said Mitch and Morgan could expect delivery on their sailboats within a month, but they'd have to take the next model up, which he named. I knew boats. That baby went for half a million bucks. If my partners put their salaries together, they couldn't afford one of them. Besides, that company didn't make sailboats. They manufactured health-care products.

"I asked my partners about it the next day. They gave me some story about this guy getting a good deal on repossessed boats. Mitch and Morgan had always been straight with me. Hell, we were fraternity brothers. I believed them."

He paused, staring out the open doorway. "Mistake with a capital M. Later I found out Mitch and Morgan had a list of people they had the goods on. People who worked for corporations we just happened to invest Eternity funds in. My partners blackmailed these guys into funneling that money out the back door in the form of luxury items like sailboats and chalets in Switzerland. Mitch and Morgan turned these around and pocketed the cash. To make a long story short, the major part of Eternity's money wasn't being invested anywhere. The stock we supposedly held wasn't worth a nickel. I uncovered the whole scheme by accident. I was sick. I went straight to the district attorney."

"Why didn't your part in this make the news?" Adrienne asked, still unable to believe he had been innocent.

"Because *I* wasn't on trial. *I'm* the one who went to the district attorney and reported the fraud. During the trial, though, my good old partners tried to make it look like I was the guilty party."

What he was saying seemed reasonable, and yet . . . "I suppose the prosecuting attorney could corroborate what you're telling me."

Nick strode across the hut to stand in front of her, his heels stirring up the dry soil as he walked. He glared down at her. "You still don't believe me, do you?"

"It's just that—"

He shook his head and lifted his gaze to the cone-shaped ceiling before boring into her with resentful eyes. "Neither did Patrice. She walked out when it hit the newspapers, and she never came back. She never listened to my side of it. You know what, darlin', I'm glad you showed your colors before I asked you to marry me."

"M-marry you?"

"Yeah. On the way back from the village today, I was eating myself out for not leveling with you sooner. I thought, hell, you haven't given her a chance. Once you tell her everything, she'll understand. Then you can ask her to marry you, and you'll live happily ever after. Wrong. You've got a problem I couldn't live with. You go through life with blinders on. You only see what you want to see. You may be long on passion, darlin', but you're short as hell on compassion. Frankly, I'd rather live like a monk."

Adrienne bristled. At the same time, his explanation was beginning to percolate through her thick, judgmental skull. If what he had told her was true, he was as much a victim of his sleazy partners as her grandmother had been. Still, she had questions.

"The newspapers said you walked away with a bundle while your partners took the rap and went to jail."

290

"A bundle, huh?" He gave a caustic laugh. "Ask the prosecuting attorney about that bundle. His name is Weinstein."

Adrienne swallowed over a knot in her throat. "Why don't you just tell me what you did with the money?"

"Because you wouldn't believe me."

"I understand how you would feel that way, but why don't you try me?"

She waited. He said nothing. "Nick?" she urged him and touched his hand.

He didn't move. He didn't respond at all when her fingers grazed his skin. He merely looked down his nose at her, the hint of a sneer on his lips. The silence was so loud it roared in her ears.

"Don't," he finally ground out, "touch me."

She pulled her hand into her lap and licked her parched lips. "Okay."

When he began to talk again, Adrienne's heart fluttered. "What assets Eternity had the courts froze. I sold my house, my car, and my cabin in the mountains. I cashed in my insurance policies and liquidated my municipal bonds. I took the money, in cash, to Weinstein." He snickered. "That was my bundle."

"Why to him?"

"For a victims' compensation fund."

Adrienne remembered her grandmother receiving a letter from somebody about such a fund, but nothing was ever said about who financed it. Adrienne had assumed it was the government. She had helped Gracie fill out the forms for her share. When the check had come, her grandmother had fallen into a state of depression. Fifty dollars. That's all she got.

A wave of nausea swept over Adrienne. Her stomach clenched into hard knots. Everything Nick was saying made sense, which was scary.

Nick walked to the doorway and paused, his back to Adrienne.

"Nick?"

"Yeah, Adrienne," he answered, and the hurt in his voice nearly killed her.

"Don't go."

"What's the use?"

Panic seized Adrienne and pulled her off the bench. She crossed to Nick and laid a tentative hand on his back. Her thoughts and her emotions were colliding like frantic birds in a cage. She only knew she loved this man, and, if what he was saying was true, she'd judged him unfairly. She blotted out her apprehension and told him plainly, simply, "I'm sorry I jumped to conclusions, Nick."

He shrugged away from her touch. "Why should you be different from anybody else? That's why I got the hell out of the States and changed my name."

"If you gave all your money to the prosecuting attorney for the victims' fund, how could you afford to come here?" she wondered. She knew how expensive her own ticket had been.

"Still the skeptic, huh?"

"Nick, please. I want to understand, but this has all been a shock to me. You should have confided in me earlier. You should have given me a chance to be fair."

"As fair as you've been this morning?" he said, slanting a hostile glance over his shoulder.

"Nick . . . ?"

"Okay, I sailed here. Are you satisfied?"

"In the *Lorelei?*" she asked incredulously.

"No, Adrienne. Not in the *Lorelei.* Even I'm not that stupid. I knew cruise ships sometimes need extra crewmen at the last minute, so I hung around the docks for a couple of days. I didn't care where in the hell I went. I just had to get away. The media were hounding my family unmercifully. If I disappeared, they'd let up after a while.

"Anyway, I found the captain of a windjammer cruise whose crew was sick with botulism. I was still a pretty fair sailor. The captain was desperate enough to sign me on. We sailed to Nouméa. I got off and met Murph. I asked him if he'd take me to the most remote island he knew. He didn't ask any questions. He just brought me here. A month later I wound my way around to the lagoon. I found a sunken sailboat out near the reef. I figured with a boat, I could fish and make a living. I salvaged her and cleaned her up. I named her the *Lorelei.*"

The *Lorelei.* The dusty remembrances from a

293

high-school literature class popped into Adrienne's mind. *Lorelei* was derived from an old German word that meant "to be on the watch for." In one story the *Lorelei* had been a maiden despondent over an unfaithful lover. She had thrown herself into the Rhine where she became a siren who lured fishermen to destruction.

Despondent over an unfaithful lover. Or a friend. Two friends. And a wife.

"The first time I hauled in oysters while sailing her," Nick continued, "I found a pearl."

"That's why you didn't want to take me scuba diving. Because you were afraid I'd find pearls, too."

He nodded.

"I can understand why you didn't tell me about your pearl project with the natives, but why didn't you reveal who you were? Didn't you think I loved you enough to get past your admission?"

"You didn't this morning, and if it's all the same with you, I don't want to talk about it anymore."

She ducked under his arm and whirled around, forcing him to look at her. "In a few minutes, I'm supposed to get on a plane and fly out of here. I may never see you again."

"Perhaps," he said, a haunted expression in his eyes, "that would be better for both of us."

They stood there, staring at each other, Adrienne afraid he wouldn't go on, Nick trying to decide if he should waste his breath.

When Nick had discovered Adrienne was missing, his world had crashed down around him. He was afraid someone—Mitch or Morgan maybe—had kidnapped her. Then he had figured out she'd simply left, without a word, just like Patrice had four years ago. Back then he'd wallowed in self-pity. But this time, he had been so angry he could have ripped palm trees from the soil.

When he had found out Adrienne could be walking into trouble, he only knew he had to save her, no matter what she'd done to him.

Since he'd entered that terminal and seen her sitting there, waiting for the plane, his heart had wrenched from its moorings. She couldn't leave. He loved her too much. But was it Adrienne he loved or the woman he thought her to be?

She looked up at him, as if she wanted to believe him. Should he give her another chance to take a swipe at him, or shouldn't he?

While he struggled with perhaps the most important decision of his life, she took his hand and squeezed it. "I've done you a terrible disservice by misjudging you, Nick."

Her voice quavered. He weakened. Damn, he didn't want her to cry, no matter how much she had hurt him.

"But you're also at fault," she went on. "You didn't trust me enough to tell me the truth. Maybe, if you had, we wouldn't be standing here, arguing. We might be back in the lagoon . . . making love."

Hearing her speak the word *love* in such a cavalier attitude angered him. "In order to make love," he tossed back, "you have to love someone. And in order to love, you have to trust. So please don't refer to what you and I did together as making love."

She glared at him. "All right, so we just had great sex. Which won't happen again, considering we only have five minutes left."

He wasted one of them trying to decide if he was going to tell her some things she need to hear. While he was vacillating, he heard a faint drone in the distance.

"Nick, please. Talk to me. I don't want to leave like this."

She was still leaving, despite what he'd told her. That meant she didn't believe him. He pulled his hand from hers and crossed his arms over his chest. "I don't know why I'm wasting my breath, but here goes. One of my reasons for keeping silent was to protect the natives. I figured if you knew who I was, you'd tell others, and soon the media would flock down here like vultures and resurrect the Eternity Health-Care scandal. They'd try to prove I was ripping off the natives when I was only trying to help them. God, Adrienne, don't you see? That's what I'm trying to do? Make up, by helping them, for being a part of what happened to your grandmother and so many others like her?"

She said nothing. She only looked at him as if someone had hit her in the head with a frying pan.

"How much do you know about pearl culturing?" he continued.

Adrienne frowned. "Not much. The Japanese are the masters, aren't they?"

"They were until recent years. Then the Australians broke their stranglehold on the market. Lately Marutea, which is not all that far from here, has produced some fine black pearls. For lack of much to do around here, I read a lot. When I found those natural pearls in the lagoon, I already knew one thing. Natural pearls don't necessarily replenish themselves. Where they have grown, though, the gems can be cultured effectively.

"Not exactly being caught up in any desire to make money, I didn't give much thought to the matter. Not until I heard the French government was opening up Ile de Fleur for foreign investment in tourism. I thought, hell! These islanders are going to be ripped off, big time. They'll lose the land they've lived on for centuries, along with their privacy, and God knows what else.

"And then it struck me," he continued. "Maybe I could help them establish a pearl culturing farm before people like Foster developed the island. I ran the idea by the chief. He said, go for it. I spoke with my dad back in the States. He put me in touch with Pierre, who bought one of the gems I found. The money financed my trip to Australia to study pearl culturing. It took me a while, but I made the right contacts. Almost everything's in place, ready to begin. As we speak, two Japanese men skilled in the more technical aspects of the business are working with the natives. Two men you *didn't* see in the village."

For once Adrienne kept her mouth shut. Maybe he was getting through to her. He went on.

"Until I was sure the natives would have a hundred-year renewable lease on the pearl culturing rights to the island's waters, I couldn't confide in anyone. Not even you. If I'd trusted the wrong person again, as I'd trusted my buddies, someone could have stepped in and cheated the islanders, and I'd have been to blame."

"You're saying, if you revealed your identity to me, I might have told Foster, and he might have passed it on to someone else."

"I think you're finally getting my drift."

A muscle in Nick's jaw twitched. He spoke with the determination of purpose. "I made myself a promise four years go. That I'd find a way, somehow, somewhere, to make up for my part in hurting those poor people back in the States."

The drone in the sky grew louder. Adrienne touched Nick's arm with trembling fingers. He wanted to pull her into his arms, but he couldn't. Her lack of faith in him had cut too deeply.

"But what happened back in the States wasn't your fault, Nick," she said, swiping at the tears with her knuckle.

"So you finally believe me," he shot back and saw a glint of metal in the sky.

Mitch and Morgan.

Adrienne might not be deserving of his love, but he couldn't let her get hurt. "You've got to clear out of here," he told her.

"But Nick—"

He bounded back into the hut, grabbed her computer and purse, and pulled her by the arm.

"Where are we going?"

"Over there, in those bushes."

"But why?"

"Adrienne, for once, will you just trust me?"

They were running now. Adrienne couldn't keep up with Nick's pace. He paused long enough to scoop her into his arms. The fullness of her breasts pressed against his chest, and he almost stumbled. Why did she have to be so soft, to feel so right in his arms?

By the time they reached the scrawny thicket, his heart was about to burst from his chest, and not solely from the effort of running.

He eased her down and struggled for breath. "I want you to lie down and keep quiet. Not a peep, understand?" He turned to start off, but she grabbed his arm and pulled him back.

"Where are you going, and why do I have to hide here?"

"I'm going back to meet that plane and the passengers Murph told me were on it."

She lifted her face, that dainty, pointed chin jutting out. A lump sprang to Nick's throat. "Who are they?" she demanded.

"My old partners, Mitch and Morgan. They got out on parole two weeks ago. And if Murph's sources are right, I don't think they're here to soak up the sun."

"Nick, wait! Don't leave. They'll hurt you."

"Nah," he said, with a forced grin, "they can't. But if they see you here, they'll figure we're connected. And what better way to get back at me than to hurt you."

"I'm coming with you!"

"No, you're not. I've got it all figured out. So far they don't know anyone's here but me and the natives, so you'll be safe."

"But what about you?"

"They won't hurt me if I can convince them I'm involved in something here they can make a lot of money on. Hell, I'll tell them I've got something worth a lot of money back in the lagoon. The pilot knows he's to pick you up. He'll wait on you. Stay here until we disappear into those trees over there," he instructed her, pointing to the path back to the lagoon. "Then run like blazes and get on that plane."

# Chapter Fourteen

Nick spun around and bolted for the terminal before Adrienne could utter another word.

*Think! What can you do to help? Even now Nick's partners might be aiming a gun at his head. Because of you!*

Lying on the ground, she pressed her fingers to her throbbing temples. Old prejudices, recent revelations, and the dictates of conscience whirled through her head in a dizzying maelstrom. The two-engine plane circled the clearing, then lined up with the runway. She choked back a sob.

*Let it crash.*

*No, you can do better than that! The pilot could get hurt, and maybe Nick, too.*

Perspiration slickened her breasts and dampened her back. The plane landed with a bounce, then flung itself down the runway, the reversed engines screaming at fever pitch.

The thicket about her came alive. Insects and birds and smaller varmints clamored over the leaf-strewn ground at the invasion of their peaceful habitat.

*We should be fleeing with them,* Adrienne thought, wishing Nick had considered that option. But no, he was trying to protect her, even after she'd left without giving him a chance to explain himself.

The plane taxied to a halt not ten feet from the terminal. The door pushed open with the rending sound of metal. Two men—one tall and dark-haired, one short and fair—jumped to the ground. A man wearing a billed cap—the pilot, Adrienne guessed—pitched a small satchel from the plane, then disappeared.

The two passengers looked around, apparently scanning the clearing. They looked straight at Adrienne. She held her breath.

Something, a spider maybe, scampered across her leg. She stuck her fist in her mouth to keep from screaming and held still, absolutely still. Her heart was beating so fast, her chest hurt.

The pilot reappeared in the doorway. The men turned back around. Adrienne carefully let out her breath and watched the pilot hand the tall man a piece of paper. Muffled sounds of voices drifted across the clearing. Adrienne strained, but she couldn't sort out the words. The tall man looked as if he was studying the paper. The pilot pointed across the clearing, in the direction of the path back to the lagoon.

*They're looking for Nick!* The coppery taste

of fear jettisoned to her mouth and burned the back of her throat.

She hoped Nick had brought his machete with him. Had he?

She scanned her memory. Had she seen that weathered, tan sheath when she had catalogued Nick's appearance in her mind?

She was almost certain she had. She breathed a little easier. Maybe Nick was waiting inside the terminal and would spring himself on his old partners, brandishing his weapon.

But every hope she had for his safety disappeared as Nick strode out of the terminal and straight to the plane.

The voices grew angry, the gestures of the three men jerky, their postures stiff. Adrienne rose to her knees. She had to do something. She couldn't let Nick stand there and risk getting killed.

Slipping the strap to her purse over her head, she crept back into the thicket, then circled to her left. When her view of the men was blocked by the terminal, she took off at a dead run across the savannah.

"Say, buddy," Mitch said, smoothing his dark hair back on his forehead and preening. Nick remembered the vain gesture only too well. "You don't look like you've been living a life of luxury the past four years."

Nick narrowed his gaze at the more verbal

of his former partners. He wanted to cram his fist down the jerk's throat and make him swallow his cocky words. But Morgan was acting suspiciously confident, and he was easing toward the satchel the pilot had pitched from the plane.

"That all the luggage you got?" Nick queried, pointing at the satchel.

"All we need," Mitch said. "We figure since you walked off with all the money, you'd fix us up with what we need. Isn't that right, Morgan?"

Morgan, the weak weasel, merely nodded.

"You know I don't have a cent of that money. I gave it all away."

"Is that right? Then how did you get yourself a sweet little sailboat?"

So his old buddies had done some detective work. It was no secret in Nouméa that Nick owned the *Lorelei.* That's why Adrienne's boss had been able to track him down as a guide. Nick only hoped no one had told Mitch and Morgan about Adrienne.

Nick wanted to steal a glance into the bushes. To make certain Adrienne had done as he'd told her. But the slightest glance in that direction might tip off Mitch and Morgan. They were too perceptive. They'd know instantly he was trying to hide something.

"I sweated blood for that boat, but you never understood the virtue of hard work, did you, Mitch?"

"Thanks to you, we've worked our butts off the last four years in that hellhole they call a prison. But no more. Whatever you've got going for you here is ours."

"What I've got going for me is clean living."

"Then by all means, show us the way, old buddy," Mitch replied, giving Nick's back a none-too-gentle shove in the direction of the lagoon.

Nick resisted the urge to slam his fist into Mitch's gut. He had to get them out of there fast before the pilot gave up on Adrienne and left without her. "This way," he indicated and took off across the savannah.

"Not so fast," Mitch said. "You don't want to lose us." Something hard and round jabbed into Nick's back. A gun. He stiffened and slowed his pace.

"Not until we take what's rightfully ours," Mitch continued with a mocking laugh. "Then we're going to show you what it's like to live in a cage, aren't we, Morgan?"

Sweat was streaking down Nick's chest. Only fifty more yards, and they'd clear the savannah. Adrienne could get on the plane and take off. She'd be safe. He stirred up the conversation to make sure he kept Mitch and Morgan's focus on him and away from that plane.

"When you're scum, you deserve to live in a cage."

Morgan whacked him on the back with the butt of the gun. A pain exploded in Nick's

305

shoulder. He gritted his teeth. He wouldn't give them the satisfaction of knowing how much it hurt.

"Then I guess you're scum, Mack boy. 'Cause we've found us another little island, just like this, and there's a sweet cage waiting for you. It's on one of those islands they've condemned because of nuclear testing. I don't know what'll get you first. The sun baking your pretty-boy skin, or the soil eating away at you. Frankly, I don't care. You can't imagine what it's like living in a cell that smells like—"

"Oh, boys."

The sound of Adrienne's voice sent all three of them spinning. Nick made a grab for Mitch's gun, but he wasn't quick enough. He watched while his old partners raked Adrienne with their filthy eyes.

"Well, what do we have here?" Mitch asked, walking a slow path around Adrienne. "Mack boy's sweetheart, maybe?"

Nick glared at Adrienne. "She's not my sweetheart."

Morgan's gaze shot to Nick, then swerved back to Adrienne. He grinned. "Hey, Mack, you should have learned to play poker with us in college. You're lying through your teeth."

"I have a proposition for you gentlemen," Adrienne said and winked at Nick.

What the hell did she think she was doing? "Adrienne, stay out of this."

"So her name's Adrienne." Mitch draped his

306

arm over her shoulder and glanced down her cleavage. "I knew a girl named Adrienne once. The best lay I ever had."

Nick lunged for Mitch. Mitch fired his pistol into the ground at Nick's feet. "I wouldn't if I were you."

"There's no need for violence, gentlemen." Adrienne slipped the strap of her purse over her shoulder and handed it to Morgan. "There's something in there you can split if you'll walk back and get on that plane."

"There isn't enough money to make me leave." Mitch blurted out. "Not yet."

"Oh, really? That's rather commendable since you probably don't have two cents to rub together. And, since you've violated your parole, nobody in his right mind back in the States would hire you."

Morgan pulled a rectangular piece of paper from Adrienne's purse. Nick recognized it as a check. He opened his mouth to protest, but Adrienne shot him a murderous look.

"That's it." She snatched it from Morgan's hand and thrust it into Mitch's.

He appeared to give it only a cursory look, but then his eyes widened, and Nick saw him swallow hard. "Fifty thousand dollars!"

"That's right," Adrienne said, circling to stand by Nick. She slid an arm around his waist and gave him a hug. It was only then that he could tell how hard she was shaking. He looked into her eyes and saw all the love

307

he'd ever wanted. He hugged her back and winced as a sharp pain cut across his shoulder.

"If you sign a paper saying you'll leave Nick—Mack—alone, forever, that money will be yours. I won't stop payment on the check. Fifty thousand dollars would go a long way in Australia or someplace where people don't know you."

Mitch handed the check back to Morgan and snorted. "We'll sign nothing. We'll get rid of you both, and the money will be ours anyway."

"How are you going to get out of here?" Adrienne asked in a sweet little voice. "Or do you plan on spending the rest of your life on this God-forsaken island?"

"We'll leave the same way we came in," Morgan answered as if she didn't have a brain in her head.

"I don't think so. I told the pilot if I didn't give him the signal in ten minutes, he was to take off without you."

Mitch waved the gun in her face. "So, give him the signal."

"Why should I? You'll shoot us either way. Now if you were to hand over that gun and sign this . . ." she dug in her purse and pulled out a wrinkled sheet of paper. She handed it to him. "I'm sorry if the punctuation isn't quite accurate. I wrote that rather hastily a few minutes ago."

Mitch read what Adrienne had handed him

308

and shoved it back into her hands. "I can't sign this. It says Mack was innocent in the health-care scam."

"And it promises I won't try to stop you from cashing that check."

Mitch looked to Morgan. Morgan shrugged. Adrienne consulted her watch. "One minute to go. I guess you'd better get it over with. Shoot us and do your best to get comfortable." She pointed over her shoulder. "You'll find two huts about an hour's hike that way. But watch out for the wild pigs and poisonous snakes."

Nick chuckled. "The lady's making pretty good sense, Mitch. It looks like you've got two choices."

"And," Adrienne said, tapping the face of her watch, "about one minute to make up your mind."

# Chapter Fifteen

With fifteen seconds to go, Mitch pitched the gun fifty feet into the savannah, then grabbed the paper from Adrienne's hand. She dug in her purse for a pen and handed it to him. Grumbling, he hastily scribbled his signature beside hers as his time expired.

She ran into the field, waving both arms over her head. The pilot acknowledged her signal by starting his engines. Nick and Adrienne followed Mitch and Morgan back to the runway and asked the pilot to witness the signature.

The sun was angling at its two o'clock berth when the Cessna streaked down the runway, then lifted to skim over the treetops at the far end of the savannah.

"I wonder if Australia's ready for them," Adrienne murmured, watching the plane until it was only a dot in the cloudless sky.

"Perhaps I'd better radio a couple of friends and have them tip off the Australian authorities to watch out for those two."

"That might be wise. But I have a feeling their pictures will be plastered all over newspapers everywhere as soon as I show this contract they signed to the American ambassador in New Caledonia."

"I'll make it up to you, Adrienne," Nick said. "As soon as you get back home, I'll ship you the rest of the pearls I've found. That should more than compensate for the fifty thousand dollars."

She spun around, hardly able to believe her ears. "I don't want your pearls."

"But—"

She tilted her head back and screamed. "Men! Why do you have to beat it through their thick skulls?"

"I know how much that money has meant to you. From the time you sold those pearls, you've been a different person."

She swatted him with her purse. "I've been a different person because I fell in love with you, and you made love to me, you fool, not because of the money."

"But I thought—"

She slipped her arms around his waist and, propping her chin on his bare chest, gave him a broad grin. "Sometimes it doesn't pay to think."

"But what about your nest egg? You just gave half of it away."

"So, we're young."

"You mean *you* are."

311

She nibbled at his chin. "I said, 'We're young,' and I meant it."

"Adrienne," he said on a sigh, "maybe you'd better tell me exactly what you mean."

Beneath her chin, Adrienne could feel Nick's heart kick up its beat. His chest was streaked with dirt and sweat, but she didn't care. He smelled like a heavenly combination of earth and sea and sun, and she loved him without reservation. She pressed her cheek to his chest and tried to find the words to convince him she would always be there for him.

"I may be making a fool of myself. I mean, I'm assuming a lot, but, well . . . as long as you want me . . ."

Nick uttered an animal-like growl and scooped her into his arms. "Want you, darlin'? Is that what you're asking? Do I want you?"

She sifted her fingers through the fuzzy blond hair on his chest and smiled up at him coyly. "Well, yes."

He bent his head and captured her lips in a deep, tongue-thrashing kiss that ignited fires of wanting deep in her abdomen. She whimpered into his mouth. He released his hold on her and let her slide slowly to her feet. She brushed against that rock-hard part of him she longed to take into her body. She prayed he would forgive her for her lack of trust in him, for now and for always.

He broke the kiss and exhaled with a shudder. "Does that answer your question?"

Her throat tightened. This time when she spoke, the words came out croaky. "How long?"

"How long what?"

"How long do you want me?"

He slanted her a cocky grin, then lifted her in his arms again.

"A simple answer would suffice," she said demurely.

He whirled around and carried her into the hut beside the landing strip. "Pick that up." With a nod of his head, he indicated his machete that lay on the bench.

"You aren't going to do anything kinky are you?" she asked, scooping up the hefty weapon.

"That depends. I just might."

She frowned. "What's this doing here anyway?"

He ducked through the opening and started across the field with her. "I left it for you, in case those two sorry characters gave you a hard time."

"But, Nick, you might have needed it yourself."

"Right. And who saved whom in that confrontation anyway?"

"We worked together."

"Yeah, right."

"We did. You didn't answer my question," she said, ducking to avoid an overhanging limb.

"What question?"

She ran a finger over the pectorals of his chest. "How long will you want me?"

"Oh, that," he replied flatly.

Until now, their playful banter had given Adrienne hope they could forget the angry words and the hurt. She bit her lip to keep back the tears. If Nick wouldn't say what he had to know she needed to hear, she wouldn't goad him.

He carried her to a grassy spot beside a gurgling stream and set her on her feet. No sooner was she standing than he began to pace.

"I can't promise you a very peaceful life," he said, frowning. "When I go back to the States, the media will have a heyday with me. It won't be easy, I guarantee you."

Adrienne watched him stride back and forth, wanting to scream to him to stop. "You'd consider going back?"

"This is hardly a proper place to raise children. I'd want them to have the best of schools and a nice house. I'd have to find someone I could trust to oversee the pearl farm until the natives can handle it on their own."

He was talking about *their* children. Hope lifted Adrienne's spirits. "Here," she said, whipping an envelope from her purse. "This might help a little."

"What is this? A letter?"

"Open it," she encouraged him, hardly able

to wait to see his expression when he did.

He slipped the cashier's check for twenty-five thousand dollars—the one she'd asked Pierre to have made out to her—from the envelope. "What is this for?" he asked numbly.

She pressed her cheek against his arm. "You've done so much for me, I wanted to do something for you. And you can use part of that to pay for the binoculars."

Nick shook his head. "What did you do with them this time?"

"You see, I got sort of ticked off when I found that letter from your attorney in your drawer, and on the way out of your hut I saw the binoculars, and—"

"Adrienne, will you just tell me where they are?"

"Well," she said, wincing, "I sort of pitched them into the lagoon."

"Did you ever play softball?"

"How did you know?"

"Oh, just a lucky guess." He smiled at her warmly and stuffed her check back into the envelope. "As for the binoculars, somehow I think you'll find a way of making it up to me." He waggled his brows. "I can think of a couple ways right now. But this—" he tapped the envelope in his open palm, then thrust it back into her hands "—I simply cannot accept."

"Oh, right. I can accept three pearls from you that were worth a small fortune, but you can't accept twenty-five thousand dollars from me. Give me one good reason why not."

"It's your money."

She put the envelope back in his hands. "So, I want it to be yours."

"You don't owe me anything. You spend it."

"I have plenty of money, and I didn't give it to you out of a sense of obligation."

"What about that nest egg you want so badly?"

"My nest egg—one hundred thousand dollars of the pearl money, less fifty thousand for Mitch and Morgan—is earning interest in a savings account in Phoenix. This is extra. And it's yours."

"No," he said flatly.

No her fifty thousand wouldn't earn interest or no he couldn't take her money? Or was there another reason why Nick hadn't reacted as she'd expected when she handed him the endorsed cashier's check? And then it hit her. She hadn't told him what the money was for!

"Maybe I didn't make myself clear," she said, feeling foolish. "The money isn't for you . . . exactly."

"That's clear as mud, Adrienne."

"What I meant was, I'd like you to put it to use for the natives. You said they have a lot of needs, like a hospital, and you've been working on this pearl culturing thing for them. I figure you must have a lot of expenses. And as for leaving the pearl farm, I spoke with Foster about it when I radioed him the other day. He just might be willing to help. He said if he decides to build his resort here and he likes it, he might retire here."

"And you?" Nick said, pulling her to sit with him on the grass. "Are you willing to take a chance? No guarantees on security with me. At least until I reestablish myself and get us situated."

In his crazy, roundabout way, Nick was proposing! Adrienne swallowed over a cotton candy ball in her throat and tried to find the words that he needed to hear. "For years, I've thought security meant money. Enough to pay my bills if I got sick. Enough so I wouldn't have to depend on anybody to take care of me. You," she said, smoothing her hand over his cheek, "have taught me that real security is knowing the one I love most loves me in return. And you've taught me to dream again."

"Good dreams, I hope."

"Dreams of you."

"Does that mean you'll marry me?"

"Are you asking me to?"

"Hell, yes!" He sobered, and for a brief moment, she thought he'd changed his mind. "Of course, I haven't had any choice for some time."

"What's that supposed to mean?" she demanded, stung by his tone as much as by his choice of words.

"That I've been caught up in a superstition

the islanders swear is not just a bunch of mumbo jumbo."

She narrowed her gaze at him, wondering if he was pulling her leg again. "What superstition?"

"Well, darlin'," he explained, in that maddeningly slow Southern drawl, "according to the natives, it goes like this. After a boy reaches the age of puberty, his marital fate is sealed in his body temperature."

"What?" she shrieked.

She caught him fighting back a grin. "The first time he runs a fever, he'd better watch out. Because the first gal he sees when the fever subsides is his intended."

"That's the most absurd thing I've ever heard!"

"You do remember when I cut my leg, I ran a fever."

She thought back to that first week and smiled at the memory. "So you did."

"After it went away, the first woman I saw was you."

"Good thing," she said with a chuckle. She laced her arms around his neck and, lying on the grass, pulled Nick down for a long, hot kiss.

When they came up for air, she wiggled beneath Nick in an outrageously suggestive manner. "If some other woman had tried to cut in on my action, I would have—"

"Thrown my binoculars at her?" he teased as

318

he slowly unbuttoned her blouse.

"Yes! And, I think you'll agree, with the practice I've had, my aim is pretty good."

"Oh, Adrienne," Nick said, laughing out loud, "life is never going to be boring with you."